W9-CEQ-737

DEVIL'S KISS

To my wife and daughters

DEVIL'S KISS

SARWAT CHADDA

DISNEY • HYPERION BOOKS
NEW YORK

For information address Disney • Hyperion Books, 114 Fifth Avenue, New York, New York 10011-5690.

Printed in the United States of America
First American Edition
10 9 8 7 6 5 4 3 2 1
Library of Congress Cataloging-in-Publication Data on file.
ISBN 978-1-4231-1999-9
Reinforced binding
Visit www.hyperionteens.com

THIS LABEL APPLIES TO TEXT STOCK

Who made thee a prince and judge over us?
Intendest thou to kill me,
as thou killedst the Egyptian?

—Exodus 2:14

DEVIL'S
KISS

1

KILLING HIM SHOULD BE EASY; HE'S ONLY SIX.

Then why the bilious, twisting feeling deep in her guts? Why the cold, clammy dampness down her back?

He's only six.

Billi waded through the spiny grass toward the back of the park. The autumnal night wind whispered to her, down here in The Pit.

What a name for a playground.

But no one played here; hadn't for years. The low fence around it had long since fallen, leaving rotten planks jutting out of the earth like crooked black teeth. The animal rockers watched her with hollow eyes, and their old springs creaked as they nodded their heads in greeting.

The boy sat on the swing, the middle one of three.

Only six.

Billi approached with a flashlight in her hand, its beam

aided by the full moon and the red lights on the Crystal Palace radio aerial. It loomed over her like a giant black spike stabbing the sky.

The rusty chains groaned as he swayed back and forth, watching her.

Maybe it's not him. Maybe he's just some normal kid.

Maybe I don't have to murder him.

He looked normal. Tatty Nike trainers, a pair of jeans with an elastic waist, and a blue and burgundy Crystal Palace top.

A local boy.

Normal, except for the marks on his neck. His white throat was circled with dark purple bruises.

Billi drew a deep breath and crossed over the old fence boundary, her heart hammering hard against her ribs. The gravel playground was scattered with litter: old cans, moldy newspapers, and brittle brown leaves that had blown down from the skeletal trees at the top of the hill. But the corruption was more than just gentle aging. All the signs were here.

Of a desolation: a place of evil. Innocent blood had been spilled, tainting the soil itself. Billi thought, if she dared to listen, she might still hear dying screams echoing in the wind, and the leaves rustling with a child's last breath. The earth seeped with a sweet oily vapor. It tinged the air, but as Billi passed the threshold it doubled in thickness, until after a few steps her lungs felt as if they were drowning in it. The few flowers and weeds that had broken through the gravel were gray and malformed. Glossy black beetles scuttled their armored bodies over the stones, and fat white luminescent worms writhed under her feet.

"Hello," said the boy.

"Hello," said Billi.

The boy looked at her. He was missing a lower front tooth, but otherwise his baby teeth formed a soft, easy smile.

Just like the photo.

I could still be wrong.

But with each step closer, she knew she wasn't. It was the bruises.

Billi stopped a few feet in front of him. The marks still held the impressions of fingers, even after all this time.

"Have you come to play?" he asked.

Look into his eyes. That's what they'd told her. Wasn't it one of the first lessons she'd learned in the Order? The windows of the soul. She'd often stared at her own black orbs, wondering what really lay behind them. Maybe only more darkness.

The boy got off the swing, and Billi stepped backward; she couldn't help it.

He looked up at her, catching the moon full on his plump, gap-toothed face. His eyes shone like mirrors, like a cat's eyes. Billi pulled off her hood and tucked a loose black lock behind her ear. She was tall for fifteen, and Alex was small for six, so she squatted down to his level, her boots creaking. She gazed into the boy's eyes, looking for something real, something alive.

But there was nothing. Just an empty reflection.

It's him.

"I'm sorry, Alex. I've come to take you back."

"How do you know my name?"

What didn't she know about him? She'd read the old newspapers, trawled through the library archives for a week. Even watched the faded eight-millimeter home movie, a flickering yellow-tinged illusion of life on a white bedsheet.

Alexander Weeks. Six years old. No. 25 Bartholomew Street. Pupil at St. Christopher's Primary School. Brother to Penny.

Last seen in 1970.

"But I just got here. I want to see my mummy."

Only son of Jennifer and Paul Weeks. Billi remembered them sitting with her dad in the church, showing him their old photo album. Telling him how they still dreamed of Alex even now.

How some nights they saw his face outside their window.

"I know you do. But you can't stay here."

She'd argued she was only fifteen, a year below age. But her dad had insisted. It was time. The Ordeal. Her last test before she was initiated into the Order.

And no one argued with Arthur SanGreal.

She'd always expected her Ordeal to be a Hot Meet. A

fight, lots of sound and fury. Why else all those years practicing sword fighting with Percy? She was finally ready for a duel against one of the real Unholy. A loony, fang-face, even an infernal, maybe. Like a real warrior.

Not this.

Not killing a little kid.

Alex took another step. "Why? It's not fair!"

The swings on either side of him rattled on their chains, agitated. Billi tensed. Goose bumps crept along her arms, even under her fleece. Alex radiated coldness.

"I know, son."

Billi spun around.

Her father strode over the broken fence and walked toward them. A flash of anger shot through her. He'd promised just to watch, not intervene. Maybe he didn't think she could do it.

Billi glanced at the boy she was about to kill, sitting small and scared on the swing.

Maybe her dad was right.

Arthur was wearing his suit, his one and only suit. Dark blue and shiny from use, the stitches strained against his compact and muscular frame. In his left hand he held a scabbard, in his right, a sword. Three and a half feet long, its pommel was a thick iron disk bearing the Order's symbol: two knights on a single horse. The broad blade gleamed ghost-silver in the moonlight. It was a brutal weapon made for hacking.

The boy looked at him. "Have you come to kill me too?"

Arthur stopped halfway between them and the fence and discarded the scabbard. His pale face broke into a smile, but it was thin and half hidden in his black beard. And there was no gentleness in his icy blue eyes.

"No, lad. You know I can't." He glanced at Billi. "You're already dead."

"It's not fair!" The swings were thrashing and clanging now, and the merry-go-round creaked to life, turning slowly, grinding its rusty axle against its corroded socket.

"The man said I could feed the birds! The man said—"

"He's been punished for what he did," said Arthur.

"Is he in Hell?" asked Alex.

"I promise you he is." Arthur's knuckles turned white as they tightened around the sword hilt.

The boy wailed. "I didn't want to die!" He held up his hands. "Please, let me stay." Crystal tears dribbled down his face, and his mouth and chin wrinkled in misery. "It's dark and I'm all alone! It's dark and I'm scared!" He stepped nearer, begging.

He's just a little boy. . . .

"No, Billi!" shouted Arthur, but too late. Billi dropped to her knees and embraced Alex. She pulled him close to her heart and—

the chill seeps into her pores, saturating her skin with ice.

Like venom, black ichor floods her veins, pumping her with Alex's despair, envy, and

HATE

that he was snatched from the sunlight by sweaty hands and crushing fingers, in the dirt and fallen leaves, never to feel the

WARMTH

he misses so much and wants more than anything, and so he sucks it from her, leaving only coldness that is brittle and bone-deep, the air out of her lungs white frost, and her

FLESH

blisters, and tears freeze on her cheeks, and she stares into Alex's eyes, black and malice-filled, remembering only the

AGONY

that he cannot forget, and it eats him, an abysmal virus that he can't contain, so she must

SUFFER

like he did, and the cold burns her heart as he infests her with his darkness, burrowing deeper and—

Powerful fingers dug into Billi's shoulders and ripped her free. Arthur tossed her away from the boy, and she tumbled to the gravel, slamming down hard on her cheek.

She was frozen, her body trembling with the deep chill.

Possession. It had tried to possess her. It wasn't Alex. Not anymore. She tried to stand, but her legs wouldn't bend; they felt as brittle as icicles.

"Billi!" shouted Arthur.

There was a loud crack as the wooden swing seat broke apart, and the two loose chains lashed out. Billi ducked as one whipped out above her, but Arthur took a blow across his forehead. The sword flew away, he stumbled, then was lifted off the ground as the chain wrapped itself around his neck and tightened.

Arthur dangled from the swing's A-frame: a perverse playground gallows. He clawed at the noose, his face turning deep red.

"Let him go!" screamed Billi. She bent forward, hoisting herself onto her feet, legs quivering like spaghetti.

But Alex wasn't listening. There was a black, savage fire inside him, and he freed a bestial howl as her dad dangled on the end of the chain. The cry sliced Billi's skin like daggers.

Alex could never have made a sound like that. No child could.

The sword stood between them, point buried into the ground, upright like a steel crucifix.

"Please, Alex!" Billi begged. Arthur's hands dropped, and he went limp.

But Alex, or the thing pretending to be a living boy, just laughed and waved his arms, a mad puppeteer with her dad's heavy body as his doll.

Billi charged, ripping the sword free in a shower of dirt and insects. Alex turned, and she kicked him in his chest, knocking him over.

Grip reversed, she held the sword above him, tip pointed down.

"God forgive me," she whispered, plunging the blade into the child's heart.

The shriek tore the sky apart, and Billi shuddered, but her fingers tightened around the wire-bound sword hilt. Black bile erupted from the wound, alive almost, saturating her clothes and face. She choked as droplets of ectoplasm splashed into her mouth and down her throat.

She drove the sword deeper, pinning Alex to the earth.

Leaning onto the pommel, she fumbled in her pocket with one hand and pulled out a small silver bottle. Her sweaty fingers wouldn't open the stopper, so she bit it off. Then she smeared the clear oil onto her fingers.

Alex stared, eyes huge, as Billi tossed the empty bottle away. She released the sword and dropped to her knees beside him.

"No, Billi! Please! I don't want to go!" He punched and screamed and scratched as she tried to hold his head still enough to mark it with the cross. He pulled her black hair and spat out stinking oily gore.

"Exorcizo te, omnis spiritus immunde, in nomine Dei Patris omnipotenti," she intoned. Locking his head still with her left hand, Billi pressed her first two right fingers on his forehead, then chin, and finally both cheeks.

"Please, Billi. Let me stay. Just a little longer," he whimpered.

Billi tried to ignore the desperation in Alex's voice. She had to finish this. *"Ego to linio oleo salutis in Christo Jesu Domino nostro, ut habeas vitam aeternam!"*

Billi leaped away as Alex's body spasmed. Bile poured out of his eyes, nostrils, ears, mouth—great jets of bubbling noxious fluid that filled the air with the stink of brutal death. Alex's cries weakened as the outpouring diminished, his body eroding before her.

"What have you done?" he hissed, eyes blazing with demonic madness.

"Deus vult," Billi whispered. It was the Order's battle cry, but right now it seemed more like a curse.

God wills it.

He gave a final scream, then the last of Alex faded away. A pale outline lingered for a moment before, in the sigh of a breeze, it disappeared. Billi stared at the empty spot. Only a black stain remained, and a vile odor. She pressed her hands against her face.

I killed him.

She'd passed the Ordeal; she should be elated. She'd trained so long and hard for this.

Instead she felt sick and hollow.

Arthur crashed to the ground, free from the now lifeless chains. He shook with a dry rasping cough, then slowly rose to his feet. He stumbled over and stood beside her, inspecting the dark outline.

"Well done. A clean kill," he croaked, rubbing his

bruised neck. Then he saw her covered in slimy gore. "Figuratively speaking."

He wrapped his fingers around his sword and worked it back and forth until it came free. He wiped the blade with an old rag, inspecting the edge inch by inch for any new nicks or cracks. Finally he nodded with satisfaction and, on retrieving the scabbard, slipped the weapon in.

"How was school?" he said.

"What?"

"School. You did go, didn't you?"

"School? How can you talk about school after what I've just done!"

"Done? What you've done is free a tortured soul. Whatever it looked like, whatever it said, that was not Alex Weeks. It was a spirit of pain feeding on the agonies this place has absorbed. Nothing more than a corrupt after-image of that poor boy's last moments." He glanced at the broken swings. "The dead should not linger."

The ground swayed as she stood, and her guts churned. She sucked in the cold night air, but something putrid bubbled in her stomach. Arthur put his hand awkwardly on her shoulder. "How d'you feel?"

She wanted to laugh. She stumbled toward the boundary, clutching her belly. The ectoplasm writhed inside her like serpents, slithering up her throat.

"I feel—"

She dropped to her knees and puked. It was black.

Her body buckled under each discharge. Arthur squatted down beside her and drew out a crinkled packet of cigarettes. “Yes, it was the same for me the first time.” He lit one. “Welcome to the Knights Templar.”

2

BILLI CRASHED DOWN ONTO THE BACKSEAT OF HER dad's battered gray Jaguar. Her eyelids began to droop the moment her cheek touched the worn leather. The seat shivered when the engine chugged into life, as though the old car needed an awakening shrug before moving. Her father was still talking, but she couldn't make any sense out of it, what with Radio 4 crackling out of the speakers and the dull drone of the engine. It was all Templar stuff he was talking about anyway, and she'd had enough of that for tonight. More than enough.

The vehicle began to rock rhythmically, and her eyes closing, Billi finally gave in to exhaustion.

* * *

She pretends to be asleep. She hears the door creak open, and a sliver of light cuts across the room and her bed. Billi keeps her eyes closed and lets her breath slip in and out, ever so gently.

The floorboards groan, despite the visitor's attempt at silence. She doesn't need to see to know who it is. A hand brushes the hair away from her face, and she picks up the familiar scent of sweat, oil, and old leather.

Dad.

"They're waiting, Art," comes a loud whisper from beside the door. The voice is deep and soft: Percy, her godfather.

The hand straightens her duvet and rests momentarily on her shoulder. Then her dad sighs and turns away. Moments later the door closes and darkness returns.

Billi waits unmoving for a minute, then slides out of bed. She's tall for her age, but slender. The floorboards don't even squeak as she crosses them. Then she's at the door, listening.

Muffled voices murmur from beyond. She can't make out any words, but there's the scrape of chair legs on bare wood and the sound of a water tap running: they're in the kitchen, downstairs.

Billi understands what she's doing is wrong, but she must know. Her dad is lying to her.

Why?

Why are there half-burned bandages in the fireplace? Bloodied bandages.

Where does he go when he thinks she's asleep?

And why does she fear he might never come back?

Billi opens the door and darts through the narrow gap. She scurries along the short corridor, crouches at the top of the stairs, and listens.

"If the boy is right, we've got no choice."

It's her dad; he sounds tired. What boy? It can't be anyone from school. None of the other parents let their children play with her anymore. Maybe it's that boy Father Balin brought last week. That skinny boy with the huge blue eyes and white hair. What was his name? She remembers.

Kay.

"A girl? In the Order? That's not foolishness, that's heresy!" The voice is hard and full of rage: Gwaine. Why is he always so angry? He and her father used to be friends.

"Art, at least give her a few more years of freedom. She's only ten," says Percy.

They're talking about her! Billi catches her breath. She wants to hear everything. She puts a foot on the step and shifts her weight onto it slowly. She takes another silent step, then another, and soon she's at the bottom, waiting beside the door.

The tap runs, and water rattles inside a kettle.

"You know what the Jesuits say," someone says, in the slight Welsh-tinged accent of her babysitter, Father Balin. "Give me a boy of seven and I'll give you the man."

There's a snarl from Gwaine. "We're not bloody Jesuits! We're—"

"Enough. I've made my decision," says her dad, and everyone shuts up. It's like they're afraid of him. Why? He's not important. He's just a porter, here at the Middle Temple, like Percy and Gwaine. He fixes things. He tends the gardens and waters the plants in the halls. Doesn't he?

"D'you think I'm happy with this? With what she'll have to go through?"

Why are they talking about her? Is she going to have to change schools again?

Peeking through the narrow gap, she sees Father Balin put the old steel kettle on the electric stove. Percy, Gwaine, and her dad sit around the kitchen table. She momentarily glimpses something metallic and bright on top of it, then Percy, who's the biggest person Billi knows, shifts his seat and blocks her view. But as the giant African moves, she spots something else. Something wrapped up in a black plastic garbage bag—something that drips blood.

Gwaine slowly grinds his head side to side like a bull about to charge. "Just because you're Master doesn't give you the right to make decisions like that, Art."

Master? What's Gwaine talking about? Master of what?

"Actually, Gwaine, being Master gives me exactly that right."

Gwaine jerks forward. "For the last nine hundred years the Order has followed the Templar Rules, ever since Bernard de Clairvaux. You can't just discard them and make up your own!"

Arthur leans back into his chair, arms folded across his chest, his fingers slowly flexing into fists, then loosening. Billi glances from her dad to Gwaine and back again. Gwaine's face is bullet-hard, his skin blotchy with rage. Her dad looks back at him, unblinking and impassive except for his cool eyes burning under his dark brow.

"I can, and I have," Arthur points to the priest. "Balin, she'll study Latin, ancient Greek, and occult lore with you."

"And religious duties of course?" asks Balin.

Arthur hesitates, then slowly nods. "Of course." He slaps Percy's massive shoulder. "Percival, weapons training."

Billi sees a thin smile on Percy's lips. He's wearing the red scarf she bought him for Christmas, but around his neck it's like a ribbon around an oak tree.

"Of course," he says. "Any preference? Swords, daggers, quarterstaff?"

"Everything," replies Arthur. "I'll teach her unarmed combat."

"Arthur, I'm begging you. Please reconsider," Gwaine says. He won't give up. "Remember what happened to Jamila."

Billi starts as he mentions her mum. The room is silent and she looks toward Arthur. He stands, rigid. Even now, five years after her mum's murder, Billi can see the pain splashed across his face.

Arthur jabs his finger at Gwaine. "History and Arabic."

Gwaine leaps to his feet, his face bright red. "Your arrogance killed your wife, and your arrogance will kill your daughter too!"

Billi screams as Arthur's fist blurs the short distance across the table, smashing Gwaine's jaw and hurling him off his stool. Gwaine crashes down hard, knocking into Balin and sending the tray of mugs into the air and down onto the tiled floor. Billi screams again as the mugs shatter and tea splashes everywhere.

But the others ignore the broken crockery and stare at her.

Chair legs screech harshly as they slide across the floor, and Arthur stands. His face is cool, blank, and frightening. He points at a spot in front of him. "Here. Now."

Gwaine struggles to stand, ignoring Percy's offer of help. "Little sneak. How long has she been listening—"

"Shut it, Gwaine," says Percy. He slides his hand over his smooth bald head, from forehead down to the back of his neck. His fingers dip into his denim collar, which he loosens with a sigh.

Billi's and Gwaine's eyes meet, and red anger wells up in her chest. He's wrong. Her mum's death was not her father's fault. He'd loved her. He'd never have hurt her. And he'd never hurt Billi. She knows what they whisper at the school gates, but it's not true. Her dad was innocent. The judge said so.

It takes forever for her to cross the room. She looks up at Percy for reassurance—nothing bad will happen to her if he's here—but his usually friendly expression is gone. Instead his face is hard emotionless rock.

She stops in front of her dad and forces herself to meet his stern eyes. When she does, she can't stop her legs from shaking.

"Why were you spying?" he asks. It's strange how when her dad is angry, his voice becomes quiet and flat.

"I . . . just wanted to know."

"What?"

Billi takes a deep breath. Everything. She wants to know everything. But where to begin? Why did Gwaine say that? Why are they talking about her like this? That's where she'll begin—with him.

"Where you go. What you do."

Arthur gazes silently at her for the longest time. It's as though he's searching her eyes for something. Finally he gives a curt nod.

"Then look," he says, "at what I do," and steps away from the table.

Billi gasps. Lying across the dark oak table is a sword. It's huge. The blade is wider than her hand, and the whole thing's as tall as she is. The pommel is nearest, and she can see that its face is engraved with an image: two knights astride a single horse. Though the blade has been wiped, traces of blood smear the polished steel.

Next to the sword is a large, long-barreled revolver. Three silver bullets are lined up next to it.

She stares at the weapons. Then turns to her dad.

"You're not . . . bank robbers, are you?"

Arthur looks scornful but says nothing. He unwraps the black package.

Billi can barely hold in the scream when she sees the severed limb within.

It's a dog's forepaw. Thickly muscled, gray-furred, with savage yellow claws as long as her fingers; the dog must have been the size of a lion!

"You killed a dog?"

"A wolf," says Arthur. "Show her, Balin."

Balin gently lifts the silver crucifix off his neck, and with it clenched tightly in his right fist, he touches the paw with his left palm.

"Exorcizo te," *he whispers, then stands back.*

Billi watches the paw. Nothing happens.

Is this some joke? She half expects them all to burst out laughing at how they've managed to scare her.

The paw curls. The thick nails retreat into the flesh, and the wiry gray hairs thin and sink into the skin. The limb twists and mutates, changing form and color. The hairs have all but gone, leaving pallid white flesh. The paw is now a five-fingered hand, and the limb no longer the front leg of a giant wolf, but the forearm of a man. Billi's entire body trembles, and her skin is coated in a chill sweat. She wants to run away and bury her head under her pillows, but can't take her eyes off the severed arm.

"Touch it," says Arthur.

"No!"

"Touch it."

Billi looks at it. It's stopped changing now. She can see that the fingernails, though overgrown and encrusted with dirt, are normal nails, not claws. The arm, the same. She stretches out her hand, wary that it might spring to life and grab her.

But it doesn't. She lowers her hand and rests it on the skin. It feels dead . . . like meat. No so different from chicken fresh from the butcher's. Cold, a bit hard, but now not an arm, just dead material. Her heartbeat, running at a hundred miles an hour seconds ago, slows down, and the shivering gradually stops.

Just dead meat.

She moves back, and Arthur wraps it up. He rests his hand on her shoulder and looks deep into her eyes.

"Fear makes the wolf seem bigger."

The predawn chill nibbled the back of Billi's neck and dragged her out of her dream. More than a dream—an old memory. Five years ago and it was still crystal sharp. She remembered Gwaine glowering at Arthur afterward, and the halfhearted apology for the accusation he'd made. But the bad blood between them lingered even now. She didn't remember much else before then. It was as if that night had been the beginning of her life. She groaned and curled up on the seat, trying to block the draft coming through the open door.

"We're home," said Arthur. "Grab some breakfast. It'll be matins in an hour."

Why? She still didn't understand why they needed to go through all this. The Templars were heretics—officially they weren't even proper Christians. But her father had told her that believing in God wasn't the same as believing in religion. Still, the prayers, the exorcism rites, and the crucifixes worked in their fight, so Billi had learned them in the same way she'd learned the sword. Prayer and blade were their tools against the Unholy.

Billi glanced at her watch: 5:33. The birds weren't even

up and he wanted her at dawn prayers? Wasn't it enough she'd spent the night fighting a ghost? She watched him open the trunk and lift out the Templar Sword. He half drew it from the scabbard, then slammed it back.

"Can't I get special dispensation? Y'know, after the Ordeal?"

Arthur shook his head. "All the more reason you should be at prayer, giving thanks."

Thanks? For being possessed? Thanks for what she did? She tried to remind herself that she hadn't killed a six-year-old boy, just a bitter malevolent spirit in the guise of a child, but it was hard. Billi slid off the seat and onto her feet, arms wrapped around her chest. It was still dark, and the cold breeze carried a hint of winter. She shivered.

"Stop that," Arthur said. "A Templar does not tremble." Their eyes met. He couldn't look down on her the way he used to—she was too tall. Maybe he wasn't really her dad. It would explain a lot; they couldn't be more different. She was like her Pakistani mum had been: tall, skinny, and dark-eyed. He was broad with a pale craggy face made hard from years of fighting, dominated by those psycho blue eyes. His hair wasn't pure black anymore—now it was heavily spiked with gray. He gave the slightest shake of his head, then turned and walked off.

Billi fought the urge to give him the finger. "Coming," she muttered.

She crossed the cobbled courtyard of King's Bench

Walk, weaving through the few cars still parked there, trailing after her dad toward their house on Middle Temple Lane. The Templars still owned a few dwellings in Temple District, and the narrow Edwardian house was one of them. The paint on the window frames was peeling, the brick-work needed re-pointing, and the roof tiles were uneven and patchy. Above the red-painted door was a small alcove. In it sat a carving of Saint George slaying a dragon. Arthur unlocked the door, and Billi came in behind him.

Her dad flicked on the hallway light, illuminating the faded carpet that led to the spiral stairs at the far end of the room.

"What, no balloons?" Billi asked drily.

"You want balloons, join the circus."

Typical. This was what he had wanted. But not a word of praise. All the other Templars had been recruited as adults. Only she and Kay had joined as children. Kay, the one friend she'd had. But even he was gone now, sent away by her father.

Billi walked along the dimly lit hallway, passing portraits of the ancient Grand Masters of the Order and scenes of famous battles. She paused by Jacques de Molay, the last Templar Grand Master, and hung up her coat on a nearby hook. There he stood, splendid in his armor and white mantle, the bright red cross upon his white tabard, hand resting on a sword.

What would he make of the Order now? A handful of

warriors, near destitute, living in secret and led by her dad, an ex-criminal and altogether rubbish parent? She shook her head. He'd make nothing of them. The original Order was long gone, with Jacques de Molay dying a heretic and Devil-worshipper, burned at the stake by the Inquisition.

It had been hard trying to understand how the Templars, created by the Church to protect it, had ultimately been destroyed by Rome. Arthur and Gwaine still argued over it. Billi would be upstairs, trying to sleep or do homework, and she'd hear the two of them shouting at each other. Gwaine wanted the Templars to "return to the fold," as he put it, to re-establish the Order as defenders of Christendom. Arthur said the Templars' job was to defend all of humanity.

Arthur disappeared into the kitchen on the first floor, but Billi continued up to the second and kicked off her boots before wandering into the bathroom. The pipes rattled as she twisted the hot tap of the bath.

While the steam rose, she inspected tonight's bruises. The one on her cheek was a fluorescent purple; there was no way she'd hide that with makeup.

Damn. The school welfare officer was suspicious enough.

The cut across her knee from Monday's sword practice had almost closed—she was lucky she hadn't needed stitches—but there was a fierce red welt across her ribs, courtesy of Percy and his quarterstaff. She twisted slowly, wincing as her muscles slid under her skin.

At least there's no broken ribs. She stared at herself until she vanished into the hot fog. Then she turned and, bone-weary, climbed into the bath.

Dressed and fed, Billi set off for matins. She'd found a box of chocolates from Percy in her bedroom, a "Congratulations on surviving your Ordeal and not being dead" present. Nothing from Dad—*quelle surprise*.

She'd hoped there'd be something from Kay. She hadn't heard from him in over a year, but surely he'd try to get in touch for this, at least. Instead . . . nothing. Not even a card or a text. Some friend. Billi kicked a can across the courtyard. Friends. She didn't need them.

She gazed up at Temple Church and, like always, paused. It stood wrapped in the dawn mist, the pale yellow and orange walls glowing like an eggshell in the weak autumn dawn. The flagstones glistened with frost, and the vaulting stained-glass windows along the high walls seemed like portals to the underworld set in gates of polished black marble.

"This way! Quickly, Mrs. Higgins." Billi glimpsed a dash of scarlet from beyond the columns of the cloisters off Church Court. Suddenly a dozen figures spewed out, led by a tall woman wearing a bright red mackintosh. She headed for the Templar column, a thirty-foot-high stone post bearing the Order's emblem.

Half past six. It must be the Monarch Tour group. Only they started this early.

The tour guide did a quick head count, then clapped her hands as if she were addressing a bunch of school kids instead of a group of white-haired tourists. She cleared her throat.

"The building behind you is Temple Church and was once the heart of the London preceptory: the English headquarters of the Poor Fellow-Soldiers of Jesus Christ of the Temple of Solomon, better known as the Knights Templar. Founded by Hugues de Payens in 1119, they took their name from their base on Temple Mount in Jerusalem, believed to be the ruins of the original Temple of Solomon. They were warrior monks sworn to protect pilgrims in the Holy Land. Originally comprising only nine men, the Order soon grew to become one of the most powerful organizations in Europe."

Hands began to wave frantically. One woman, with pale blue hair and silver framed glasses, pushed her way to the front of the crowd, arms flapping.

"We'll find you a bathroom in a minute, Mrs. Higgins," said the guide. "This church was consecrated in 1185, but has been extensively modified since—not least of all by the Luftwaffe, who bombed it in 1941. But it was from places such as this that the Order declared its crusades and holy wars. Yes, Mrs. Higgins?"

The woman pushed her chin up.

"They say the Knights Templar found treasures in the Holy Land. Is that true?"

The guide snorted. "There are hundreds of conspiracy theories and legends regarding the Templars, but the truth is very mundane. They were a highly trained, fanatical military force, sworn to defend Christendom, that grew very rich and very envied."

Billi suppressed a laugh. Fanatical wasn't the half of it. A Templar wouldn't retreat until outnumbered three to one. He would accept no ransom nor allow himself to be captured alive.

"What happened to them?" shouted someone from the crowd.

The guide looked up at the two iron knights on top of the column. "The first Temple of Solomon was built in 960 BC to house the Arc of the Covenant. By the time of the Crusades, when the Templars established their base in Jerusalem, the original temple was long gone. Still, whispers sprang up about occult treasures they were said to have found during excavations of Temple Mount."

Billi watched as the tourists leaned closer. Everyone loved a good conspiracy.

"Enemies, both within the church and outside of it, said they were black magicians, others said they had made pacts with devils and other supernatural beings. How else to explain their meteoric rise?"

Oh God, what rubbish. Billi couldn't believe people still thought that. The Templars were sworn to *fight* the Unholy, not to ally themselves with them.

The guide pointed at the church. "But it's clear the Templars had heretical leanings. This was to be their undoing." She turned back to the crowd. "On Friday the 13th, October 1307, the entire Order was arrested. Its Grand Master was brought before the Inquisition, and the Templars were tried and found guilty of heresy and Devil worship. Then they were exterminated."

"But I thought some of them escaped," continued Mrs. Higgins as she gazed around the courtyard. Billi's ears pricked at the question. Was it her imagination, or did the old woman look at her?

"Rumors. Only rumors. The Knights Templar are ancient history now." The guide clapped her hands again and moved through the crowd, back toward the cloisters. "Quick now. We've got to be at Buckingham Palace in thirty minutes."

How many times had Billi heard that story? A hundred? A thousand?

Some of it was true, of course. The Order had been formed to defend the Holy Land, but that battle had been lost long ago. Their war wasn't for Jerusalem, not anymore, but for mankind's soul. Their war was against the supernatural evil that preyed on humanity. A war they called The Dark Conflict.

The Bataille Ténébreuse.

Their endless, unwinnable war.

Billi watched the party head back up to Fleet Street and

their waiting bus, all safe in their cocoons of ignorance, unaware of the shadow war being fought around them. A cold wind carried twisting ribbons of mist across the flagstones, like restless ghosts. She stood alone in the cold, but the presence of the old knights lingered in their great preceptory. Who but she, her father, and a few others still remembered the reasons they'd died, or the sacrifices they'd made? Billi pulled her coat tightly around her. Would her own spirit haunt these stones one day? After all, what was the first rule, the first law of the Knights Templar? What was the promise made to a knight when he took on the bloody mantle of the *Bataille Ténébreuse*?

You shall keep the company of martyrs.

3

VOMIT-WORTHY. IT WAS THE ONLY WAY TO DESCRIBE HER day, and it was barely lunchtime. She'd fallen asleep during geography and earned herself another detention. She'd made up an excuse about her math homework—better than telling Ms. Clarke she couldn't even remember being given any. How could she? Every evening was bloody Latin, ancient Greek, and occult lore—the hierarchy of Hell—and every morning was weapons practice and unarmed combat. Maybe the reason homework always slipped her mind was because of the countless blows to the head she'd received over the last five years. Fifteen and punch-drunk. And these were meant to be the best days of her life.

She'd been excited at first, being part of something big, mystical, the stuff of legend. Being part of the Knights Templar and their secret war against the enemies of mankind. The Unholy.

The beast within: mortals with the heart of the wild.

The hungry dead: corpse-eaters and blood-drinkers.

The ghosts: spirits of pain.

The devils: tempters of humanity.

And the Grigori: dark angels.

But soon she was lying to her friends, missing classes, gathering bruises and cuts, drifting apart from the other children. The cruel rumors about her mum's murder emerged, quickly circulating around the lonely playgrounds. When she'd brought her troubles to Arthur, he'd dismissed them. She was a Templar now—that was all that mattered.

So she learned to keep the teachers' concerns at bay; she hid the worst injuries, she didn't get so many black eyes now, and managed most days without nodding off at her desk. But Billi was drifting through her school years like a ghost, barely awake in class, her whole life absorbed by other duties. Could she have said she wanted out? To be normal? Have friends? Have no more bruises? No more nightmares? No. Her dad would never allow it.

Billi gazed down the line at the food counter, her stomach rebelling against the stale, lukewarm odors rising from the faded boiled carrots, the gray-looking gravy, and the assortment of fried and coated offal. The shrink-wrapped sandwiches looked no more appealing; their corners were curled and their fillings smeared under the plastic. All that was left was the fruit basket: a couple of wrinkly apples and bruised bananas.

I should be at home. She felt flushed and clammy; maybe some of that ectoplasm was still there, bubbling away in her guts. The line shuffled along, and Billi picked through the sandwiches. The least offensive ones were cucumber on white bread. She took them and the two remaining bananas. She added a bottle of water and, tray balanced on one hand, dug into her blazer pocket for her lunch voucher. She handed it to the cashier and looked for an empty seat.

"Oh look, it's the free-meal freak," said someone to her left. Someone she recognized.

Just fan-tas-tic. Like her day wasn't bad enough. Billi turned toward the voice.

"Lovely to see you too, Jane," she replied. "I see you've got your hench-bitches with you today. Didn't realize the zoo had day release."

Jane Mulville leaned against a dining table, her skinny legs blocking Billi's path. Michelle Durant and Katie Smith, her bottle-blonde clones, stood on either side.

"Jeez, what happened to your face?" asked Jane. Despite the foundation, the bruise on Billi's cheek still shone through.

I really don't need this, not today, thought Billi. She could rearrange Jane's face with minimal effort, and sometimes, like now, the urge to flatten that dainty little nose was nigh irresistible.

"It's her dad, I bet." Katie giggled. "He's way mental."

Billi's gaze dropped to where Jane's legs still barred her way. "Do you mind?" she asked.

"Yeah, we mind a lot, SanGreal. Why they haven't expelled you by now, I don't know. Doesn't say much for the standards in this school that they let the likes of you in." She looked Billi up and down. "I mean, even the other weirdos here don't want anything to do with you."

"Have you met her dad? Not surprising she's turned out this way," said Katie.

Jane smiled. "Is it true, SanGreal? That your dad killed your mum? That's what they all say, isn't—"

Billi's tray clattered on the hard wooden floor, the sharp noise instantly silencing all the background hubbub. As one, the students in the hall fell silent.

They still believed that old lie, that her dad had murdered her mother. But then, would they believe the truth? That she'd been killed by *ghuls*, the hungry dead? That she'd died protecting Billi, leaving bloody handprints smeared over her bedroom door, where she'd been hidden? No, they'd never believe *that* truth.

"What did you say?" asked Billi. Her question was barely above a whisper. Her hands free now, they curled themselves into tight, solid fists. In the silence, her breathing seemed loud, and she could hear the blood thundering in her ears. "Sorry, Jane, I didn't quite catch that." She spoke slowly, pronouncing every word. She assessed Jane's features, not as a seamless whole, but as an assembly of disjointed, breakable parts. The tiny nose, the perfect teeth, the dainty chin. It would be so easy.

Katie and Michelle took small steps away from Jane, sensing the threat of violence radiating from Billi. The hall, silent already, now stopped breathing. Jane's hands trembled, but she braced herself against the table, the fingers beneath her red nails going white as they pressed against the shiny Formica surface.

"Billi!"

Billi was spinning at the shout when a pair of arms wrapped themselves around her. She tried to free herself, but all she could make out was a thick mass of silvery-blond hair as the person embraced her. She finally pushed him off.

"Miss me?" the boy asked. He was tall, knife-lean, and albino-white. Any paler and Billi would have had to stake him.

"Kay?"

He winked.

Billi stepped back. It couldn't be. He'd been such a scrawny bag of bones when he'd left. Now he was taller, and the wispy beginnings of a beard collected on his chin. His sapphire-bright blue eyes hadn't changed.

"Look who's back, the Thin White Puke," Jane butted in. Kay turned toward her.

"Jane, what an unpleasant surprise." He frowned. "You put on weight?"

Jane paled. It was probably the most insulting thing anyone could say to her. Kay looked her square in the eyes and Jane quieted. Once the merest glance from her would have cowed him. This was new.

Kay's frown twisted into a cruel smile. "A few pregnancy pounds around the hips."

"What?" gasped Jane, groping her belly. Katie and Michelle leaned closer. So did the six other students around the nearest table. This sounded good.

Kay continued. "It's Dave Fletcher, isn't it?"

Jane backed away, knocking over the plate of beans and mashed potatoes that Michelle was holding. The slimy orange sauce covered her skirt and slid slowly down her black tights, smearing them in grease. Kay held out his hand. "Congratulations. You'll make a beautiful couple."

Jane screamed and ran. Katie and Michelle stared open-mouthed, then turned and ran after her. There was a long silence, then the hall erupted. Jane Mulville was pregnant!

Kay bent down to retrieve Billi's sandwiches.

"She's really going to have a kid?" Billi asked. She watched him stand up, still shocked over the change. Not just physically, but the way he carried himself now, the way he'd just handled Jane.

"In a few months." He handed over the slightly dented packets. "Care to join me?"

He acts like he's never been away.

He shrugged. "But now I'm back." He turned and walked to a table in the corner of the hall.

Billi bit her lip. Stupid mistake. Kay wasn't just a Templar, he was an Oracle.

A psychic. Reading minds was the least of his abilities.

"Didn't anyone tell you it's rude to peek?" she said as she dragged out a chair to face him.

"You never answered my question, Billi."

"What question?"

"Did you miss me?"

"A year, Kay." Billi didn't look up from her meal; it was the only way she'd keep her temper. "And did you even once try to get in touch?"

"Billi, you know why Arthur sent me to Jerusalem." His lips tightened before he spoke. "I had to learn how to control my abilities."

"And it took every waking minute? Why? Were you in special-ed class?" She ripped open the packet. The sandwiches looked even more lifeless. She sighed. "No. I haven't missed you. You might be surprised to learn that the universe doesn't actually revolve around you." Billi bit into the limp bread. Yummy: cardboard flavor. "When did you get back?"

"Few days ago."

"And you didn't bother to tell me?"

"I had work to do. For Arthur."

So even her dad hadn't told her.

"Once, Kay, us being friends was more important than us being Templars." All those nights she'd snuck over to his house to stay with him until dawn, missing training because of the nightmares. The trouble he'd gotten into helping Billi with her Latin translations, or making up stories at school about how she'd gotten that fat bruise or cut lip. Billi raised her gaze from her food to Kay. He had changed, and not for the better.

Bloody Kay, she thought.

He stood up.

"Same old Billi," he said.

4

THAT EVENING, BILLI MARCHED UP THE STEPS TO Father Balin's house. So Kay was back. So she wouldn't have to sit by herself in class anymore. Big deal. She'd managed the last twelve months just fine without him.

To think, they'd found Kay through social services. She remembered him arriving just before her training had begun. A stick insect of a boy, all nerves and jumping at shadows, nightmares every night and talking to things that weren't there, or at least things normal people couldn't see. And the fits that he never remembered, spouting out all sorts of gibberish in God-knows-what languages. He'd freaked her out big-time telling her about the ghosts he'd spoken to in her bedroom. No wonder he'd been palmed off from one foster home to another. But that wasn't unusual. Powerful psychics always had disturbed childhoods: visions, poltergeist activity, strange apparitions; it would spook most families. Unless the psychics were taught how to harness their powers, they'd eventually be driven mad. How many potential Oracles had the Templars lost over the years? How many had ended their days screaming in asylums, the voices in their heads drowning out their own thoughts?

Father Balin lived in the Chaplain's House, an elegant Georgian building with whitewashed walls, guarded by a tall iron fence, immediately adjacent to Temple Church. Billi walked along the garden path, between two lines of rosebushes, and knocked on the black-painted door. The smell of garlic and roasting peppers breezed over her the moment it opened. Father Balin smiled as he saw her.

"Italian tonight?" asked Billi. "What's the special occasion?" Like she didn't know. She'd survived her Ordeal and gotten a box of chocolates. Kay'd come back from a year's vacation and they were throwing him a party.

"Miss SanGreal. I'd been wondering when you'd turn up." The old man stepped aside. "Kay's here."

"I know." Billi rolled her eyes. *Kay's here*. Big deal. Balin perched his glasses on his bald head. Publicly, he was all that remained of the Templars. As priest of Temple Church, he performed all the normal services and day-to-day operations of the church itself. His official title was The Right and Reverend Master of the Temple, but to the knights he was their chaplain, in charge of religious duties.

"Thought you'd be more pleased than that, Bilqis." Only Balin used her proper Islamic name.

The noise of rattling pans, plates, and cutlery came from the kitchen. Percy passed into the hallway carrying a bowl of steaming spaghetti. He winked at her before ducking his head under the chandelier and entering the dining room to the sounds of chatter and further rattling. Billi followed him in.

Moonlight shone in through the windows facing the garden, but the knights were too busy consuming the hot food to admire the colorful collage of plants, shrubs, and flowers that were the priest's masterwork. Billi squeezed onto a chair between Percy and Kay.

Along with Father Balin, there were only four others present: Gwaine, Percy, Kay, and her dad, all elbow to elbow around the small dining table. The rest of them were out in Dartmoor, hunting a loony: a werewolf. Ever since the Bodmin Accord, following Arthur's defeat of the werewolf pack's alpha male, lupine kills had been limited to sheep and the odd cow. But one had gone rogue, started attacking backpackers and hikers. The Templars had gone out to hunt it down. Pelleus was leading the mission, backed up by Berrant, Gareth, and Bors. Billi remembered Bors boasting how he'd skin the werewolf and have its pelt for a rug. The guy was a psycho, but what else would you expect from Gwaine's nephew?

Her dad sat quietly, flicking through a pile of newspaper clippings on his right, and occasionally glancing at the laptop on his left. Gwaine looked up but swept his glance past her as if she didn't exist. Gwaine was Arthur's second-in-command: the seneschal. He was a grizzled old warrior with cropped iron-gray hair and small, suspicious eyes settled deep within wrinkles. By all rights he should have been the Templar Master after Uriens died, not her dad. Gwaine had recruited Arthur and couldn't accept that his squire was now his master. Billi knew the old man was waiting in the wings for his chance to take command of the Knights Templar. He just needed Arthur to die first.

Billi caught a look from Kay, who rolled his eyes; there was no love lost between him and Gwaine, either. Gwaine thought Oracles were only one step away from witches, and the seneschal had Old Testament views on witches.

Thou shalt not suffer the witch to live.

"Any news from Pelleas?" asked Arthur, his eyes still on the screen. Percy sucked up a string of spaghetti before replying.

"Just a whole lot of dead sheep so far. He and Bors are checking the farms, Berrant and Gareth are on the campsites. Reckon it's a nomad passing through, causing trouble."

The beast within. Even a single werewolf was deadly. That's why her dad had sent half the Order. Half! She glanced around the table. Excluding Balin, who wasn't part of the fighting Order, that made nine, just nine of them against the Unholy, against all the supernatural evil lurking in the shadows. And the Knights Templar had once numbered in the thousands. But nine hundred years of endless war had taken its toll. Why did they fight on, in a war that could never be won? Because it was God's will? Billi didn't believe that, and she knew Arthur didn't either. But he said someone had to fight the Unholy. Billi just wished it wasn't her. Now, with so few of them, all it would take was one bad day and that would be it. Wipeout. It had almost happened ten years ago, during the Nights of Iron.

When her mum had died.

Why couldn't Billi remember her? She'd been five, so she should remember *something*. There were just vague images, distant feelings, and an idea that she'd been happy . . . nothing solid. But she knew from the others that the Nights of Iron had been twelve days of horror. The Templars had been hunted down by *ghuls*, starting with the old Master, then Lot the Oracle, and so many more until only Arthur and a handful were left. Arthur's leadership had taken him from a lowly sergeant to Templar Master, but at a terrible cost. A few *ghuls* that had survived Arthur's purges had found his home and murdered his wife. Was it so terrible that Billi had blanked it out?

"What have you got, Art?" asked Percy. Arthur handed over some photos. Billi caught a glimpse as they crossed the table. Bite marks on someone's neck.

"Our Hospitaller brothers took this. A girl fainted outside the Auto de Fe nightclub last night. Thought it might interest us." Arthur and the older knights still referred to their contacts within the St. John's Ambulance service as

Hospitallers, even though they were no longer active in warfare. When the Templars had been hunted by the Inquistion, members of the Order had been hidden within the ranks of the Hospitallers, in honor of the blood both orders had spilled together over the centuries. But now the Hospitallers were sworn to the path of healing, not battle. Even so, some of them aided their brother warriors in gathering information on "unusual" attacks or injuries. Like vampire bites.

A stake and bake, thought Billi. Just as long as she didn't have to do it. The last thing she wanted was to waste a night hunting the hungry dead in some derelict graveyard. This was her last chance to get in her math work, or it would be detention until Christmas.

Percy inspected the photos. "The girl alive?"

"Yes, just." Arthur looked around the table. "Let's nip this one in the bud."

Percy passed the pictures to Gwaine. The seneschal flipped through them slowly.

"We could use some help," he said. "I've got men who'd be ideal—"

"No," Arthur snapped. The two men stared at each other, and Billi saw the way Gwaine's hand unconsciously touched the bread knife. Arthur certainly did.

"You want to add anything, Gwaine?" asked her father.

Gwaine abruptly shook his head.

Billi looked at Kay, and it was obvious he was thinking the same thing.

What was that all about?

"Any idea where he'd be laired, Art?" interrupted Percy, breaking the threatening tension.

Arthur shook his head. "No. But I want you and Percival to find him. Tonight." Then he turned to Billi.

"Now that Kay's back, we'll begin your training in psychic defense." He looked over at Kay. "How's tomorrow?"

"Ideal, sir." Kay straightened in his chair as he addressed Arthur. The stiffness in his back suddenly reminded Billi how much taller he now was. But it wasn't just the height, it was his manner. The nervousness was gone, the fear. Maybe he'd only seemed small because he'd acted small. Billi noticed the focus he had—there was no more stuttering when he addressed her dad or the other knights.

"Good. Eight o'clock at Finsbury Park. You know where to take her, Kay."

Psychic defense? With Kay? Was he really that good now?

"But, Dad, we agreed I'd have the next three nights downtime after my Ordeal. To catch up on homework," Billi said. It wasn't like she was asking for time off to enjoy herself. Oh no, having fun was not in the Templar Rules.

"Not important. You train with Kay." Arthur collected his clippings and slid them back into his folder. "Any other business?" Gwaine gave a curt twitch, and Balin mouthed a silent no, but Percy stood up.

"Just two things, Art." He raised his mug high. "First,

welcome home, young Kay. Life's been exceedingly boring without you. I'm looking forward to hearing all about Jerusalem." Billi didn't miss the way the others looked at Kay, different from the way they used to, before he mattered.

The wise and mighty Oracle. She was surprised they weren't all on their knees in adoration. Pathetic. Then Percy grinned at Billi. "And I'd like to propose a toast to the newest member of the Order. Only fifteen and, if you'll excuse the vernacular, totally badass. Won't be long before we're calling you Master." There was a snort from Gwaine, but Percy ignored it. "To Bilqis SanGreal."

Good old Percy. Always looking out for her. More than once she'd wished he was her dad, instead of just her godfather. The others rose, Gwaine last of all. Even Arthur lifted his teacup slightly.

"To Billi!"

Then Arthur clicked the laptop shut and placed his folder on top of it. "Well, if that's all, I'll leave you to your duties." He tucked them both under his arm and walked out. Balin and Gwaine followed moments after, while Percy helped Billi and Kay stack up the plates.

"What did Gwaine mean about having men?" asked Billi.

Percy scooped up a pile, then paused. "Gwaine thinks we're under-resourced."

"Well, he's right," said Billi.

Percy's eyes narrowed. "But he wants to recruit from the Red Knights."

Billi stopped stacking. The Red Knights were nothing more than a bunch of thugs who used religion as an excuse to go around beating up immigrants. They saw themselves as natural inheritors of the Templar mantle, fighting for Christendom, but their only agenda was terror. Gwaine had tried to use them a year ago on a vampire hunt. Half had fled, the other half had been eaten alive.

"No way that's going to happen. Not with Art in charge," Percy added, almost sounding as if he were trying to persuade himself. He shrugged his shoulders and popped the last sausage into his mouth. Then he lowered his head down from where it almost touched the ceiling to the level of the two squires.

"Play nice, kids," he said. He eyeballed Billi for a long moment, then left.

Kay began lining up the blue china teacups on a tray. Billi didn't help.

"So you're going to teach me some Jedi mind tricks?" She waved her hand limply like a conjurer.

"You heard what your dad said. Don't worry, I'll go easy. I could help you with your homework afterward, if you like."

"Actually, I don't like." He couldn't just turn up and think everything would go back to how it used to be. She couldn't let him know the truth.

That she'd missed him.

5

IT WAS SEVEN THE NEXT NIGHT WHEN BILLI EMERGED from Finsbury Park Station. Cold drizzle fell, and the gutters were stuffed with soggy leaves, causing swollen puddles on either side of the road. She flicked off her hood and spotted Kay by the bus shelter. His black woolen cap was pulled down to his eyebrows, and his silvery hair seemed to glow under the stark fluorescents of the shelter.

"You're late," he said.

"Detention. Again." She shrugged. "But didn't you get my message?" She tapped the side of her head. "I thought it really hard. 'Kay, I'll be late. Kay, I'll be late—' "

"You think this is a joke?" He stood and turned up the collar of his coat. "Let's get a move on. I've wasted enough time already."

They walked down the high street lined with shops hidden behind metal gratings and graffiti-coated roller shutters. The only open shop was the liquor store. A bald man with tattooed arms folded across his hefty stomach stood at the door, a growling pit bull at his heel. It barked at them as they passed, and pulled at the heavy chain around its neck. They turned the corner, and Billi saw it ahead—Elaine's Bazaar—lit by a lone streetlight.

It was a pawnshop, and had been there since the nineteenth century. The three golden orbs that hung above the door had paint flaking off them, but they were the originals. Heavy steel bars covered the dusty windows, displaying hi-fi equipment, DVD players, a set of chrome weights, and a kid's bicycle; the flotsam and jetsam of a thousand bankruptcies and repossessions.

It was also the Templar reliquary.

All these years and she hadn't been here once. But why would she? This wasn't the domain of warriors. It was the domain of sorcerers.

Here lay hidden the last of the treasures of King Solomon. Billi couldn't believe this old hovel was home to one of the greatest magical artifacts of the ancient world. But that was the point—who would ever suspect it?

Billi's mind flashed back to one of the lessons with Balin. When the Inquisition launched their attack on the Order on that fateful Friday the thirteenth, the Grandmaster, Jacques de Molay, had managed to smuggle the Templar treasures, including those found at the Temple of Solomon, to the Order's fleet, docked at the French port of La Rochelle. The fleet sailed out that night. One ship turned up in England, and the knights went into hiding, continuing the *Bataille Ténébreuse* in secret thereafter. Billi's Order was descended from those few knights.

The other ships vanished from history.

The ground floor was dark. A single window was lit in the flat above. Kay rang the bell, and after a few moments the window slid open and an old woman stuck out her head, her gray hair a tangled mess.

"Piss off!"

Kay stepped backward into the glow of the streetlight.

"Elaine, it's me, Kay!"

The woman stared, mouth hanging open.

"Kay?" Suddenly she grinned. "Kay! I'll be right down!"

Billi waited in the doorway as Elaine came downstairs and unlocked the door and then the steel mesh gate.

"My sweet angel! C'mere and give us a kiss!" She threw her bony arms around him and planted a fat wet one on his cheek. Billi saw him go rigid as the old woman's lips slurped freely.

"Hi, Elaine," he said, blushing. They stood in the unlit doorway of the run-down old shop. The wallpaper was faded and peeling, the paint of the ceiling had crumbled into tiny flakes, and the carpet was worn down to wiry threads. Elaine admired Kay, her legs apart and hands on hips like a pirate captain.

"As handsome as ever; the girls must be dropping at your feet."

Billi pushed past Kay into the cluttered shop. "Yes, dropping dead," she said. It annoyed Billi intensely how Elaine, who acted like a cranky old witch with everyone else, turned all soppy with Kay. Just because she'd been in charge of his early training.

"Brought Her Majesty, I see," Elaine scowled. She had the face for scowling: weathered, wrinkled, and stained by fifty years of heavy tar cigarettes. Billi had given up trying to figure out why Elaine didn't like her. She slid past the old woman, found the light, and switched it on.

Junk filled the interior. It had accumulated without any sense of organization: there were battered old trunks, doorless wardrobes, a penny farthing bicycle, and a thousand other useless treasures. They'd probably been in this shop for generations.

"How was Jerusalem?" asked Elaine. "Who did you work with? Rabbi Levison?"

Billi smiled to think what the early Templars would make of their secrets being protected by a Jew. But after the last Templar Oracle had been killed, the Order didn't have anyone psychically trained to guard the reliquary. Gwaine had gone mental when Arthur had nominated Elaine, but Arthur was Master. The old religious war didn't concern the Templars anymore, he said. After all, hadn't the Order been destroyed by fellow Christians? Since then, the only thing that had mattered was the *Bataille Ténébreuse*. But why did Elaine stay? She hated Gwaine with a passion and barely had a kind word for any of the other knights, even Percy. Was it just loyalty to Billi's dad? How did he make people love him when he treated them so badly?

"Him, and others," replied Kay.

"Like who?" Elaine's eyes narrowed with curiosity.

"The Sufis on the West Bank. Spent a month with the Nestorian monks in the Sinai. I learned a lot, Elaine." He glanced away, embarrassed. "About how emotions cloud my focus."

"More than I could ever teach you," said Elaine. She had some psychic talent, but wasn't in the same league as Kay. No one was. Her skills in tarot, astrology, and the occult had come from years of hard work. Skills Kay had been born with. She sighed. "But I suppose this ain't a social call?" She fished out a battered packet of Benson and Hedges from her faded pink dressing gown.

"You suppose right," said Billi. Elaine lit up a cigarette, wrinkling her eyes against the first bite of bitter nicotine.

"C'mon, then, I haven't got all night." She shoved aside a stuffed bear to reveal a door set deep in the wall. She fished out a key from the cord around her neck and needed both hands to turn it in the lock.

The door groaned open. Steps led down into a basement, thick with the smell of slow decay. Elaine flicked the brown Bakelite switch, and there was a hum before the bulb came to life, gradually filling the catacomb with a soft golden glow. Ahead of them stood a large black cabinet. The dim light shone on its bronze hinges and on the ornate patterns laid on its surface with tissue-thin gold leaf, silver, and mother-of-pearl. The images were faded, but Billi could just make out the imps, demons, animal-headed monsters, winged nightmares, and celestial hordes at war across an ebony field. In the center, where the two door leaves met, was a large corroded copper disk, broken in half, bearing a six-pointed star.

The Seal of Solomon.

The mystical ward was the first defense against demons, devils, and angels, the creatures of the Ethereal Realm.

Billi felt a chill as she stared at it. She'd read the earliest Templar diaries, of how Hugues de Payens had found the cabinet and the treasure inside soon after the end of the First Crusade. How he'd taken it and made the Knights Templar the most feared organization in the medieval world. She'd often wondered how exciting it would be to see the treasure for herself. But now, with it in arm's reach, Billi realized it wasn't excitement buzzing in her heart. It was fear.

"It's in there, isn't it?" she whispered. The black cabinet seemed to shimmer, as though it radiated light from within. The chill deepened, and Billi wrapped her arms around her body. What lay behind those ebony doors had been both the source of the Order's power and the reason for their near annihilation by the Inquisition.

"The mirror?" Elaine nodded. "Of course. Where else

would it be?" She turned to Kay. "So, any luck with, y'know, next week's lottery numbers? Or the Grand National winner?"

Kay shook his head. "You know I can't do that. Prophecies aren't my thing."

She paused and looked at him. "No, of course not."

Kay dusted off a stool and slung his coat over it.

"This'll do." He stretched out his arms. "Thanks, Elaine. We'll give you a shout when we're done." Elaine looked at both of them, then nodded and turned away.

Billi waited until Elaine had left. "Why are we here?"

"To help you." Kay pointed into the corners of the room. Billi squinted in the gloom and could just make out markings on the top row of bricks, all the way around the ceiling. They were in cuneiform, the oldest writing in the world, and looked similar to the patterns on the black cabinet. Talismanic protections from *maleficia*: black magic. Kay rummaged around in his coat pocket.

"This chamber is psychically sealed, which prevents anything from being detected. It also dampens any supernatural or psychic powers. Gives you a bit more of a chance."

"Chance?"

He tossed a small red packet to her. Billi caught it: a pack of playing cards. "Shuffle them," he said.

"I didn't know we were here to practice your magic tricks."

"No tricks." Kay's lips tightened into a thin line, and

Billi spotted him rubbing his palms on his trousers. Maybe the old nervousness wasn't completely gone. Billi peeled off the shrink-wrapping and gave the deck a cursory mix.

"No. Shuffle them properly. Use the table."

Billi reluctantly did as she was told. She spread the entire pack over a small coffee table and swirled them around until they were totally jumbled.

"What exactly is the point of this?" she asked.

"Various types of the Unholy have the power to . . . influence thoughts. They can take command of our senses, our memories. Remember what happened with you and the ghost of Alex Weeks?"

"How d'you know about that?" Billi spun around to face Kay, her eyes narrow and sharp.

"I'm an Oracle, remember?"

She bristled. Obviously nothing in her life was private anymore. Could he just dip in and out of her head whenever he liked?

Kay motioned for her to collect the cards and turned his back on her. "I'll teach you to strengthen your mind against undesired intrusion."

"Like yours?"

He sighed. "Just pick a card. Hold it in front of you but try not to think about what it is. Think about anything else. Try to prevent me from seeing the card through your mind."

Billi picked a random card off the table. "Tell me when."

"Three of clubs. Next."

"I wasn't ready!" She threw the three onto the floor. She took the next and held it in front of her.

"Five of diamonds. Next."

"Wait!"

"Four of diamonds. You did shuffle them properly, like I told you?"

Billi shuffled them again. *Right, think about anything except the card.*

"Queen of hearts. Next."

Damn it, this isn't working.

"Don't swear; concentrate on the cards."

She cut the pack twice, a third time, and snapped one out—

"Ace of spades. Next."

"You're not giving me a chance!"

Kay spun around. "Why should I? This isn't a game, Billi! If we were in a fight, would you back off? Take it easy? No, you'd go for the kill." He looked into her eyes, searching her face. "Of course you would. Start again."

"I'm not playing this game," Billi said. Who did he think he was? Her dad? She threw the cards, which scattered into the corners of the room.

"You are such a child," he said. "You don't like it, so you're going to leave, is that it?"

Kay put his hand on her arm, but Billi stepped away.

"Do that again and I'll break it," she said. "While you've been off on your holidays, d'you know what I've been doing? Getting beaten up, getting bruised, battered, and cut. All for the greater glory of the Knights bloody Templar. He wants me to be just like him, Kay." Billi pictured her father's face, hard and forever judging. "He wants it so badly."

"I'm sure he has his reasons, Billi."

Reasons? The reason was simple: her father wanted her to be a Templar. They fought, they struggled, they suffered, and they bled. But she could never bleed enough, not for her dad. He pushed her harder and harder, and she had no choice. Not like the others, not like Kay. *He* wanted this life. She didn't. She'd been given no choice, no praise, no affection, and definitely no reason.

Billi zipped up her jacket. She wasn't going to waste her time here anymore.

"Where are you going?"

She raised her hood over her head. If she rushed she'd still be home before midnight. "You're the psychic one; can't you tell?"

"Stop." The door ahead of her slammed shut. The table beside her began to shake, hopping up and down, and the old swords on the walls clattered against each other.

His wild talent. Telekinesis. This was what first alerted the Templars to Kay's abilities. When he'd been angry as a child, objects had flown across the room.

"Stop it, Kay." Billi felt a coldness seep into the chamber, and goose bumps rose over her skin as the weapons that hung on the walls clashed and fought each other, held by phantom soldiers. Kay's emotions were getting the better of him. Their eyes met.

Kay sighed. The table settled down, and the swords stopped rattling. Billi looked at him.

His jaw was set hard, and he slowly wiped the sweat off his forehead. He'd lost control.

"What is it you want from me, Billi?"

"What makes you think I want anything from you? I've passed the Ordeal. Have you?"

She might as well have slapped him, the way he reddened.

"You know Oracles don't have to pass the Ordeal. We're too . . ."

"The word you're looking for is 'afraid,' isn't it?"

"I am not afraid." But he looked uneasy.

Now he knows how it feels, Billi thought.

She'd been afraid all those times in the past year when he hadn't been there, when she'd needed him. Well, she didn't need him now—not when *she* was searching for vampire graves and following werewolf tracks, and *he* was tucked up at home. Afraid.

"I said, I'm not afraid!" The table flipped and smashed itself against the wall. Billi flung her arms over her head as she was showered with splinters.

When she lowered them, Kay was standing in front of the black cabinet. His fingers traced over the seal.

"You don't know what I can do," he said, eyes fixed on

the six-pointed star. "You think waving a bit of steel around and beating people up is all that matters." His fingers curled around the edge of the door leaf. "You have no idea." He opened it.

What on earth was he doing? Billi grabbed his arm.

"This is stupid," she said. "Don't do it."

Kay snatched his arm away.

"This room's safe, Billi. The wards will protect us." He pointed at the carved symbols on the edges of the wall. "Stop anything from getting out."

He drew out a dark blue velvet box, the type that might contain a necklace. He flicked it open.

Lying inside was a simple, highly polished copper disk, about seven inches in diameter. The Templar seal had been delicately engraved on its surface, and the edges were slightly corroded and green-tinged, but otherwise it glistened in the low light. Kay stared at it and slowly sat down on a stool, holding the box from underneath. He laid it on his lap, then gently touched the copper surface.

It rippled.

The Cursed Mirror.

The last of the Templar treasures. Legend had it that King Solomon had used it to perform his great magics. In Islamic lore he was a master of spirits and commanded angels and devils, all through this mirror. John Dee, the Elizabethan sorcerer and Templar Oracle of his day, had apparently contacted the Ethereal Realm through it. Heaven and Hell had opened up to him. But nobody had that sort of power anymore. Nobody. Kay wouldn't achieve anything. But seeing the cold emptiness of his eyes, Billi felt a prickling chill run through her.

"I'm not joking, Kay. Put it back now."

"I'm just looking," he whispered, more to himself than to her. As his fingers stroked the metal surface, his eyes rolled back, revealing the whites. He let out a long sigh, then slowed his breath to the slightest whisper.

The mirror shimmered, and soft sparkling trails of colored lights followed the path of his fingertips like oil in sunlight. The surface swirled, and Billi thought she could see into dark distant depths within, as if gazing into an infinite whirlpool. The streams of light threw out spinning patterns, and the walls and ceiling became tapestries of chaotic color. A small smile turned the edges of Kay's lips. Billi gazed at the kaleidoscopic display, hypnotized by the ever-transforming melange of reds, yellows, oranges, greens, golds, and so many other twisting tinctures that she became dizzy, but she couldn't take her eyes off it. She wanted to laugh, to cry; she'd never seen anything so beautiful. It was as though the walls, the world itself, were falling away into a universe of color and grace. She turned to kiss Kay for showing her something so utterly amazing.

Kay sat there, his body quivering and froth bubbling on his lips. His teeth were clenched together so hard his gums bled, tainting the froth pink as it dribbled down his chin.

The air around him trembled like a desert mirage, and as the colors spun faster and faster, Billi saw shapes forming from the hurricane of light. They were indistinct, vaguely humanoid, but growing and becoming more solid by the moment. She could see arms, legs, heads taking on definite human proportions, fingers growing on the blobs for hands.

Who summons us?

The voices echoed in her head, and out of the light she saw eyes, bright and keen, peering out at her.

We come. Welcome us.

"Stop," Billi whispered. She gazed around, awestruck.

But Kay didn't hear. His eyes were squeezed shut and he was lost in some distant realm, his mind and soul roaming. More shapes began to coalesce, growing distinct and taking on human form.

Call to us and we will come.

Suddenly furnace-hot air roared from the disk. The wards along the walls glowed an unbearable bright white, and the forms began to take features. Billi saw the black silhouettes build faces, eyes, noses, mouths smiling with delicious eagerness, and voices raised and multiplying until the cacophony became unbearable—

The door crashed open and Elaine charged across the room. Billi saw her mouth widen into a scream but was deaf to everything but the cries piercing her mind. Elaine swatted the mirror out of Kay's hands. He fell backward as the disk spun into the air, crashed against the wall, and rattled on the floor until it finally came to rest.

All the lights had vanished, all except for the dull glow of the single bulb above Elaine's head. Kay lay on his back, staring wide-eyed at the ceiling, panting like he'd run a marathon, his body dripping with sweat, and his white hair lying plastered against his scalp. He forced himself up, though his legs looked as though they were about to give way. Elaine stared at him, eyes wide with shock. She touched his face, checking to see that he was okay, then slapped him. A row of thin red marks rose on his cheek, but he hardly noticed.

Around them the engraved wards glowed an intense red, like bricks just out of a kiln, then dulled and, with a hiss, cooled back to their usual brown clay. Billi's ears echoed with the sudden silence.

She'd been wrong. She'd thought that sort of power no longer existed. She looked at Kay as he swept his hand through his sweaty hair. Their eyes met, and his burned with feverish excitement. In four hundred years no one had picked up so much as a radio signal with the mirror. No one since John Dee, the Templars' greatest Oracle.

Greatest, that is, until now.

6

"I DON'T BELIEVE IT," SAID ELAINE. HER HANDS WERE still shaking when she poured the tea. "Those wards should have held."

They'd retreated upstairs into her living room. It was the complete opposite of the ramshackle shop below. The furniture was modern, plain wood without frills. A row of track lights sparkled in the clean white ceiling. The only decoration was a menorah on the windowsill and two large reproduction paintings. The first was a Caravaggio, of Abraham about to sacrifice his son Isaac. An angel on his left stays the knife hand. Billi was caught by the mix of terror and determination in Abraham's face. What must he have felt, asked by God to kill the one he loved above all others? The second was Islamic calligraphy. The name of Allah entwined to form a circle.

"My mum had a picture like that," said Billi.

"It *is* your mother's," said Elaine, catching Billi's curious look. "What? We were friends, you know."

Billi didn't say anything. She hadn't known.

Elaine handed them each a mug. Then she pulled out a stiff-backed dining chair.

"What just happened?" asked Billi. She took the mug and realized it wasn't only Elaine's hands that were shaking.

"Kay opened the portal to the Ethereal Realm," said Elaine. "And almost let something through."

Billi stopped mid-sip. The Ethereal Realm was the spirit world beyond the physical universe. The domain of the brightest and darkest of entities. In it lay the domains of Limbo, Hell, and Heaven itself. She could see the shock in Kay's face.

"Almost let *what* through?" asked Kay.

"What do you know about the Grigori?" Elaine said. Billi hadn't thought it possible for Kay to become any whiter, but she was wrong. He went ashen.

"The dark angels," he said. "The watchers."

"They're mentioned in the Book of Enoch." Elaine looked at them both. "You've heard of it?"

Kay gave a slow thoughtful nod.

"It's one of the Apocryphal texts," he said. "Early Christian lore deemed . . . too dangerous to go in the Bible."

"Not long ago you'd have been burned at the stake for even reading it," said Elaine.

"Why?" asked Billi. She knew the Grigori were angels

of retribution, and part of the Unholy. But they hadn't been encountered in hundreds of years, thousands even. They weren't considered a serious threat anymore, not like *ghuls* or werewolves.

Elaine continued. "It discusses the true nature of angels. There are three classes of them." She pointed to the Caravaggio. "The *Malakhim*, the messengers. They're led by Gabriel and are the most common form of Ethereal being. But there are two others. Each given their specific role in testing mankind." Elaine looked at Billi. "Did your mother ever tell you the Islamic story about Satan? About Iblis?"

Billi frowned. There were hundreds of stories, and though she could barely remember some of them, there were others that stayed deep in her bones.

"When God created Adam," Billi said, "He asked all the angels to bow down before the new creation. Satan, or Iblis in the Quran, refused. He said he bowed only to God."

"Very good. Satan showed both his disobedience and his loyalty to God. He was then given the role of tempting mortals, to test them." Elaine raised her head. "He took with him other angels who likewise thought mankind didn't deserve its special status as first among God's creatures. Those angels became the devils."

"And the third class of angels? The Grigori?" asked Kay.

"The watchers." Elaine glanced at the door as though she half expected someone, or something, to burst in just because she'd spoken their name. "They were the judges.

Sent to Earth to teach Man righteousness and to punish him should he transgress. They were . . . are led by the Angel of Death himself." She got up and walked over to the Caravaggio. She drew her finger around the face of the young boy, arms held behind his back, the look of utter terror on his face as his father raised his knife, ready to slit his throat. "The Grigori are the most terrible of God's angels. Two hundred of them descended on Earth. It took only three to destroy Sodom and Gomorrah. It was they that unleashed the Flood."

Billi shivered at the thought. "What happened to them?"

"They were summoned back to Heaven," answered Kay. "But not all went. Seventy rebelled. They turned their back on Heaven and cut off their wings."

Elaine smiled, impressed. "They'd grown too fond of the Material Realm. And why not? Beautiful, powerful, immortal, they were in every way superior to humans. They thought they should remain on Earth and rule over us. They became monsters, tyrants. Feared. Loved. Worshipped."

"Bloody hell," said Billi.

"No. Bloody Earth. The watchers ran amok. Righteous justice became righteous slaughter. They threatened to turn the Earth into a charnel house." Elaine left the painting and crouched down in front of Kay. "It was King Solomon who eventually defeated them. Given perfect wisdom by God, only he was strong enough to trap the Grigori. In the Cursed

Mirror." She shook her head. "It's a portal into the Ethereal Realm, a doorway if you will. And that's where they are to this day. All of them but one."

"The Angel of Death," said Kay. "The right hand of God."

Elaine nodded. "Too powerful for even King Solomon to bind, only he escaped. Vastly weakened, to be sure. But not in the mirror like his brethren."

"So he's been looking for it ever since," said Billi. "And if he ever found it, he'd be able to get back all his powers *and* free the others, right?"

Elaine's fearful expression was answer enough.

"So that's who we saw, wasn't it?" said Kay. "The banished watchers trapped in Limbo?" He sank his head into his hands. "Oh my God. I thought I'd just try to make contact with the Ethereal Realm. To see if we could hear something."

"Oh, we heard something all right," said Billi, her anger spilling out over her fear. "I told you not to do it, but you didn't listen; you thought you'd show off. For God's sake, Kay, you could have freed them."

He looked up, his face drawn. "But I didn't, did I? Nothing escaped. The wards—"

"Are apparently useless," snapped Elaine. "I should have checked, but I never suspected you'd be that strong." She put her hand on Kay's shoulder, and Billi caught the mixture of awe and dread in the old woman's face. Kay, who used to be afraid of shadows, was now able to contact the agents of God Himself. He had powers they couldn't measure or imagine. Elaine was right to be afraid. They should all be afraid.

"Lot, the last Oracle, carved those wards, and I assumed he'd done a half-competent job." She looked out the window, eyes narrowed as though searching the darkness beyond. "But no, no one got out. I'm sure of it."

"So what has happened? Isn't it all okay?" asked Billi, unable to hide the desperation in her voice.

Elaine's eyes didn't leave the window. "The cry went out, Billi. Those trapped in the mirror have lingered in silence for so long, and Kay has allowed them to call out." She turned, and she wasn't just scared, she was terrified. "And what if someone heard."

Who had heard? One of the Unholy? Another Ethereal? Arthur was going to go crazy when he found out what Kay had done. It wasn't like they didn't have their hands full already, what with the werewolf attacks and vampire bites. Still, for once this was not her fault, though that didn't make the chill go away as she recalled the fear on Elaine's face.

The night had been seriously insane. Billi just needed to get out of there. She left Kay and Elaine to repair the wards. She was going home. Billi ran across the road; she had five minutes before she missed the train, and she wasn't going to waste another minute.

She slapped her card down on the reader and raced down the white-tiled tunnel toward the southbound platform. If she was lucky she'd be home by one, an early night for her. The air rattled with the noise of the approaching train, and she leaped up the steps two at a time.

Bloody Kay! She wished he'd stayed in Jerusalem. It would have been safer. And what was he trying to prove? How powerful he was? The boy was dangerously delusional. Billi saw the train doors opening at the far end of the corridor and picked up her pace.

She slipped through the doors just before they shut, and collapsed down on an empty seat, trying to catch her breath. She closed her eyes, but instead of darkness she saw the afterimage of the chaotic patterns and dancing lights that had radiated from the mirror. Billi pressed her fingers into her skull to stop the dizzying sensation. It took a few minutes for the colors to fade and the spinning in her head to settle down. She leaned back and sighed. She'd catch a short nap now and depend on her internal clock to wake her at Holborn. It was a ten minute walk back home from there.

But sleep wouldn't come. All she could think about was what Kay had done.

Who did he think he was? Obi-Wan Kenobi? True, he wasn't the same scrawny geek he'd been before, but he was still Kay. And that meant weird. How could she have forgotten?

Billi fished out her iPod and plugged in the small white

earbuds. She cranked Nirvana up to the maximum volume and let the music drown everything out. All she wanted was a break from her Templar duties—and from Kay.

The tracks ticked over, and she was just relaxing into the steady rhythm of the carriage rocking back and forth, when the sudden slamming of a door made her eyes flick open and her muscles tense.

They'd come through the interconnecting carriage door and made their way toward her. There were three of them, swaggering like they owned the place. Two dropped down either side of her, the third opposite, his legs as wide apart as his grin. She slid her gaze up and down the carriage and lowered the volume on her iPod. It was empty except for them.

"What you listening to?" the one across from her asked. Billi flinched as his fingers brushed the back of her hand.

What was this? Bully Billi Day? Maybe if she acted dumb they'd leave. Three to one were bad odds, even for a Templar. She said nothing, just lowered her eyelids a fraction. The one on her left slid his arm over her shoulders.

"C'mon, guys, it's late. I just want to get home." She knew it was hopeless to appeal to their good sense. They didn't look like they'd recognize good sense if it kicked them in the teeth.

"Sure you do, just after you give us your 'pod." The boy on the left grabbed for her music player.

Billi jumped up, twisted her wrist, and drove her right

palm heel into his face, smashing his nose with a satisfying crunch. An instant later her foot snapped out into the stomach of the thug opposite. He gasped and curled up in agony. Billi spun sideways, but the third tackled her and they both crashed down, Billi winded by the impact as he landed on top of her. No time for finesse, she had zero room to maneuver, so she slashed at his face with her nails, her fingers hooked like talons. He fought to keep her from getting his eyes, punching her clumsily during the scuffle. Then he reached into his waistband, and out came a knife.

Terror shot through her veins. The blade wasn't long, but getting dead was suddenly on the agenda. She tried to grab his wrist, but got a cut across her hand instead. Distracted by the shining steel blade, she didn't block the next punch; it caught her square on the cheek and suddenly Billi had lights exploding in front of her eyes. The knife came in and she couldn't stop it. There was a scream.

But it wasn't hers.

Billi blinked as she stared up directly into the overhead light: the thug was gone. The edge of a dark coat brushed her face as someone stepped over her.

"He's got a knife," she croaked, still dizzy from that last punch. But Billi turned to see the thug drive the blade into the new combatant. The guy blocked the attack and grabbed the wrist, twisting it sharply. The knife spun away. Then he kicked the attacker's feet out from under him, smashing him down on the floor.

The guy paused, then turned to Billi and held out his hand.

"Let me help you up," he said.

"I'm fine." She didn't need his help. Not now, anyway. The train was slowing, and Billi gripped the side of the seat to steady herself while looking for the three would-be muggers. One was rocking on a seat, bent double after the kick to his guts. The second had a nose sitting at right angles to the rest of his face and was crying as he tried to halt the blood. The knife man groaned on the floor. It had taken all of ten, maybe fifteen seconds.

"I've never seen anyone move so fast," she said.

The guy shrugged. "Not too shabby yourself."

The train came to a halt. Holborn.

"I've got to go," Billi said. She stumbled a few steps toward the door, the ground swaying under her feet even though the train had stopped. She was more battered than she'd thought. A pair of hands lifted her up by the arms.

"I'll just help you out, okay?" he said.

Billi nodded reluctantly.

He led her off onto the platform. The doors closed behind them, and the train rattled away. Billi watched its lights disappear into the darkness. She turned and looked up at her rescuer.

He was tall with raptor's eyes, slanted and amber almost, half hidden under unkempt black hair. Under his coat, a

T-shirt was taut over his muscular torso, and a tattoo of spiky vines climbed from his right hand to his throat. The thorn along his jaw stretched as he smiled. Billi didn't think he looked much older than she was.

"Shall we call the police?" he asked, breaking the silence.

She'd been staring. *How embarrassing.* She shook her head, trying to turn away from the boy's gaze. "Not worth it."

The last thing she needed, or the Templars needed, was the police sniffing around. "And anyway"—she couldn't help a wry smile at the memory of the thug's face making contact with the floor—"I think you've shown them the error of their ways."

"Can't take all the credit, Miss . . . ?"

Billi held out her hand. "Billi."

He gazed at it for a moment, then reached out. Billi felt a shiver as they touched. Getting weirder, she thought. But not in a bad way.

His fingers wrapped around her hand.

"Mike."

7

"Y'KNOW, I CAN GET HOME BY MYSELF. I'M NOT some damsel in distress," Billi said as she and Mike walked along the Strand. There was no one else out, just a garbageman collecting trash bags from outside the shops.

"And I'm not a white knight," Mike replied. "But it's on my way."

Billi stopped at the gatehouse just as it began to drizzle. In it was the black door that led to Middle Temple Lane. . . home.

"You live in there? I thought that was just for lawyers and stuff."

"What makes you think my dad's not a lawyer?"

Mike laughed. "No lawyer's daughter fights like that."

Billi pulled out the key. "He's a porter. Part of the deal is that you get a place to live. So there's always someone around if the lawyers run out of gin or something." She turned around and offered her hand. "Anyway, thanks."

Mike didn't take it. "Billi. Short for what?"

"Bilqis. My mum was Pakistani."

"Was?"

"She died when I was five." She shook her head, dismissing the memory before it took hold. "I don't much remember her." She unlocked the door. "Listen, I really, really appreciate what you did. But I'm all right now. My house is just down there."

Mike glanced at the door. "Then it's good-bye." He smiled briefly. "See you around." He turned and walked away.

Billi watched him, torn. The guy *had* just saved her life.

She never invited anyone home. Hadn't for years. Too many secrets, too many little lies she'd have to make up, the pretense of being "normal." That's how her dad had taught her. She was a Templar. Friendships were a dangerous luxury.

"Wait!" Billi ran after Mike, catching him at the corner just before he'd be gone for good. "Wait."

He stopped, and Billi skidded to a halt, barely avoiding colliding into him. "I'm sorry," she said. Now what? *Oh, just say something, Billi, don't just stand there like a moron.* "I'm sorry. It's raining."

"That's hardly your fault," he said, holding down a smirk.

"What?" *Oh, that was a joke. Damn. Should have laughed.*

Billi took a deep breath. "Come in for a minute. I owe you a cuppa at the very least."

There, not so hard after all. Mike's golden eyes narrowed as his lips curled. Was he laughing at her?

Then he nodded. "Thanks. That would be nice."

Billi led him down the dark tunnel-like alleyway. They passed the courtyard beside Middle Temple Hall and reached her front door. Her heart raced as she unlocked it. Inside it was dark, and Arthur's heavy jacket was missing: he was out. Billi sighed with relief.

"The kitchen's upstairs," she said.

Mike inspected the paintings of ancient warriors and battles that lined the hallway. He stopped in front of one.

"What's this?"

"Waterloo. An ancestor fought there." She pointed out a crowd of besieged soldiers in blue. "For Napoleon."

"Family of heroes, eh?"

"Glorious losers, more like."

Once in the kitchen, Billi got busy with the kettle. She could feel his eyes on her back and tried to act cool and casual. Why was it she couldn't remember where anything was? She opened most of the cupboards before she found the one with the mugs, and then had to empty it out to find any that weren't chipped. There were a few tea bags left in the tin, and just about enough milk in the carton. She sniffed it discreetly. It smelled okay. She had to grind the sugar out of the bowl using a knife as a chisel, but eventually the water was boiled, and two steaming cups were down on the table.

Billi dragged up a stool and sat across from Mike. She was suddenly painfully aware of the faded tablecloth, the yellow-stained tiles, and the lopsided cabinets. The linoleum on the floor was torn, revealing the warped floorboards, and there was a fold of paper wedged under one of the table legs to stop it from wobbling.

"I'm sorry. Bit of a mess," she mumbled, embarrassed.

"Just needs a lick of paint," said Mike generously. "You're dad's obviously not into DIY."

Paint wasn't going to cover it up. This wasn't anyone's home. It was a place of Templar business, and she just happened to sleep here. She glanced at the wall. What had happened to the photos? She couldn't even remember when they'd been taken down. There used to be loads of her, Dad. And Mum. All gone now.

"My dad's not very handy. Not that he's around much." Billi almost slapped her hand over her mouth. It had slipped out, and suddenly she wanted to take it back. But she slowly looked up at Mike, this stranger, and there was something in his face, something familiar. Like she knew him, and he knew her.

"Sounds hard." He sighed. "I know how you feel." He was gazing away, far away. "My father and I . . . don't speak anymore. I left home ages ago."

"Do you miss it?"

"Every day." There was something familiar and so sad

about him, that Billi wanted to reach out and touch his face. His eyes sparkled like a lake under the sun.

A crash made Billi jolt out of her skin.

Tea splattered over the table as she looked up to see Arthur standing at the doorway. He'd dropped a heavy army backpack at his feet.

"Who's this?" Fiery embers crackled in his gaze.

He's been fighting. She shuddered to think of what might be in the bag. She had to get Mike out.

But Mike was already up. He crossed the room and held out his hand. "I'm Mike."

Arthur ignored it. He went to the sink and began washing his hands.

"It's late," he said. "We need to talk, Billi."

Billi was mortified.

"Thanks for the tea," said Mike, smiling and apparently unconcerned by her dad's rudeness.

Billi jumped out of the chair. "I'll show you out."

She took him downstairs and out the front door. She checked over her shoulder to make sure her dad was well out of earshot.

"I'm sorry about that. My dad's a bit funny with strange visitors." Mike raised an eyebrow as Billi realized what she'd said. "Not that you're strange. At all." *Oh God, what is wrong with me?* Mild concussion during the fight. Had to be.

"You're a strange one yourself, Billi," said Mike. "Most girls would be pretty freaked out after a night like this. You sure you're going to be okay?"

The rain was heavier now. Billi spotted a glistening drop roll down Mike's neck, getting tangled in the thorn tattoos.

"Yes, yes. You'd be surprised how rough some of the lawyers get around here." She shifted awkwardly at the door. "Well, thanks for everything. Y'know, for saving my life and all."

Oh, that was so totally cool. Stop speaking. Now.

Mike grinned. "Shame I never got to finish my cuppa." He looked toward the kitchen window on the upper floor. "Why don't we try that again, somewhere else, maybe?"

He's asking me out. At least she thought that's what he was doing. Boys almost never came anywhere near Billi, let alone asked her out. Her dad's reputation made sure of that.

Not sure how to respond, she just nodded. Mike handed her his mobile so she could enter her number, and she was instantly aware of the touch of his hand on hers, surprisingly warm despite the cold rain.

Billi's fingers stumbled over the tiny keypad, and she had to take a deep training breath to calm herself enough to get the stupid digits right. Mike inspected the screen before flicking his mobile shut.

"Then I'll see you soon, maybe?"

"Yeah, maybe." She only just managed to get the words out.

Mike waved before retreating into the darkness, his shape fading into the hazy gloom between the pools of orange under the streetlights. Then he was gone.

Billi lingered, watching the sparkling raindrops catch the lamplight as they fell like gold over the cobblestones.

Back in the kitchen, her dad had emptied out his Bergen. Newspaper covered the table and he was wiping down his *kukri* with an oily cloth. After the Templar sword, the wide-bladed Gurkha knife was Arthur's favorite weapon.

Billi could barely look at him as she came in. "We were just having tea."

"People like that only complicate things."

"People like what?"

"Like that. Boyfriends."

Billi turned abruptly and faced the sink, hoping her dad couldn't see the telltale redness of her face.

"He's just a friend."

Arthur just looked at her. "Elaine told me what happened." He put down his knife. "Are you all right?"

Billi almost fainted with shock. Was her dad *concerned*? Her tongue momentarily died on her. She nodded.

"Good. I need you focused. There's work to do," he said.

How stupid. Not concerned at all. He was just worried she wouldn't be fighting fit.

"Nothing ever matters to you except this bloody Order." Billi grabbed the side of the counter, digging her nails into the old wood, trying hard not to explode. "You don't want me to have anything else, do you?"

Arthur's face was impassive. He didn't bat an eyelid.

Billi walked away toward her bedroom; she was so tired now.

"I did not choose this life," she said. But before she could leave the room, she heard his reply.

"None of us ever do."

8

A FEW DAYS PASSED AND STILL NOTHING FROM Mike. Her dad had won again. He bullied everyone, and now he'd scared Mike off, and with him, a chance Billi might have had for a social life. She should just accept it.

But she couldn't. She kicked off the duvet. This was not the life she wanted.

She leaned over to her bedside table and flicked open her mobile for the millionth time, hoping some text or message might have come while she'd been asleep. Nothing. Damn it! She shouldn't be surprised: who in their right mind would want to go out with a girl with a psycho for a father?

She slid out of her pajamas and into her tracksuit. It was six a.m.; the birds outside hadn't even woken yet, and here she was, too angry to sleep. There was only one solution.

The catacombs ran under the entire Temple district.

Secret warrens, tunnels, and chambers had been excavated by the Templars of old, and all record of them had conveniently vanished over time, so only the knights themselves were aware of their existence. There was even a secret entrance to the underground Fleet River, unbeknown to all above. Few realized how the ancient bones of the city slept under the steel and glass towers of modern London. Billi entered the underground armory and switched on the lights. The harsh white fluorescent tubes glowed along the walls, illuminating the ancient bricks, the low vaulted ceiling, the cold flagstone floor, and the weapons. It had once been the Templar ossuary; even now the bones of the ancient knights rested in crudely carved alcoves along the walls. After all this time, Billi still felt a chill when she entered the gloomy chamber, under the gaze of those old bones. In a hundred years would her own sightless skull sit there watching some new squire training, perhaps with the very same weapons? She shivered, and it wasn't because of the cold.

The smell was a dusty mix of seeping damp, oil, and polish. How many thousands of hours had she spent down here? Last August she'd hardly seen the sun. She'd returned to school in September as white as a ghost. During that month she'd worked with a whetstone and cloth on weapons maintenance. All those nicks and cuts, and bruises and black eyes, all those strange looks in class—all those excuses.

Oh, I tripped.

I ran into the door.

Fell down the stairs.

A vase dropped on my head.

The dog/cat/goat bit/scratched/kicked me.

She walked along the row of swords, all neatly stacked on wooden racks. There were Scottish claymores, German bastard swords, French rapiers, Indian *patas*; deadly steel from around the world. She needed to master all of them. Arthur had taught her there was no glamour in weapons: they were tools, no more, no less. Even the *katanas*, the very souls of the samurai, sat beside the crude and battered bronze *khopesh* swords. Billi snatched up a *bokken*, a Japanese wooden practice sword. Templars didn't train with modern kendo equipment; with armor and hollow bamboo sticks. Percy thought nothing trained reflexes better than the risk of serious injury. The heavy cedar stave of the *bokken* was lethal. She turned the weapon slowly, loosening her wrists, getting the blood pumping, building up speed as she started with jabs, cuts, parries, and slices against imaginary opponents. She twisted, turned, dived, darted back, forward, her feet sliding and leaping across the cold stone. Fire burned in her veins as she slashed off arms, heads, cut open arteries, and burst apart hearts. The *bokken* reacted before she thought, as though alive in itself. The dance was pure instinct, completely formless. Billi lost track of time as she moved across the empty floor, mesmerized by the unending motion of the wooden blade. As she swung it at an invisible target, her eyes closed and she felt a breeze, a wrong breeze, and stopped.

She turned to the steps and saw a shadow descend. Her dad stopped at the edge of the practice area, dressed in a black T-shirt and a pair of faded gray sweatpants.

Why wouldn't he leave her alone, just for a minute?

"Don't stop," he said.

"I've just finished. It's all yours." She couldn't bear to be stuck in the same room with him.

Arthur picked a *bokken* from the rack. His wrists clicked as he repeated the same warm-up exercises that Billi had just done.

"Percival says you've come a long way this year." He stopped in the center of the armory. "Show me."

Fight her dad?

It had been a long while since they'd fought, especially now that Pelleas taught unarmed combat; her dad was too busy. They'd occasionally have mock duels when Percy wasn't available. But for some reason this, this felt different.

Arthur stood, legs apart, slightly bent, slightly springy, in the low guard: hilt waist high, sword tip pointed up at the target's throat.

Fine, if that's what he wants. Billi came forward, moving into high guard, the standard position against her dad's stance, and primed for the principal blows to his unprotected head. Speed and control. The essence of the mock duel was to strike fast and pull the blow at the last possible second. Maybe she could pull it a moment too late? The image of her dad with a big purple bruise on his forehead brought a smile to her lips. She took long breaths, subduing her rapidly beating heart and taking control of the adrenaline bubbling in her body. They were several feet apart.

"Do you hate me, Billi?"

The question was so unexpected that she faltered, and in that second her dad attacked without hesitation. He feinted with a jab, drawing Billi's sword down, and then he slammed his blade hard across hers: the fire-and-stones cut. The impact jarred her arms, and Billi loosened her grip to let the energy dissipate. But Arthur sensed the weakening grip, his tip darted up, and with a twist of his wrist, Billi's *bokken* leaped from her hands, and she watched it spin in the air, then clatter to the ground.

"Well?" Arthur asked.

"Well what?" Billi furiously shook the sting out of her hands; such a simple trick and she'd fallen for it!

"I asked you a question. A simple one."

Simple. Was he crazy? Billi stared at her father, straight into those bright, fierce, blue eyes, and wondered again if he really was her dad. The similarities began and ended with the black hair. They said she was more like her mother. Not as beautiful; she had her dad's genes to thank for that. He'd never been handsome, and over the years the broken nose and the crisscross of scars had only made him uglier—and easier to hate.

"Why should I hate you?" She walked away from him

when she said it, just in case he could read her face. She picked up her sword. When she turned around, he was waiting, low guard again.

"For ruining your life." He gave a slight shrug. "That's what you think, isn't it?"

"I'm a Templar; that's all the life I need," she intoned.

"Sarcasm is the lowest form of wit."

"What if I do hate you?"

Now it was Arthur's turn to hesitate.

Billi smirked. *Let him deal with that.* But the smile withered. Did she? Did she really hate him, or had she just come to hate this life? She shook her head and took the high guard again.

"Why do we have to be part of this?" she asked. "We've been fighting the *Bataille Ténébreuse* for almost nine hundred years and have gotten nowhere." That was it, wasn't it? The waste of all those men and lives for something that would never end. There were only nine of them. "There aren't any Templars in Wales. It hasn't been overrun by demons, has it?" She paused. Why did they bother? Why did she live this life when it didn't make any difference?

"We're Templars. We have a duty to be vigilant." He focused his attention along the sword.

"Against what?" She tightened her grip around the hilt; she wasn't going to fall for the same trick twice.

"Against the attack no one else sees coming."

Billi swept down, and Arthur drew his blade up and

parried, barely, but enough. Billi jabbed, then let the battle guide her, no thought or strategy, no plan, just the subtle shifting of moves, positions, attacks, and parries. He was stronger, she was faster. Attacks came deadly and close, but in the gaps between seconds, Billi moved and would knock a blow aside or launch one of her own. They crossed the armory floor, back and forth, back and forth, neither giving the other a moment's respite. Billi drew in close, hilts jammed together, and her dad smiled.

Then head-butted her.

Sparks filled her vision and she couldn't keep upright. The ground pitched suddenly, and Billi tottered backward.

Her dad caught her.

"You bastard," she whispered, shaking her head clear. She checked her nose. If it was broken . . . No, not even bleeding. But her eyes were watering heavily. "Bastard."

If she hadn't hated him then, she hated him now. He couldn't even fight fair! He lowered her to the ground, then squatted down beside her.

"You hate this life, don't you?"

"Yes! Of course I do!" Billi wiped her sleeve over her face; the tears just wouldn't stop. She didn't want him to think she was crying for any reason except for his head-butting her.

Arthur nodded. He gazed at the *bokken* in his hand. "Good. You ought to."

Billi shook her head again. She wasn't hearing right. "What?"

"You're right, Billi. There's so few of us, but we keep the darkness at bay. Why? Because we're ruthless. We bring nightmares to the monsters." He leaned closer so he could whisper it. "Fear is a powerful weapon."

Billi froze. She'd never felt so cold in her life. Her heart must have turned to ice. Arthur stood up; he didn't look at her.

"You need to be ruthless. Nothing can stop you from fulfilling your duty. One day you'll have to make a terrible choice, and pity will fill your heart, and you'll hesitate. You'll think there has to be a better way." He sighed. "But sometimes there isn't. You'll be up close, you'll feel a person's warm breath on your face, see the glow of life in their eyes, and know you have to end it. Like you did during the Ordeal." He pulled Billi up. "You hate what we do; you're right to. Who would want this life? Sometimes we must do terrible things, make huge sacrifices. But we must. Because the alternative is so much worse." He cupped her face and leaned forward. Billi tensed and thought he was going to kiss her forehead, like he used to a long time ago.

Or maybe head-butt her again.

Instead Arthur dropped his hands and turned away. "Tidy up. When you're finished, I've got a job for you."

9

BILLI EMERGED FROM THE TIDE OF KIDS WASHING OUT of the school gates, her backpack slung over her shoulder, to find Kay waiting. He was perched up on the high wall like a crow, wrapped in a black coat and scarf.

"What's going on?" Billi asked.

"Read this," said Kay as he passed Billi a sheet of paper. It was an e-mail from the head of the children's ward of some hospital. She scanned it. Four kids had died in the last two days. Their hearts had simply stopped. The autopsies had brought up nothing. Each child had been in for minor operations: a couple of tonsillectomies, and one, Rupresh Patel, for an ingrown toenail. But it didn't seem much to go on.

"Dad thinks it's something supernatural?"

"That's for us to find out."

* * *

The main building of China Wharf hospital, a six-story Victorian structure, reeked of decay. There was a damp odor clinging to the walls, green mold coated the drainpipes, and the wooden window frames were rotten and cracked. The hospital never saw direct sunlight; it was forever cringing in the shadows cast by the titanic towers of nearby Canary Wharf. A couple of sallow-faced patients sat in wheelchairs, numbly staring up at the glass-face bastions of wealth. Beside them a trio of weary nurses clustered together under the entrance canopy having their cigarette break.

"Let's go to work," Billi said, and walked through the automatic doors.

They pushed their way through the outpatients reception area. Every seat was filled, and almost every patch of floor space was too. There were lots of kids, some in strollers, others being cradled by their parents, while a seriously harassed-looking registrar was trying to control the dense mass and prioritize the worst. It looked like something out of a third-world news story. Billi plowed through the crowd toward the elevators. Kay hadn't moved. He stood in the middle of the room, eyes narrowed.

"What's up?" she asked.

Kay frowned. "Do you hear something?"

Billi concentrated. "A bunch of screaming kids. Why?"

He shrugged. "Can't tell. Maybe nothing."

"Fine. Let's get a move on."

Kay had checked the building plans off the Web; the

children's ward was on the top floor. They slipped into the elevator with a party of visitors. Kay pulled out a box of candy wrapped in a bow. If anyone stopped them, they'd say they were visiting a friend.

They watched the indicator light ping up floor by floor. Through a pair of large wooden doors they entered a grim series of rooms. Someone, a long time ago, had tried to decorate the walls with scenes of cartoon characters, colorful rainbows, and portraits of cheerful patients. But over time, and through lack of care, patches of damp discolored the ceiling tiles. The smiling figures had developed sickly, cancerous skin as the paint had aged, flaked, and yellowed. It was where Billi'd had her Ordeal—there was something tainting this place. Billi shook her head. She was getting as paranoid as her dad. This was just a run-down hospital, short on funds. It wasn't a desolation. She peered up and down the corridor.

There were four wards on either side, then the special care unit containing a regiment of occupied incubators, with the maternity unit beyond.

"You check down there"—Kay pointed at the west end of the ward—"and I'll look here. Give me a shout if you see anything strange."

Billi had expected there to be some life, some ambient noise of natural childish laughter and excitement. But there was none. A single ward nurse sat at the viewing station, almost hidden behind the high battlement of the desk. In the staff room beyond, Billi could hear *EastEnders* crackling through the speakers of an old telly, and there were two other nurses within, lying almost comatose in their armchairs, each staring dumb-eyed at the flickering screen.

It was *all* strange, but there was nothing she could pin down and warn Kay about. Billi moved down the corridor, fighting down the feeling of unease.

From their beds the children seemed listless, while others watched Billi with icy distrust.

What was she looking for? There were beds, there were sick kids. What else did she expect? It was a hospital. Another one of her dad's paranoid fantasies. She couldn't see Kay; where had he gone? She wanted to wrap this up and go home.

"Excuse me, dear, but are you a visitor?" A ward nurse had appeared from nowhere. "These children need rest, and if you're not visiting, you should leave." She spoke with a weary firmness, not harsh, but certain.

Billi pointed at a door and headed to it. "I'm here to see"—she got closer and noticed the sign, REBECCA WILLIAMSON—"my friend Becky. Just for a minute." And she went in.

The lights were off and the curtains drawn, but there was enough illumination from the pallid glow of the monitors to see a girl asleep in the bed. She was small, seven or eight, with a drip in her arm, a pulse sensor taped to her finger, and a breathing tube threaded through her nose. Her hair was thin, and Billi could see her skull, the skin thin and lined with blue veins. Billi would wait here a minute then sneak out to find Kay.

The girl opened her eyes. When she breathed it sounded as if she were trying to suck in air against the will of her body.

"Hello," said the girl. Her voice was fragile and weak.

Billi wanted to leave, but she looked into the girl's eyes and saw the life burning fiercely within. The girl wanted to do something besides wait in the dark. There was fight in her.

"Hi . . . Rebecca."

Rebecca let out a long breath, then with great effort, drew in a new lungful. Her skinny body trembled under the sheets.

"Are my mum and dad here?"

"No, I'm sure they won't be long, though."

The girl started crying. Her head jerked slightly and tears bubbled then trickled down. There was hardly any sobbing, just a feeble panting sound. Billi looked around the room and found a box of tissues. She passed Rebecca a handful. She watched as the girl limply lifted them, and the effort to wipe her face exhausted her. The damp tissues floated to the floor.

"I'm sorry," said Rebecca. "I'm afraid."

Billi didn't know what to say. Comforting the sick was work for Hospitallers, not Templars. She just stared at the way Rebecca's skeletal chest rose and sank. She could see the ribs beneath the white nightdress.

Rebecca turned to face her. Her focus settled on the silver crucifix around Billi's neck. "Do you believe in God?"

Did she? Billi touched the cross more out of habit than faith. She'd spent half her life praying to Allah, the other half to Jesus. She'd asked her dad early on how she should pray. Arthur's answer, for a Templar Master, had been a heretical one. He didn't know, and thought God, whoever He was, probably didn't care.

"I . . . suppose."

"Why?"

Billi looked at the dying child, at how her brittle fingers gripped the sheets. "I guess there has to be a reason for why the world's the way it is. A reason why"—she listened to the terrible sucking noise as Rebecca fought on—"a reason why bad things happen."

Rebecca closed her eyes. "My mummy never used to pray"—her breathing settled into the shallowest, quietest ripple—"but she does now, all the time."

"Billi?" Kay's head appeared around the door. "I've been looking everywhere. . . ." He looked at Rebecca, eyes widening. He came in and grabbed Billi's arm.

"Leave. Now."

"What is it?"

"We've got to tell Arthur," said Kay. He was already backing away, dragging Billi with him. He was terrified. His eyes darted into the corners of the room, into the shadows.

Billi tugged her arm free. "Stop freaking. What is it?"

Kay looked like he was going to run; instead he took Billi by the shoulders and turned her around to face the sick girl. He stood behind her and covered her eyes with his hands. Billi felt their coldness on her eyelids.

"What are you do—?"

"Look." He separated his fingers, letting the sight slowly filter in. Billi blinked as the cobwebs of reality gently tore apart.

The lonely child sat shriveled in a bed wrapped in shroud-white sheets, gazing at Billi with maggot-filled eye sockets, while things wriggled under her tissue-thin skin. Grotesque skeletal flies sat feeding off dripping, oozing flesh, and rank odors and putrescent vapors wheezed out of the girl's lungs. The child breathed through an opened mouth lined with yellow teeth loosely bound to decayed, blackened gums, and her slime-coated tongue hung limp over her white lips.

"No," Billi whispered, backing away from Kay, shaking her head free of the hideous image. She stumbled down the corridor, battling the bitter, metallic bile climbing up her throat. Kay caught up with her and pulled them both through the doorway into the stairwell. Billi leaned against the wall, teeth clamped together, and waited for the nausea to pass.

"What is it? What's happening to her?" She'd never seen anything like it. She couldn't remember anything like this in any of the old manuscripts, the old Templar diaries. Kay squeezed her, his chest touched her back.

"I don't know." He turned back toward the door. "But I think this is only the beginning."

Billi called her dad while Kay got them tea. They'd found a greasy spoon café off the high street, empty but for some old guy with a beard stirring his coffee endlessly and muttering at a blank spot on the wall. Faded posters of Caribbean beaches and white Alpine mountains decorated the walls, corners curled and colored from cigarette smoke. She couldn't get through; the phone went straight to messaging. She'd finally gotten Percy. He'd told them to sit tight; he was on his way.

When she went back in, Kay had their tea and a bun waiting. He clutched the mug tightly, but his fingers still trembled.

"You okay?"

He smiled weakly. "Been better."

"What's happening to her?"

"It's a sickness, a disease. The necro-flies are penetrating the Ethereal Realm and slowly eating her soul. I could see her aura, but it was barely there. Once they've done it and the soul is totally consumed, the body will just die."

"Can't you do anything?" she asked. Her stomach twisted at the memories of those flies. Kay didn't even look up.

So the little girl was going to die, and there was nothing

they could do about it. Billi thought about her just lying there blankly, gazing at the ceiling. That was how it was going to be, a small pointless death, and her last memory, the one she took with her to the grave, was going to be of a lightbulb. Maybe Arthur would know of a way to save her? Hold on: hadn't she read somewhere that people could live even without their souls?

Kay's eyebrows arched as he sensed her thoughts. "Without her soul it's better that she dies, Billi."

She tried not to think about the little boy from her Ordeal, Alex Weeks.

Kay leaned across and tilted her chin up gently so she had to look at him. "Billi, without a soul we lose that one part of us that's divine, the breath of God. The path of the soulless leads only to damnation. Only the vilest, most evil person would consider it."

"Or the most desperate." Billi couldn't get Rebecca out of her mind.

"Without a soul, a void is left that creates a terrible, endless hunger. One they'll try desperately to fill."

"With blood." And so the legend of blood-drinking monsters had been born. The Templars still had one of the biggest occult libraries in Christendom; only the Vaticans rivaled theirs, and that was because they'd stolen much of it from the Templars themselves.

Kay nodded. "The taste of a person's soul lingers in their life blood, in their flesh. The hungry dead feed on that. It sustains them for a while, but the taste is never enough. Then they kill again. And again. Each time, the blood they sup on becomes less and less sustaining. The worst are reduced to eating corpses."

Vampires. Nosferatu. Lamia. All cultures had their own name for the hungry dead. The Templars used the old Arabic word.

"*Ghuls*," said Billi. "You think Rebecca will become one?"

Kay shook his head. "I don't think so—you need to choose to surrender your soul to become a *ghul*, that's clearly not what Rebecca's doing." He frowned mockingly. "But don't you pay any attention in Occult Lore? Balin must be pretty disappointed."

"Hey, I pay more attention than Bors."

"You must offer your soul willingly, to someone capable of consuming it, an Ethereal. It's usually a devil, and it then passes some of its own essence into the now soulless body. It's not an easy transfer. It takes a lot out of the Ethereal; even a single trade can weaken one for years. That's why these sorts of deals aren't that common. Otherwise devils would be creating *ghuls* all over the place."

"So you sell your soul. For what?"

"For wealth. Power. Immortality." Kay stared out the window. "Nothing important."

Billi looked at his reflection, half lost in the darkness beyond.

Ghuls. They'd been behind the Nights of Iron. But she knew that all these things came with a price. Immortal didn't mean unkillable. Not even a *ghul* walked away from having its head chopped off. It was one of the main reasons the Order still trained with hacking weapons. Modern firearms didn't stop *ghuls*, but an ax through the skull did.

"How can you stand it?" she said. "To see such things?" She'd been shaken badly, but Billi knew even the horror she'd witnessed was a faded and weak image of what was really happening to the girl. Kay would have seen it ten times more clearly. If that was what his gift gave him, she was thankful she wasn't an Oracle.

"You have to take the good with the bad." He smiled, but the smile was drawn and desperate.

"Meaning?"

Kay sat, looking at his mug. "You don't know." He looked up at her like he was going to say something, then dropped his head again. "Not everything I see is ugly."

"What else? You can see people's auras, right? What are they like?"

Kay stretched out his arms, his fingertips spread as far as they would go. "They're amazing things, Billi." He smiled to himself, and Billi couldn't believe it was Kay. The smile was so sincere, so full, she felt almost ashamed she'd seen it. It was too personal. Someone's secret smile. "It's not the colors that are amazing, but the brightness. Sometimes, Billi, sometimes we shine so very bright." He folded his arms back around himself. "It sort of restores your faith in things, y'know?"

She felt warm in his smile, watching his open face. Why couldn't she see the world like that? "Kay, you are *très* strange."

"But in a good way, right?"

Billi laughed. Maybe some of the old Kay was still there after all. "Oh God, d'you remember when we convinced Bors that you could predict the future? Told him how he was going to die within two weeks unless he repented all his sins?" It had been a bad time. Bors, the eldest squire, had taken it on himself to torment Billi endlessly, never pulling his blows during sparring, even sending her to the hospital when he'd almost broken her arm. Billi had told Arthur, who had merely sniffed and said if she couldn't handle Bors, what use was she?

Kay nodded, tears running down his grinning face. "It was great, wasn't it? Breakfast every morning. Him doing all our Latin homework, all the weapons maintenance." Billi looked into his blue eyes and was caught by the deepness of their color. She fell silent, her laugh snatched away.

Billi's mobile rang. *Saved by the bell.* She pulled her gaze away from Kay. She didn't recognize the number.

"Hello?"

"Billi? It's me, Mike."

Mike. She couldn't believe it. Nothing all week and he calls now?

She looked awkwardly at Kay. "It's . . . not a great time, Mike." Any second Percy was going to come barging in, probably with half the Order in tow. Kay hadn't taken his eyes off her, so she gave him a half-frown and walked away from the table.

"You busy?" Mike asked. "Just thought we might have that tea. There's a great café around the corner from you. Interested?"

Billi hesitated. After what she'd seen at the hospital, she knew things were going to heat up back at the Templar preceptory. She needed to keep her nights free. Then she thought back to how her dad had treated Mike—had treated her, even—and made a sudden decision.

"Yeah, I'd love to."

They made plans to meet the next evening, not far from the Temple. Billi snapped her mobile shut and waited for her heart rate to slow down.

She'd made a date. It had been easy.

Then why was she feeling so flustered? She put her mobile away and wondered if this wasn't the beginning of something new: something of her own outside of the Templars—beyond her dad's control.

"Who was that?" asked Kay. He was just behind her. Not at the table like he should be.

"Just a friend."

"Who?"

"For God's sake, Kay, you are not my keeper!" As soon

as she said it, she wished she hadn't. She saw the darkened look. *I have no time to pander to his fragile ego.* He'd left her by herself for a whole year, and now he'd just have to deal with the fact that she had a new life.

"You don't need to pander to my anything," snapped Kay.

"You prick." And just when she was beginning to like him again. Well, she was an idiot.

Kay held his palms open. "Look, I couldn't help it. I can't just turn it off and on like that. I didn't mean anything by it."

"Get lost." She wrapped her scarf twice around her neck and crossed over to another table. She'd wait for Percy there.

As Percy collected them, Billi made sure she got in the front seat so she wouldn't be near Kay or even have to look at him. She didn't need to be psychic to feel his eyes boring into the back of her head, but she refused to budge even when he accidentally-on-purpose shoved the back of her seat.

God, he was so irritating! If he could steal into her mind at any time, how could she trust him with anything? Or keep her feelings to herself?

Billi concentrated hard on trying not to think anything at all, and certainly not about Kay.

She heard him huff with frustration. Maybe her being angry helped block him out. Good. She could stay angry at him for a long, long time.

They pulled up at King's Bench Walk and went to the Chaplain's House, where they told Percy and Balin everything they'd seen. Billi was surprised that her dad wasn't around, but didn't comment. Kay remained with Father Balin, so Billi wandered home with Percy.

"Where's Dad?" she asked as they reached her front door. Percy frowned and looked down his huge chest at her.

"Can't say, sweetie. But he'll be back in the morning."

"What's going on, Percy?"

He shrugged. "Don't know for sure, but we'll get to the bottom of it. Now you get some rest." He pushed the door open for her and left.

The hallway walls seemed to close in, trying to trap her. The ancient faces of the past Templars peered down as she walked by. She hung up her coat beside the portrait of Jacques de Molay and glared at him—the Order's last Grand Master. De Molay was seen by the Templars as a hero. A martyr. He'd been burned alive, willingly going to the fire because he believed in the Order and refused to abandon the Templars. But Billi didn't want to be a hero. And she certainly didn't want to be a martyr. She wanted to be normal. She wanted to hang out in cinemas, go to clubs, go on dates. . . .

She *would* see Mike tomorrow. The Templars had managed without her for the last nine centuries; they could manage for another night. She turned her back on the old Grand Master.

The kitchen was empty but for a cold cup of tea Arthur had left. She opened the fridge, but there was just a packet of sausages and a pint of skim milk. Even now she couldn't bring herself to eat pork. Maybe Gwaine was right: once a Muslim always a Muslim. So Billi poured herself a glass of milk and went to bed.

10

"BILLI, WAKE UP."

Billi shuffled under her duvet. Was someone knocking at her door?

"Wake up, sweetheart."

She wiped her hair out of her face and found her clock. 4:15 a.m. She rubbed her eyes. Yes. 4:15 in the morning.

The knocking became urgent.

"Get up, you lazy squire. Immediately."

"Percy?"

The door opened, and Percy switched on the light. Billi grimaced at the glaring brightness.

"Ah, the princess awakes at last. Get dressed. Art wants you down at the church, like right now."

"What's going on?"

"Something important."

* * *

They were all there. Arthur had sent word and they'd all come back that very night. He'd called a council of war.

In the round of Temple Church stood nine chairs. High-backed, engraved with ancient images of war and faith, they'd been arranged in a loose circle lit only by candlelight that flickered on the grim faces of the men that sat there. Thin ribbons of smoke spiraled from the candles into the lofty dark ceiling. Beyond this circle was gloom.

Billi took her seat. Kay was beside her, his face impassive but eyes bloodshot. He obviously hadn't slept. On her left was Bors, the other squire. He glanced at Billi, his eyes hooded and lips curled in slight disdain. At twenty he was the second biggest warrior in the Order. Next year he'd qualify as a knight, and he clearly resented still being seated among the squires.

Arthur's hands gripped the armrests. Behind his chair stood Father Balin, pale as a midnight ghost. He wasn't part of the fighting order so did not have a seat. But as the chaplain he had a right to be present, even at a council of war. To Arthur's right was Gwaine; as seneschal he took the next most honored position to the master. On Arthur's left was Percy, the Templar Marshal, the Master of Arms. Billi looked around the circle at the others.

Pelleas seemed tired. His right hand was wrapped in a bandage, and he struggled to keep straight in his chair. Hunting werewolves was his area of expertise, but this hunt must have gone badly. No doubt she'd hear all about it soon enough. But that can't have been why the council had been called; they were used to dealing with werewolves. Beside Pelleas sat Gareth, the Order's apothecary, or medic. He nodded briefly at Billi. He seemed relaxed, but his fingers fiddled nervously with a short length of black feather—fletching from his signature weapon, the bow and arrow.

Berrant sat opposite him, between Gwaine and Kay. The youngest of the knights, he polished his glasses on his sleeve before sliding them back onto his straight narrow nose. He was the Order's computer expert and hacker. He was also one of the deadliest duelists alive. His high cheekbones gave him a sunken, skeletal appearance in the shadowy light.

"Where's Elaine?" asked Pelleas. Billi checked over her shoulder to the pew where Elaine usually sat, but it was empty. Being Jewish, she couldn't be a member of the Order; but given that Arthur had summoned them all, it was odd she was missing.

"She's busy," said Arthur. He looked toward Kay. "The Oracle has something to tell us."

Not *Squire Kay* anymore. *Oracle.* Chairs creaked as the others all turned to Kay. Billi watched him steady himself before speaking. He was the same age as her, but his responsibilities were a hundredfold greater now. The Templars were counting on him, and this was his chance to prove his worth.

"Billi and I witnessed a girl, Rebecca Williamson, having her soul devoured."

Father Balin crossed himself, and a long silence followed Kay's statement. Percy and Arthur exchanged a concerned glance, and Billi wondered why. What did they know?

"How?" asked Gwaine. "What will become of her?"

Kay shook his head. "She won't become one of the hungry dead, if that's what you mean."

"You sure, boy?" Gwaine hardly deigned to face Kay, his contempt barely concealed.

Kay's eyes locked on the seneschal, and there was steel in his gaze. The old man held it, but not for long. Arthur watched and leaned back into his chair.

"Explain," he said.

"A *ghul* can only be created voluntarily. To become one, you need to renounce all that is holy and give up your soul through your own free will." He sighed, and Billi wanted to say something. He looked so tired. "That's certainly not Rebecca's case. She's fighting it all the way."

"So she might survive?" asked Balin.

"No."

Gareth tucked his feather behind his ear. "And what of the other children?"

Billi stiffened. She'd forgotten. There had been four others besides Rebecca.

"They've been cremated. We don't need to worry about them."Arthur was chillingly matter-of-fact.

"We're avoiding the key issue," Berrant said, straightening his glasses. "Who's behind it, and are these five the only ones?" He lifted up three fingers. "Soul-taking can only be done by an Ethereal, an angel. We all know that." He counted them off. "Either one of the *Malakhim*, or a devil, or a watcher."

"A devil, surely?" said Gwaine.

Billi shot a look at her dad. Was this to do with the mirror? His face was stony blank.

"But it's a direct attack. The devil would be breaking his covenant." Balin stepped into the circle of chairs. "The devils are tempters. They can only lead Man off the path of righteousness to commit evil. They can't perform evil directly." He gestured to Kay. "What the Oracle describes is a violent attack."

"A covenant?" Billi muttered to herself, confused.

Balin heard. Billi fought the urge to sink into her chair to escape his frown. Maybe Kay was right—she should have paid more attention in occult lore.

Balin frowned at her. "Each class of angel, Bilqis, is bound by an immutable law, a covenant." He went into lecturing mode, nodding to himself as he recounted the facts. "The watcher must pass over and spare the household where a sacrifice has been made; the *Malakhim* can only deliver God's Word. To change even a syllable would lead to their utter destruction. Likewise, devils, as powerful as they are, cannot directly cause harm. They will tempt you, persuade you to kill your brother, but they cannot wield the knife themselves."

"It's not the work of a devil," said Kay. "We're dealing with a watcher."

"How d'you know?" asked Gwaine suspiciously.

"Because I used the Cursed Mirror."

Gwaine leaped from his chair and pointed accusingly at Kay, but Billi couldn't hear what he was saying because everyone was shouting at once. Balin stood in the center, his mouth agog. Gwaine barged past him, and Percy sprang up to protect Kay.

"SILENCE!"

Arthur's word froze time. No one moved except to look at him. He stayed seated, but his eyes met theirs, and each one of them, including Gwaine, returned to their chairs. Balin seemed to wake from a trance and, after straightening his cassock, moved back to his place behind the Templar Master's chair.

Arthur stood up and walked to Kay. He put his hand on the boy's shoulder, and a pang of jealousy shot through Billi's heart.

"The damage has been done," said Arthur, seeming almost resigned to what might lie ahead. "Nothing escaped, of that we're certain. But still, it's more than a coincidence that a day after the mirror's been used, we have a watcher destroying souls. It seems he's not strong enough to attack indiscriminately. We suspect it's only by touch. He marks his victims, and that's what attracts the necro-flies from the Ethereal Realm."

"Wait a minute, a watcher?" Balin interrupted. "Then we know who he is, Arthur."

Of course they did. There was only one free watcher.

"The Angel of Death," whispered Percy.

"Oh this just gets better and better," said Gwaine. "God's killer himself."

Arthur ignored him and carried on. "He'll be after the mirror. But he's weak—most of his ethereal powers are still trapped in it. Have been since the time of Solomon."

"And should he ever get his hands on it, he'll regain all his former powers and all his former mates," said Percy. He grimaced. "Sixty-nine very pissed-off watchers led by an archangel. Not great."

Billi thought about what Elaine had told her and Kay, about what the Grigori had done the last time they'd been free. Bloody Earth.

"But why attack these kids?" asked Balin.

"To draw us out." Arthur looked around the circle. "After all, he needs to find us to find the mirror, doesn't he?"

"And where is it now?" Gwaine's voice was scathing.

"Safe. We've reinforced the wards around the reliquary. It's invisible to supernatural detection."

"First you let that fool of a boy tamper with it, and now you trust something this important to Elaine? Don't be stupid, Art," warned Gwaine.

"I do and have. I'm setting up around-the-clock

watches on the China Wharf Hospital. That girl isn't dead. We're going to protect her."

"And use her as bait, yes?" said Billi. If Rebecca was still hanging on, the watcher might come back and finish her off—tear her young soul from her. Billi looked into her dad's eyes. They were dead of compassion. Utterly ruthless. Was there anyone he wouldn't sacrifice?

"Yes. Bait. Berrant has hacked into the hospital files. Each dead child was the eldest sibling. Firstborn."

"Christ Almighty," muttered Pelleas.

Billi stiffened. She was firstborn. "So this sickness . . ."

She didn't even dare finish her sentence. So Arthur did.

"Is the Tenth Plague."

11

Billi couldn't concentrate on anything the next day. She sat there trying to listen to the lesson. Trying to be part of something normal like everyone else in the room. But she'd been forced into knowing, and being part of such terrible things made the possibility of a normal life—a life outside the Order—move farther and farther away from her.

There'd been so many questions, but Arthur hadn't any time to answer them. They were to set up a rotation watch on Rebecca at the hospital, and leave the rest to him.

She checked the time. She had three hours until her shift. But before then, Billi was going to live her own life.

There weren't many familiar faces at the local café, Milano's, by the time she got there. She recognized a couple from her year, but fortunately none from her class. She glanced around the low-lit tables: no Mike.

Billi bought a latte and a blueberry muffin, then hid herself in the corner, deep in the dark red armchair facing the door.

She flipped her mobile open and shut nervously. Was this an actual date? She wasn't sure. It felt like one, but Mike had been so casual about it

She looked around the café. This was home to the popular crowd from school. Pete Olson, the school sports star, all toned pecs and gelled hair, stood with Tracy Hindes, who was giggling like an imbecile and wearing a flimsy red dress that would have given Arthur a cardiac if Billi had worn it.

Billi wondered if this was how girls were meant to behave on dates. Was that what Mike was expecting? She began to feel distinctly uncomfortable. Maybe she shouldn't have come after all. She grabbed her phone and was just getting up to leave when she saw a girl stumbling out of the bathroom door. She was wiping her tear-swollen face with a long stream of toilet paper, which dragged thick black lines of mascara down her face. Billi's heart sank as she recognized her.

Oh no.

Jane Mulville stared back, horrified. Then she stormed over.

"What d'you think you're looking at?" Jane snarled. She rubbed her red face, smearing her mascara further, creating big panda eyes. "Think it's funny, do you, you freak?"

At one time, Billi would have stood up and just knocked her face in, but she sat there, curiously sorry. Jane was fifteen and pregnant, and absolutely everyone knew.

"Listen, Jane, I'm really sorry, but . . ." But what could she actually say to make it any better? "I'm just sorry."

God, that was exceedingly lame.

"I just bet you are," Jane spat.

"Is everything okay?"

It was Mike. She couldn't leave now.

He shook the worst of the rain from his dark curls.

"Hi, Billi. Sorry I'm late."

Mike slung his coat over the sofa opposite her. She had forgotten how good-looking he was. The forest of black tattooed vines and spiky thorns crept out from underneath his T-shirt up toward the nape of his neck, where his skin was still glistening wet from the rain.

"That's okay," she mumbled, not knowing what to do with Mike smiling and Jane glowering. Maybe now would be a good time for the ground to open up and swallow her.

Mike held out his hand to Jane. "I'm sorry, I didn't catch your name." The smile remained, transfixing Jane. Billi knew how she felt.

"Jane," she whispered. She backed off, eyes wide and Mike's hand untaken.

"Good to meet you, Jane." He nodded toward the door. "I think your friend's waiting."

Dave Fletcher stood by the door with Jane's white coat over his arm and a jealous stare directed at Mike.

Realizing she'd been dismissed in favor of Billi, Jane turned to her. "Just stay away from me, freak." She smiled maliciously at Mike. "And you'd better watch out for her dad. Wouldn't want him slicing up that pretty face of yours." Then she stalked off and out the door with an attention-grabbing crash.

"My mistake," said Mike, watching the pair leave. "Not a friend."

"No, you could say that." It was, in fact, the understatement of the year. "Thanks for stepping in. I'm, um . . . glad you're here." *Oh no, did I really say that out loud?*

Mike gave her a long slow smile, his golden eyes shining with amusement. "So am I."

Normal. It was a normal conversation. Nothing about Templars, about plagues and watchers. Nothing but the sort of conversation normal people have. Mike told Billi a bit about his dad, who sounded so much like hers. Strict, judgmental, and pushy. She asked about the tattoos, and he laughingly said he'd been born with them.

"When I came in and saw you with that girl, you looked like you were going to totally rearrange her face." Mike made a mocking fist. "Who taught you to fight like that?"

"My dad."

He raised his eyebrows. "Wow. I thought most daddies wanted their daughters to become ballerinas, not bouncers. Normal boring stuff." He tilted his head across the table so his bright eyes were close. "But there's nothing normal about you, is there?"

"I assume that's a compliment?" Billi frowned. She wasn't used to all this . . . flirting.

"I'd never insult you. I'd be too scared."

His hands were on the smoky glass tabletop, his fingertips an inch away from hers. *Just the tiniest touch forward . . .* Billi hesitated, trying to summon up the brazen courage the other girls in the café seemed to have no problem with.

Too late. Mike leaned back in his chair and moved his hands onto the armrests.

Billi didn't quite know where to look.

"What did Jane mean about your dad?" asked Mike, breaking the awkward silence. "Overly protective, is he?" There was a hint of a smile, but Billi's heart still sank.

He didn't know. Not about her mum or her dad's trial. What should she tell him? Billi looked down at the dark glass and saw her gloomy reflection. If she didn't tell Mike, he'd pick up the malicious rumors soon enough.

"Y'know I told you that my mum had died?" She looked up at Mike and could see how his face had subtly changed. The laughter was gone. "I didn't tell you how. She was murdered."

"Jesus, Billi. I'm sorry." Totally attentive, Mike's gaze

locked hers. Billi closed her eyes; she couldn't think with him looking at her like that. "There was a break-in at our house. Mum was stabbed. She died."

She was lying; she had to. This was the official story.

"Did they ever find out who did it?"

She shook her head. "It's more complicated than that. The police arrested my dad. He was tried for her murder."

Mike leaned over and put his hand on Billi's. The tenderness of his touch took her by surprise. His skin was as soft as cream.

"Why did they think your dad did it?"

There were so many reasons, except for the truth. No one would believe it had been the work of the Unholy. But it was easy to believe a man like her father, a soldier who'd been court-martialed, a man who'd spent a year in a psychiatric hospital suffering from post-traumatic stress disorder, might turn into a murderer.

"The police just wanted to solve the crime. My dad was an easy suspect." She looked up at him hopefully.

Mike smiled gently, but there was something holding him back.

"He didn't do it, Mike."

"No, of course not. I believe you." But she could see he wasn't really looking at her, not directly. He was looking at her bruises, the one on her cheek from the Ordeal, the one on her forehead from her dad's head-butt.

Did he believe her lies? She couldn't tell.

"My dad's a hard man. And he wanted me to be like that too," said Mike as he unconsciously trailed his finger along a thorn on his neck. "He had plans for me, wanted to control every minute of my life. That's the thing about parents, isn't it? They don't really want you to live your own life; they want you to correct their mistakes."

"What happened?"

Mike laughed bitterly. "Whatever I did, it wasn't good enough. He just wanted more and more." He spoke again, so quietly it was almost a confession. "So I left."

He caught her gaze, and his amber eyes flashed with pent-up frustration. Billi couldn't look away. It was like having all her own feelings reflected back at her.

The bell chimed, and Billi caught the unmistakable dash of white hair under a black woolen cap.

Kay.

He came straight over.

"Billi, you're needed." He looked at Mike, and the suspicion was obvious. "Now."

"Kay, I'm busy. Can't it wait?" She felt strangely guilty. *But I'm not doing anything wrong!*

Mike stood up. He was actually a few inches shorter than Kay, but his bulk and physical presence made him seem bigger. Billi hoped Kay wouldn't do anything stupid. As far as she knew, Kay couldn't fight a marshmallow.

"Another friend of yours?" said Mike.

"Yes," Kay snapped.

"So am I." He took a step closer to Billi. She didn't miss the way his arm brushed hers, and neither did Kay.

Kay edged forward. "Funny, she's not mentioned you."

Billi took Kay's elbow. "Outside," she snapped. She looked at Mike. "I'll just be a minute."

Billi had to drag Kay from the café. He stood with his hands buried in his pockets, occasionally glancing back at Mike over his shoulder.

"How did you know I was here?" asked Billi.

"D'you know what time it is?"

Kay shifted awkwardly and tugged at his hair. Billi understood.

"You read my mind," she hissed.

"Oh come on, Billi. You've been thinking about Milano's all day, practically shouting it out. I couldn't help it."

What was Kay going on about? They'd only been talking for about an hour. She checked her watch.

That can't be right.

"Oh yes it is," said Kay. "You should have been on duty ages ago."

"Then why didn't you just call me?"

Kay shifted uneasily. "I thought it best I come tell you."

"No, you thought it best to come and spy on me. To see who I was with."

He stepped back, frustrated. "We used to look out for one another, remember?"

"Used to. Not anymore. Now I look out for myself.

What d'you think I've been doing for the last year?"

Kay jerked his head in Mike's direction. "He's not one of us, Billi. You're a Templar and you've got bigger responsibilities than hanging out in cafés."

"Jeez, listen to you, Kay. You sound just like my dad."

"And what's wrong with that?" he snapped.

Billi gritted her teeth. Kay was the sort of Templar Arthur wanted. Devoted and blind. He just didn't get it. The pointlessness of it all. The *Bataille Ténébreuse* was a fool's quest; why was she the only one who could see that?

All she wanted was to turn around, go back to Mike, and not think about the bloody Templars just for one solitary evening. She shook her head. She obviously wasn't going to be allowed even that.

"Just give me a minute."

"Now."

"Just give me a minute!" Billi shouted. Kay almost said something, then turned away.

Billi wandered back into the café.

"I have to go, Mike."

"You in trouble with your boyfriend? Sorry, I didn't realize."

Boyfriend? Kay? "No! It's just . . . my dad wants me home."

Mike put his hand on her shoulder, but she gently pushed it away. She'd never have any peace, and it wasn't fair to get him caught in the middle.

"Good-bye, Mike. I'm sorry." *Yes, really sorry.* She glanced over at Kay fuming by the door. She hated what he was turning into: a Templar through and through.

"Listen, Billi. If things are hard at home with your dad, I understand." He smiled. "Been there, done that, if you know what I mean." He took her coat and helped her put it on, a curiously old-fashioned gesture that took her by surprise. Billi could feel Kay's blood boiling from here.

Good.

"Just give me a shout if you want a break. Get away from . . . whatever," Mike added.

He leaned forward, and their faces were a few inches apart. She could see her reflection in his golden eyes. Mike's neck muscles tensed, and she stared at the long curve of his throat down into his T-shirt. She stepped away, flustered. Suddenly it was all too hot and stuffy in here.

"I'll see you around, Mike."

He just wanted more and more. Billi couldn't get Mike's words out of her head. She sat in the back of Berrant's van, hunched over the small monitor, watching the corridor of the children's ward in ghostly black-and-white.

Gareth was sitting in the driver's seat, under a blanket, eyes half closed. He'd stir every few minutes, take a sip of black coffee, then drift off again.

More and more. No matter how much time she dedicated to the Templars, her dad always wanted more. Did he treat the other knights like that? She couldn't even have a few hours to herself without the Order smashing it all up.

And Mike understood. The only thing good about being on watch was that she could relive their date in her mind. She really wanted to see him again. But how? Her dad would never let her go. The harder she worked, the more responsibilities he piled onto her. She was trapped.

So I left.

12

BILLI GOT HOME AFTER THE WATCH AND WAS ASLEEP the moment her head hit the pillow. She made it through the next day only because it was Saturday. She thought about calling Mike but seemed to have left her mobile in Berrant's van. And anyway, what use was it? The more she thought about how her dad dictated every minuscule aspect of her life, the more she thought about what Mike had said—about leaving.

Evening came around too quickly, and Billi crossed the dark courtyard and made her way down into the catacombs.

The armory was alive with the clatter of weapons and thumping of punches and kicks. Billi chucked her bag into a corner and found a spot to do her warm-ups. Even Kay was here; that was a first. He was red-faced and absolutely soaked in sweat, practicing unarmed combat with the hulking Bors. There were no weight categories in real fights, so

Arthur made everyone train against each other. Billi winced as Bors slammed his shoulder into Kay's chest, catapulting him across the practice mat.

"He won't be much good as an Oracle if you knock his brains out," said Billi. Bors just grunted; when it came to Oracles, he felt the same way Gwaine did. Kay lifted himself off the mat and waved at her. She ignored him.

She looked around the catacomb. Still no Arthur, and Percy was at work fighting Pelleas. Percy wielded a heavy ax as though it were made of balsa wood; Pelleas, bandages gone now, darted under and between blows, weaving a web of steel with his rapier and main-gauche. Gareth sat on a stool, carefully wrapping fresh fletching to a quiver of arrows. An array of arrow heads lay on the table, along with armor-piercing bodkins, barbed tips, even forked rope-cutters. All brightly polished and razor sharp.

Pelleas broke off and stepped away, so Billi lifted up a quarterstaff. The straight six-foot pole was about as thick as her wrist and made of heavy oak. It was oiled and smooth from years of use. Billi raised it over her head and listened to her shoulder blades click.

"Whenever you're ready," she said. She slid the staff through her loose grip and waited. Percy dropped his ax and reached for one of the *bokkens*. It looked half-size in his hand.

She went into guard, holding her weapon waist high, the end pointed at the center of Percy's chest.

"Where's Dad?"

Percy circled around her. He held the sword in a single grip and tapped it against her quarterstaff. "Out. Where else?"

"Nice of him to mention it."

Percy snorted. "Why would he do that? You know Art."

Yes, why would he? She was made to miss out on her own life for these watches and training sessions, but her dad could do what he bloody well liked.

"Has he always been like this, Percy?"

Percy had known her dad since they'd served in the Royal Marines together. He'd been best man at her parents' wedding and had been chosen to be her godfather. If her dad had a friend, it was this man in front of her. Percy slowly took the sword in a two-handed grip. Billi watched his fingers flex around the hilt.

"Like what, honey?"

"Selfish and heartless?"

Percy stopped dead. His grip tightened, and Billi saw his jaw stiffen. Then he took a deep sigh, stepped back, and focused his attention on his weapon.

"We'll start with light sparring. Upper-body cuts first." He shifted his position to high guard.

"Percy, didn't you hear me?"

"Left strike to head." His gray T-shirt was stretched thin across his tanklike chest. He slid his right leg forward, grinding his bare foot into the floor and setting himself in, rock hard and immovable.

His *kiai* shout shook the stones, and Billi swept up her staff, and even though she blocked the attack, the impact knocked her to the ground. Her hands stung. Percy stood over her, sword tip directed at her throat.

"More flexibility in the shoulders; absorbs the shock better," he said.

Billi didn't get up.

Percy paused. He tucked the *bokken* under his armpit and lifted her to her feet. He stood in front of her, and his brown eyes softened.

"Billi, I wish it could be different. But Arthur has no choice." He glanced up, checking that no one was near, then leaned down so he could whisper, "But never doubt he loves you."

Then he put away his wooden sword and left.

Two hours later Billi was in the kitchen, clearing away dinner, when Arthur came home. He dropped his backpack against the washing machine and went to the fridge.

"You were late for watch," he said.

Oh, nice to see you too, Dad.

"Yes. I'm sorry."

"I thought I'd made myself clear, right here." He pointed at the spot in front of him. "About you wasting time . . . socializing."

So Kay had told him about her date. Some friend

he'd turned out to be. "I wasn't wasting my time."

His eyes narrowed and his fingers tightened around the fridge handle. He stood, eyes locked on hers, and Billi marked the paleness in his face.

"What exactly do you think this is?" he asked. "Some sort of game? That you can drop out of anytime you like to go holding hands with some boy?" He slammed the door shut, and the table jumped. "Yes, the training's hard, but it's for your own good."

"My own good? This has nothing to do with me! The Knights Templar—it's all you. Everything's about *them* and *you*. You don't care about *me*."

Arthur stared back at her stonily, but didn't deny it.

"You are a Templar, Billi. Never forget that. We—you—have no choice. Deal with it."

He turned his back on her.

Percy had been so wrong. Billi slammed the front door and wiped her face. She had to get out. She didn't care where, just out.

"Hey, SanGreal."

Billi spun around. Mike stood in the shadowy doorway behind her.

"For God's sake, Mike, you almost gave me a cardiac." What was he doing here at this time of night?

He pulled out his mobile. "I tried calling."

Damn, her mobile was still somewhere in Berrant's van.

"Sorry, but I lost mine."

Mike came closer. "So it wasn't because of our talk? I'm sorry if I got too personal. It's none of my business."

"No, it's nothing to do with you. It's just . . . things aren't that great with my dad." Gross understatement.

Mike saw her tear-stained face. He bit his lip, and Billi could see he was struggling not to say something. He just nodded slowly. "You okay?"

Billi stared at her door. The paint was worn and flaking. She turned toward Mike. God, she so desperately wanted to run away from all this.

"Let's get out of here," he said, almost reading her thoughts. "I want to show you something amazing."

13

THEY MADE THEIR WAY ALONG THE DARK STREETS into the City. It was dead at this time of night. Though the oldest part of London, it was a maze of narrow alleys and glass towers, old bones with fresh new flesh. The unlit wine bars, dull pubs, the monolithic Victorian banks, the glass-and-steel skyscrapers, they all jostled and pushed at each other, vainly reaching for what little sky there was.

Mike brought Billi to a building site. Barbed wire topped the whitewashed boarding, and floodlights cast their stark white glare over the skeletal black frame of a half-erected tower. Billi stopped in front of a display board.

"Elysium Heights," she said. She followed the spine of the building upward. It looked like the skeleton of some ancient giant, reaching out of his grave and grasping for Heaven. The sky hung low and brooding over it, like an angry thought. "Why would anyone want to live up there?"

"Because it's beautiful," said Mike. "Haven't you noticed how you can't see the dirt from up high?"

Billi shook her head. "It's unreal. Living up so high, it just cuts you off. But some people might want that."

"Want what?"

"To be above everyone."

Mike smiled. "You might feel differently once you've seen for yourself." He made his way to the gates. "Follow me."

The gate was chain-link, and Mike scrabbled up and over it in seconds. He dropped down on the opposite side. "Come on."

Trespassing. It was trespassing.

"No. This is stupid, Mike. Come back."

Her dad would flay her alive if she got caught.

Mike looked up at the tower. "We'll be quick. I've done it before, Billi. Up there you get a different perspective on things. Your troubles don't seem to matter so much."

She shouldn't do it. She should be a good little girl and obey her dad.

Billi hooked her fingers into the chain-link and jumped over. She stumbled as she landed, but Mike caught her. His arms lingered around her, and Billi could sense his strength, just held in check.

Then he straightened her up and moved farther into the dark.

Prefab offices and temporary sheds were scattered across the muddy playing field–size site. Tractors, bulldozers, and yellow trucks stood idle and menacing like dormant monsters. The harsh floodlights threw deep shadows, as well as glaring brightness, and it didn't take long for Billi to get lost in the labyrinthine alleyways between the piles of cement and steel.

"This is it." Mike stopped beside the goods hoist. The steel cage took men and materials up and down the building, fixed to the side via a rickety-looking yellow scaffold.

Billi stared awestruck at the scale of it all. A light rain had begun to fall and she blinked to clear her eyes of the raindrops. The frame rose out of huge concrete columns, each a couple of feet wide. A complex web of steel beams climbed higher and higher into the darkness.

Mike pointed up. "The view is awesome."

"You've been that high?" What was he trying to prove, taking this sort of risk? Billi stared upward, and her head swam.

Mike looked into the sky. "Oh, much higher." He lifted up the steel cage door of the elevator.

Billi followed him and slammed down the gate. Mike took hold of the red handle and pulled. The elevator trembled as it shook itself free of the earth and climbed.

The city spread out under her. The roads were golden ribbons twisting through the diamond-sparkling darkness, the buildings glowed in the floodlights, and the Thames wound through it all, black as marble. The wind-wrapped raindrops stung her cheeks, and the cold air electrified her skin. Higher and higher they rose, while the elevator rattled and shook, and the gears on the scaffold shrieked. The city and all her problems were so far below. Mike was right: it *was* beautiful.

The elevator halted with a jolt.

Mike rolled up the gate. "Follow me."

"Are you insane? I'm not going out there!"

"C'mon, Billi. I'll take care of you."

Billi hesitated. No one had promised her that before.

She walked to the edge of the elevator. The floor was only half cast. Here by the elevator it was broad and thick concrete, but beyond, where Mike was heading, it was just a matrix of beams with small solid patches filled in, like a massive crossword. She gazed down and had to clutch the side as her head swam with vertigo. There wasn't much between her and the ground, six hundred feet below. She slowly crossed the solid section of floor, keeping well away from the edge.

But Mike was already out there. He stood waiting for her, standing on the narrow flange of an I beam, maybe less than three inches wide. The wind howled through the steel, cut and sliced by the metal so it sounded like voices screeching in the dark.

Mike proceeded to a ladder and started to climb up. "The view is to die for."

"I bet it is," said Billi, but Mike didn't hear her.

She put a foot out on the beam. It wasn't wide, but she'd

worked on narrower in training. She'd take one step at a time, not rush; concentrate and try not to worry about the rain. Or the gently swaying tower. Or gravity.

One foot, then the next, she worked her way, shuffled her way, to the ladder. It was farther from the elevator platform than she'd thought, or at least it seemed that way. But she reached it, her hands gripped the ladder rails tightly, and she could see it was clamped firmly to the vertical column. Maybe she'd just stay here for a while. Until they finished building the tower.

"We can go back down if you're scared. I don't mind." Mike looked back down the ladder at her.

Scared? Billi scowled. If only Mike knew what she did at night. She started climbing up. Her fingers were freezing and she had to force them to close around the rungs. But she climbed.

Mike stood at the end of a beam, suspended alone in the sky, his coat flapping in the wind like the wild wings of a giant bat. He was lost in the sight of London below him. Billi could see the pale white dome of St. Paul's and the gleaming lights of the city laid out beneath the heavy black sky. And Mike, poised above it all. The wind whipped at his unbuttoned coat and tussled his hair. He stretched out his arms, daring the elements. The moon broke between the barrage of clouds, and Billi caught his almost serene look. His face was turned upward, his eyes closed, his skin pearly-luminescent and flawless.

"Come out here to the edge," he said.

"The view's fine from here, thanks. Be careful." Like that was a great piece of advice. She held on to the column. The tower was definitely swaying.

Mike shook his head. "I can't fall. I've never fallen."

"It may not be up to you. Accidents happen. Earthquake, sudden wind." She wasn't helping, but she thought he was an idiot to be up there. "Things beyond our control. *Force majeure*. Acts of God."

Mike stiffened. "Why is it they call them that? Acts of God?"

"Call what?"

"Disasters. Catastrophes. When something terrible happens, it's always an Act of God. Why is that?"

Billi started to feel nervous. Mike obviously had as much stuff to deal with as she did. But this *really* wasn't the place to be doing it. "Come back, Mike. Let's talk on the ground." But he wasn't listening. He leaned out. It looked like he was ready to jump. Or fly.

"I'll tell you why. It's when people are afraid, they turn to Him. They remember that their lives continue purely because of His whim." He snapped his fingers. The crack was as loud as a gunshot. "Lives that could end in an instant."

This sounds like seriously crazy talk. Billi reached out, one hand on the column, the other stretched toward his back. "Mike . . ."

"It takes a terrible thing to remind people of their obligations to God. The more terrible, the better. Wouldn't it be something if that happened?"

"What happened?"

"Something so terrible that everyone returned to Him. To fill the churches on Sunday instead of Ikea. To fill the mosques, the synagogues." He spread out his arms. "An Act of God that would restore faith."

Billi hung on to the steel. It wasn't the cold night that made her shiver.

"Mike—"

"Your father, he'll make you suffer, you know that."

Billi said nothing. Mike was crossing the line. . . . That was her business. She wanted to get down. The wind picked up, and invisible claws pulled at her. She wrapped herself tightly around the column.

"You owe him nothing, Billi." Mike stroked the long spike along his neck. "Help me, Billi, and I'll make you free." He turned to her, those golden eyes peering down at her like an eagle's. Predatory and surging with power now. "Where's the mirror, Billi?"

Billi's blood went cold. It couldn't be. Mike stood up, and the black coat spread out, not like wings of a bat, but like those of an angel. A dark angel.

"Betray him, Billi. For what he's done to you. For what he did to your mother."

Jesus, she'd been such a fool! Billi cast around; she had

to get down. If she could keep him talking she might have a chance to escape. The ladder wasn't that far. She reached out with her left hand.

"My dad didn't kill my mum." Her fingers touched the bare wood.

"I know, Billi."

"What?"

Mike leaped.

He launched himself out into the sky, and he seemed to halt, impossibly, at the apex of the jump. Then he dove down and slammed into the beam next to Billi. The ladder shook loose and fell away, and Billi tottered on the narrow edge before she came off, touching only empty air. Her heart froze and she flung out her arms, staring in horror as the ladder disappeared in the darkness. Terror robbed her voice of air, and all she could do was stare as the lights blurred and the sky turned and the wind screamed in her ears.

OhGodohGodohGodohGod—

Mike's hand locked around her left wrist, and she almost dislocated her shoulder at the sudden halt. He held her effortlessly with one hand. Their eyes met, and for the briefest moment, Billi thought he was going to let go. Instead he let her dangle. Billi felt her left shoe slide off, and the air tickled her foot.

"I know he didn't kill her." His eyes lit up, and there was nothing human in them. "I did."

19

BILLI FELT LIKE SHE WAS ON THE RACK AND HER ARM was being ripped from its socket. She could barely focus through the blinding agony as she swayed, high above the city, hanging from Mike's grip.

"The mirror, Billi, it's all I want. Tell me where it is, and I'll let you go." He laughed at his weak joke.

Billi groaned. Hot waves of pain raced along her arm and down her spine.

"My brothers and sisters have been imprisoned long enough." He tightened his grip, and Billi screamed.

"No," was all she could say. The ground, so far below, revolved slowly, sickeningly.

Mike's face was twisted in demonic rage. It was as though his face was wax, and had been pressed against a red-hot plate. Rivulets of flesh trailed his cheeks, the skin sagged under his eyes, and his mouth widened, nearly bisecting his face. He caught her looking at him, exposed, then the moment passed. Suddenly he was back to the friendly human Mike. But the mask had slipped and his true self had been revealed.

The Unholy.

How could she have been so stupid?

"C'mon, Billi." He smiled at her, trying on that charming, handsome illusion that now made Billi's stomach churn. "I've been searching for it for centuries. Came close a few times, like back when the Inquisition was hunting you all down. But the Templars went into hiding, deep, deep underground. For a while I thought the mirror was lost forever. After La Rochelle. You have no idea how long I've roamed the world looking for those boats."

Rumors, all those rumors about what happened to the Templar fleet. Billi caught a glimpse of Michael's quest. How many centuries had he spent fruitlessly searching for the Templar treasures?

"I almost had it, ten years ago." He raised Billi up so they were eye to eye. "Would have got it if it hadn't been for your mother."

The Nights of Iron. In spite of the pain, Billi couldn't help but listen, awestruck.

"But they were *ghuls*. The Templars were attacked by *ghuls*."

Mike pointed to himself. "Created by me. You'd be amazed at how many people would sell their souls for a little immortality." He let out a sigh. "Twelve nights of war and bloodshed. It was glorious. I killed Uriens. Crushed his skull between my palms, but he wouldn't tell. If he didn't know how to live like a Templar Master, he knew how to die like one."

Billi gritted her teeth and forced herself to look around. Maybe she could reach another beam or drop to the floor below. There was a ledge about five feet away. But a glance told her it was hopeless. The only solid ground was six hundred sickening feet below her.

Mike winked. "And when I found out Arthur had stepped into Uriens's shoes, I came to your home. Thought I'd hold both you and your mother hostage. Force Arthur to hand the mirror over in exchange for his darling wife and sweet daughter."

Fire blazed in Billi's eyes. She was staring at her mother's killer. Every fiber of her burned with hatred. Mike didn't seem to mind.

"Your mother looked at me with those very eyes. So black and so full of hate. If it's any consolation, she fought till the very end, defending you, hidden in the bedroom, with her life's blood." He smiled at the memory. "Who'd have thought she'd have so much blood in her? It was all over the door, on the walls. Everywhere." He sighed. "But she just wouldn't play along and sit tight. I was almost sorry to kill her. Especially since it was clear that you alone wouldn't be enough to make Arthur hand over the mirror.

It occurred to me, after ending your mother's life, that the pair of you had been left at home defenseless, and yet still no Arthur. . . . He obviously didn't care about you. Just like he doesn't care about you now. So I left you sniveling under the bed."

"No, that's not true," Billi whispered. No matter what her dad did to her, he had to love her. She was his daughter! But as she dangled in the icy winds, Billi felt doubt sinking into her heart. Mike leaned closer.

"See? You believe me, don't you? And this is the man you want to protect? You owe him nothing, Billi." Mike squeezed her wrist. "I only let him go last time after leaving our little party and discovering he'd killed all my *ghuls*. I decided then I would wait and rebuild my strength for this very special moment. Now it's your turn, Billi. Tell me where the mirror is and you'll be free. Free of your father. Of the Templars. Just tell me."

"I'll tell you something. You're scum. Murdering scum," Billi hissed. Mike's eyes darkened, and for a split second Billi felt his grip loosen, and her heart jumped. But then he scowled and instead squeezed her wrist so hard she could feel her bones about to crack.

"I am Michael, the Angel of Death. It was I who rained fire on Gomorrah. It was I who stalked the streets of Egypt and slew the firstborn. I cast down Satan. I and I alone." He stared at her with a mixture of pride and anger. "I will bring people back to the light. I am God's killer, and I will not be judged by the children of clay." He shook her wildly. "Where is the Cursed Mirror?"

"So you and your wingless siblings can unleash the Tenth Plague? I don't think so. I don't even understand why." She thought about Rebecca and the others he'd managed to infect with his touch in the hospital. If he got his hands on the mirror and released his brothers and sisters, the death toll would be immense. Britain would become a mausoleum overnight. "They're innocent children."

"Then rejoice, for they will soon be in His kingdom. Do you know, Rebecca's mother prays constantly now?"

He knew? He knew they'd been to China Wharf hospital? Oh God, what a fool she'd been.

Michael leaned closer. "Just think how much harder she'll pray once Rebecca dies. Think of the thousands, millions of prayers and souls I'll send to Him after I release the Tenth Plague." He looked up into the cloud-swollen sky. "God cannot ignore me then." He reached up with his free hand while gazing into the darkness. "He will take me back. He must."

Billi spat at him. Her muscles were numb now; all she felt was a dull ache down her arm. Her feet hung over empty air, and she knew she was going to die. Michael had killed her mother, and that hatred overcame the fear. He wiped the spittle off his chin and laughed.

"A fighter, just like Jamila. I like that." He swung her in long arcs like she was a rag doll. Billi thought she'd overcome the pain, but a blaze of fresh agony ran into her shoulders and down her back, and she couldn't help but let out a short scream. Michael continued, "I knew you wouldn't tell. Two stubborn parents; no wonder you've turned out this way. Totally pigheaded." He smirked and turned his head, though his eyes were still on Billi. "Isn't that true, Kay?"

Billi's eyes were blurred with tears, but she could still see Kay standing at the lift. He stared at them, horrified.

"Run!" Billi screamed. What was he doing here? Oh God, he was going to get himself killed.

Michael tutted.

"Now, now, Billi. That's not very nice. Kay's come to save you. How . . . heroic." Then Michael showed her something: her mobile. "You left it at the café. I just texted him, and now here he is. Sweet, don't you think?"

"Let her go!" Kay edged his way across the beams to a flat cast square of floor. He was scared, but there was a tight grimness to his face.

"I want the mirror, Kay. Tell me or you'll be soaking Billi up with a mop and bucket."

She felt so helpless! She *was* so helpless. She thrashed out with her foot, but it just shot wildly in the air, striking nothing. How could she have fallen for it? Fallen for Michael? It had been a con from the beginning.

"All right, all right," said Kay. He was at the edge of the ledge. "I'll show you where it is."

Mike swung Billi toward the ledge, and her stomach flipped as she tumbled through the air. Then she smashed into Kay, and the two of them rolled, banging heads, elbows, and knees, over and over on the cast floor.

Billi couldn't move her left arm. Ten thousand pins and needles stabbed and poked her muscles, and it felt like her arm was on fire. The sky spun overhead and she gasped for air. But she had to get up. She wasn't going to be beaten by the man who had killed her mother. She rolled over, and Kay was beside her, groaning.

"Jesus, Kay. How stupid are you?"

"But I thought you texted me. You wanted to meet me." He got to his feet and held out his hand. They both saw how it trembled.

"Here?" Billi gripped it, and Kay steadied himself as he helped her up. "Like under the big sign saying *trap*?"

"I wasn't the one dangling off the side of a skyscraper."

Billi spotted a toolbox pushed up against the wall. "Listen," she whispered. "When I move, I want you to dummy left. Leave Michael to me."

"I can fight."

"Trust me, you can't. Just dummy left, okay?" But Kay's face was rigid. He wanted to fight. Billi wanted to slap some sense into him. "Dummy left."

"Okay," he said finally.

Billi crossed over to the toolbox and pulled out a large wrench. Her left arm dangled uselessly by her side, but she raised the tool high with her right. Somehow she had to stop him. Michael paused, watched her grit her teeth and stride forward. Kay darted in on the left, but Michael didn't respond. Billi brought the wrench down with all her strength. Michael still didn't respond. The wrench head, a square chunk of steel, shattered the side of his skull.

Michael buckled but didn't fall. Billi gaped at the deep wound oozing thick blood. It clung to his hair, and the top shoulder of his coat was sprinkled with red droplets.

But then the bleeding stopped. The gap of broken bone began to re-form, and the deep dent bulged back into shape. Within seconds the bone had repaired itself and the skin began to seal, leaving only a thin pink scar. That too vanished within seconds.

"Is this how you dump all your boyfriends?" asked Michael. Then he struck. Billi tried to block, but her left arm wouldn't respond. She ducked under the hammerlike fist, but it caught her dead center in the forehead. Sparks exploded around her, and she felt herself falling. She collapsed, and edges of darkness crept into her vision, gently turning everything black.

Arms half lifted, half dragged her, and she felt soft warm fabric against her face. Billi's mind drifted in and out of consciousness, and deep down a small part of her screamed for her to wake up. She couldn't. She was trapped in this nightmare and couldn't get herself out. She moaned in despair.

A voice filtered through; someone she didn't recognize. A door slammed and an engine rumbled to life. "Oi, your girlfriend's not going to puke in my taxi, is she?"

"Don't worry, sir. She's just had one too many drinks," said Michael. "Isn't that right, Kay?"

There was a strained murmur. At least Kay was with her. She let the blackness take her again.

Billi . . .

15

BILLI STUMBLED OUT OF THE TAXI. KAY GRABBED HER before she fell. She tried to stand, but the ground pitched and rolled, and her sense of balance was precarious.

"This is it?" asked Michael. He didn't sound impressed. "The Templar reliquary?"

Billi glanced up. Oh no. Elaine's Bazaar. Kay really had brought them here. Her fingers dug into his shoulder. What was he doing? The lights were out in her apartment. Was Elaine in? Maybe Billi could shout a warning.

No, it was too late now anyway.

The three of them stood by the shop door. Michael took the handle, and with a sharp pull ripped the lock and the surrounding wood out.

"After you," he said, half bowing in mock gallantry.

Kay went first, Billi next. Michael kept his hand on her neck, prompting her with a squeeze as she tripped in the dark.

"The door to the basement's at the back," said Kay.

What was wrong with him? Didn't he realize what would happen if Michael got the mirror? *Oh God. Was he doing this for her?* She shot a glance at Kay. He just stared ahead, devoid of emotion. If only she could think of something. Billi's fingers wound themselves into fists as Michael pushed her along. They stopped by the stuffed bear, and Billi caught Kay's eye. They couldn't just let Mike get the mirror so easily. But Kay twitched his head once and heaved the animal out of the way, revealing the basement door.

Michael ripped out the lock of the small door, too. Surely Elaine would have heard that? Maybe if she screamed out a warning, Elaine might—

Michael's fingers tightened around her throat. "Don't do anything stupid," he whispered. But his voice was tense, excited. The mirror was almost in his grasp. Then Kay switched on the light and they descended.

The reliquary was as cluttered as before, but there were fresh changes. The wards on the walls were cleaned, recarved, and reinforced with long rows of painted calligraphy and reams of parchment. There was barely a square of wall without some symbol painted onto it or sheets of prayers stuck there. It was like her dad had said: the magical protections had been improved.

A lot.

Michael's attention wasn't on the walls; it was on the large black-lacquered cabinet. He peered closely at the broken Seal of Solomon on the door leaves. His eyes, those brilliant amber eyes, now burned with demonic hunger. He tossed Billi aside, and she collapsed against the wall.

She'd been so wrong. So wrong. He'd charmed her and tempted her, and she had given in to that temptation. And now they were here. A watcher brought right into the Templars' reliquary.

Michael ran his fingertips lightly along the bronze circle, as though he'd expected it to be red hot. But the cool metal didn't reject him, and he smiled.

"Solomon, you old fool," he said to himself. Then he took the two bronze handles and pulled the doors open. "At last."

He reached into the cabinet. When he turned back he held the dark blue velvet box, and his eyes were on that alone. He raised it toward the light. "Soon, my brothers, my sisters." He flicked open the latch and gazed in. He stared and stared, and Billi saw his face darken.

"I don't like games, SanGreal," he said. He spun the box around.

It was empty.

"Where's the mirror?" Michael asked.

"Far from here, Mike." A shadow formed on the steps and slid into the dimly lit chamber. Arthur walked in. "I moved it the minute I knew your pitiful siblings' cries had been heard." He glanced over at Kay. "We thought you'd come looking for it sooner or later."

Billi stared at Kay. Was that why he'd brought Mike

here without a struggle? Because he knew Arthur would be waiting?

Arthur had the Templar sword in his right hand and a small silver crucifix hanging from his left fist. He stopped at the bottom of the steps, but he was in easy striking distance. Mike tossed the empty box away and grabbed an old sword off the wall.

"Arthur SanGreal. D'you know, Billi, they say Satan himself only fears two things in all of existence? The judgment of God and Arthur SanGreal. Tell me, Arthur"—he stepped behind Billi to keep a safe distance between himself and the Templar Master—"what did you do to make even the Devil afraid?"

"Come here and I'll show you," said Arthur, edging forward.

She'd fouled up beyond measure in trusting Michael. Maybe Kay had been right not to tell her.

"He killed Mum," she said. Arthur ignored her, but his eyes narrowed and his fist tightened around the sword hilt.

"Do you miss her, Arthur?" Michael's smile was twisted and foul. "She's waiting for you. In Hell."

Kay grabbed Billi and together they pressed themselves against the wall, hand in hand, watching.

Arthur's sword moved like a lightning storm, far faster than Billi could follow. Michael parried as they clashed, and the hammering steel echoed loudly within the underground chamber. In the poor light their movements were a blur. Her dad's face was cold, impassive, and intensely focused. He didn't watch anything but Michael's eyes, judging his attacks, ripostes, and blocks on instinct and the touch of the blades. The dark angel's concentration was no less, but he never lost that arrogant smile, even up to the end. Then their hilts caught just for a second. Arthur twisted his wrist sharply and Michael's blade snapped. They stared at each other, the fight over, sweat dripping off them both in heavy beads. Then Arthur stepped back and slashed his blade downward, catching Michael at the back of his neck. His head slipped off, bounced a couple of times, then rolled into a corner. The body swayed, sank to its knees, and finally fell forward.

Billi stared as the blood began to pool around the severed neck. The body lay there on its front, arms on either side. Dead meat. Michael's skin was already turning pale as the blood drained from it. Arthur pulled a dusty sheet off a table and threw it over the corpse. "Call Percival. We need a cleanup."

"Wait a minute," said Billi. She couldn't take her eyes off the head. Its eyes stared up blankly. "You sure he's dead? I caved his head in an hour ago and that didn't stop him."

Kay stood beside her. "He's dead, all right. We've reinforced the wards down here. Michael's powers should have been negated once he entered the reliquary."

"You planned this?" Anger swelled in Billi's throat, and she gritted her teeth to keep it from escaping.

Kay lowered his eyes, unable to meet hers. "I wanted to tell you, Billi, but Arthur thought—"

"Percival and I have been rotating watches on this place for the last week, not knowing if anyone would come." Arthur sounded strangely hoarse. "Though I was surprised that your boyfriend turned out to be the Angel of Death."

She thumped her dad on the chest. "You told Kay about your little scheme and not me? You don't trust me at all, do—"

Arthur dropped his sword and bent over. She hadn't punched him that hard. He coughed and spat a bloody glob onto the floor.

"Dad?" Billi put her hand on him; what was wrong?

His face was pallid and he was gasping for breath. Billi pulled open his jacket and saw the dark red stain spreading on his shirt.

"Billi," he said, frothy pink foam dribbling from his mouth. His stomach was slick with blood, and only now did she see the tear in his jacket. He smiled weakly, then collapsed.

Billi grabbed him, but he was heavy, and she stumbled back as his legs failed him. Kay rushed beside her, and they eased him down onto the floor. His body shook as a spasm of coughing overtook him, the bubbles of blood-flecked spittle darker now.

"Call an ambulance!" she shouted.

The wound was just below his ribs, to the right. It had missed his heart, but the froth meant it must have punctured a lung. He was drowning in his own blood.

But it looked so small! She tried to cover the injury, but her hands just slid all over the place because of the blood. Each time he breathed, a grotesque sucking sound came from the hole. Her fingers trembled over his cold belly. The blood looked so black under the dim light, and there was so much of it. She couldn't stop it. He was going to die. Oh God, what had she done? Kay stood beside her, giving the ambulance service their address. Then he flipped his mobile shut and joined her.

"You have to plug it, Billi," he whispered. Arthur struggled to keep his eyes open; they were fluttering and hugely dilated.

"Tape, get me some tape," she snapped at Kay.

He searched the chamber frantically, emptying out a desk, and found what she wanted: a reel of tape and a sheet of plastic. When she turned back, her dad was unconscious. She could just hear the sticky hissing as air bled out of his lungs. She bit off strips of the tape while Kay squared the plastic and laid it over the hole. Her dad was nearly white, and his breath was only the slightest breeze. She took his hand; she didn't know what else to do. It sat in her palm, cold and limp. Billi squeezed it as tightly as she could. No, he had to live.

Then she heard something humming: her dad's mobile.

She found it in his pocket and flicked it open. She recognized the number immediately.

"Percy, come quickly! It's Dad!" She looked at the pale sweat-soaked face. "It's my dad."

"What happened?" Percy's voice was tense and the line crackled.

"He's been stabbed. It's bad, Percy, really bad. An ambulance is coming."

"An ambulance? Billi, you know you should have checked with me or Gwaine. The rules—"

"Dad's dying! I don't give a damn about the bloody rules!"

"All right, Billi. That's all right." She could hear him talking to someone . . . *Who? Gwaine?* "What happened?"

"We're at the reliquary. Dad's killed the watcher." She forced herself not to look over at the headless body in the corner.

"There's a body there? Listen, Billi. You've got to move Arthur."

Move him? She couldn't. What if he started bleeding again?

"Percy, he has to stay here." She was kneeling beside him, with Kay opposite her. Arthur's eyes were closed and his face was calm. Her eyes were pooling with tears, but Billi imagined the slightest smile on his pale lips. She sobbed. Was this what she wanted?

"No," she whispered. It wasn't.

There was a long pause on the other side. "Billi, you've got to understand. Your dad's just murdered someone. That's how the police will see it. You need to get him out. It'll be prison otherwise."

Jesus, this is insane. But Percy was right. She looked at Kay, and he nodded. "Okay, Percy. But be quick. Be quick."

"I'll be there in five." The line went dead.

16

SOMEHOW, BETWEEN THEM, THEY GOT ARTHUR outside, and soon Billi heard the unmistakable roar of Percy's motorbike. True to his word, he got there in five. The wheels screamed to a stop before them; he tossed his helmet onto the ground and ran to their side. Only then did Billi let her dad's weight fall and, with Percy, eased him to the ground. They folded Percy's biker jacket under Arthur's head and finally shifted him onto his side and into the recovery position.

"Hang in there, Art," Percy said as he took his pulse. He put his hand on Billi's own. "Now listen, we've got to get our stories straight. Nothing complex. What have you got?"

Kay pointed at the broken door. "We'll say we were walking with Arthur when he saw someone trying to break into the shop. He crossed the road, there was a fight, and he fell." Kay looked over at Billi. "We were too far away to get a good look at the attacker. Average height, average build. Just average."

Percy nodded. "That'll do. Got it, Billi?" She couldn't believe it; they were making up stories while her dad was dying.

"Got it," she said, her throat dry.

The ambulance sirens and lights brought people onto the street. They loitered outside on their porches and in doorways, coats slung over their pajamas and nighties, watching the paramedics bundle out of the ambulance and around Arthur. Percy pulled Billi back to let them work, and then the police arrived. The next few minutes were a blur of questions, flashing lights, and conflicting emotions. Her dad had been stabbed. She fed the police the story: the mugger, a scuffle, and then him collapsing. No, she couldn't really remember what the mugger was wearing, or what he looked like, or which way he fled. The police constable soon got weary and took down her details; they'd be in touch.

Billi joined her dad in the ambulance, holding his hand while the paramedic hooked him up to the portable monitors. Percy hugged her. Kay stood some feet away.

"I'll be right behind you," said Percy.

"What about Mike?" she asked.

"I'll take care of it. The others are on their way." He squeezed her one last time. "You just look after your dad."

By morning they'd moved Arthur out of the operating room

into a hospital bed. Billi stared at him; he'd turned old overnight. The dawn sun was weak, giving him a corpselike pallor. He seemed tiny and pathetic in the hospital bed—ugly yellow tubes dribbled out of his mouth and nostrils. His eyelids were half closed, those bright blue eyes, usually full of power and life, were now just dull, empty glass.

Had she brought this upon him? If she hadn't been so consumed by hating him, maybe she would have realized Mike was the dark angel. And now her dad was lying here.

This is all my fault.

Billi forced herself to look at him. His breath was a thin wheeze, followed by a brittle sucking. The sound tortured her ears as much as his pale face did her eyes. She hated hospitals. The smell of pre-warmed food and antiseptic, the rattle of steel-framed beds. She looked at her dad's white hands, how thin the skin seemed now, and how blue his veins. She reached out and took them, frightened by their coldness. They were limp and damp. She squeezed as hard as she could, begging for some reaction. Just the smallest twitch, the slightest sign.

Please, one sign. Just one.

There was a knock at the door.

Kay entered.

"You okay?" he asked. He held out his hand and hesitated, as though unsure if he should touch her or embrace her. Billi stared at his hand until he lowered it. "I'm sorry."

"You didn't know?" she asked.

"Know what?"

"About Michael being the watcher?"

Kay shook his head. "No. How could you think that? I would never have let him near you, Billi."

"So you weren't even strong enough to see who he really was. Read his aura or something?"

"You can't just read them like that. It takes a lot of effort." He looked uncomfortable. "Anyway, I don't go spying on everyone I meet."

"No, just me," Billi snapped.

That wasn't fair. She knew it wasn't. But she had to blame someone. She wanted to believe it wasn't her fault, but try as she might, she knew this mess was hers alone.

Kay stepped closer. "Billi, don't torture yourself over this. No one could have known—"

He'd heard her thoughts.

"That I would lead a dark angel straight to the mirror?"

But that's what she'd done. No matter how she tried to justify it, she'd led him there. And Kay had saved her. Some Templar she was turning out to be. The longer she stayed, the more harm she would do.

"Where's Percy?" she asked.

"Downstairs with Gwaine and the others. They're waiting for you."

"They're all here? Why?"

She caught Kay's guilty expression, just before he turned away to look out the bedroom window. And then she understood. "Jesus, they can't wait, can they?"

They were there because Arthur was dying. They were there to select his replacement. The knights couldn't allow the Order to be leaderless, could they? Well, sod them. Let Gwaine become Templar Master. The Order had brought her nothing but misery. First her mum, now her dad. She looked at her dad, sallow and suddenly so old. Nothing was worth this sort of sacrifice.

A vain hope sparked in her. Maybe if . . . no, not if, but when—when Arthur recovered, Gwaine would have proved to be an excellent Master, and Arthur wouldn't be needed. Maybe if the burden of the Templars was lifted, Arthur might become a normal dad. He might even love her. It was a cowardly thought, but she'd always imagined her dad as being invulnerable, and seeing him like this made her choke with fear. Billi had thought she hated him, but she didn't. She couldn't. He was all she had.

"He's a tough nut, Billi. He'll make it." Kay put his hand on her shoulder. "You'll make it."

She poured herself a glass of water. "How did the cleanup go?"

"Best you speak to Gwaine about that."

Billi stood up. Kay's tone set off alarm bells. "What's going on, Kay?"

Kay grimaced, checked that the door was closed, then whispered, "Billi, something went wrong. There was nothing in the basement. Michael's vanished."

* * *

So much for all the pomp and grandeur of establishing a new Templar Master. Once, the inner conclave of senior knights would have met at Temple Church, to hold prayers and all-night vigils before choosing who would lead them. Now they were going to vote on it in the hospital cafeteria.

Gwaine sat at the head of the white Formica table. He looked calm, but nothing could hide the eagerness in his eyes. With Arthur dying his dream was nearly fulfilled.

All because of her.

Percy stood up and hugged her.

"How's the old man?"

Billi didn't know what to say. Dying? She buried her head in Percy's chest. Then he offered her a seat at the table. There was a cup of tea waiting.

Bors looked up briefly from his bacon sandwich, then went back to tearing it apart with his teeth, chomping loudly. Berrant lowered his glasses and smiled at Billi, while Father Balin clicked through his rosary. Gareth and Pelleas were there too. Kay sat down beside her.

"Now that we're all here, I think would should get down to business," said Gwaine. "First, the debrief. Kay's filled me in, and I've reached a conclusion." He spread out his hands. "It's clear that Michael was destroyed. The body's disappearance isn't unusual. As an Ethereal being, he simply evaporated back into it when he died."

"But what about Arthur's sword? That's gone, too," Kay said.

Gwaine shrugged. "Contaminated by Ethereal blood, it would've probably disintegrated also. Simple."

"It seems too simple. . . ." said Balin. He shook his head. "I don't know. What did Elaine say about all this?"

Gwaine scowled. "We can't find Elaine. Or the Cursed Mirror." He looked around the table. "But we can't solve that tonight. We've other business to discuss."

"Aren't you forgetting something?" snapped Percy. "First we should pray for Arthur's speedy and complete recovery, don't you think?"

Gwaine glowered at him, then cleared his throat. "Of course. Father, if you'd be so kind?"

They bowed their heads, and Billi prayed. She prayed her dad would live and that this would never happen again. It had been too close, and next time she could get someone killed. There could be no "next time."

After a minute Gwaine lifted his head. "To business. It's simple, really. With Arthur out, I formally request command of the Poor Fellow-Soldiers of Jesus Christ and the Temple of Solomon."

"Temporarily," said Gareth. He was right: Arthur was still alive, so Gwaine could only be acting Master. Gwaine grimaced and looked around the table.

"I know we all love Arthur, but we must accept that his methods are high risk. Look what happened tonight. I've . . .

plans regarding the Order. We need to rebuild our strength. Recruit new members."

Percy's eyes narrowed. "Like who?"

Gwaine turned away from Percy and addressed the others. "The Red Knights."

There was a long silence as the knights looked from one to another, absorbing Gwaine's idea. Eventually it was Balin who spoke.

"There's no way Arthur would allow it. The Crusades are over."

Berrant nodded in agreement. "The *Bataille Ténébreuse* is not against fellow men, only the Unholy."

Gwaine raised his hands. "I know they're somewhat overzealous, but they could be guided. Trained and tempered." He looked at Percy. "They're no worse than Arthur was when I recruited him."

"Arthur didn't go around burning down mosques," Percy replied.

Gwaine glanced at the others, hoping for support. Instead, all he got was cool looks. "Okay, we can discuss the Red Knights another day. But the question remains: Will you declare me Master?"

He looked around the table. Balin sighed, but bowed his head. Bors nodded eagerly, the fat juices dripping off his chin. Gareth and the others agreed. So did Kay, even though he knew Gwaine would make his life hard. He was a Templar, and there were the rules. As seneschal, it was

Gwaine's right to lead the knights and Kay wouldn't let his feelings get in the way. Percy just shrugged and they looked at Billi.

"Just one thing," she said.

"This isn't a deal to be negotiated, squire. It's yes or no," said Gwaine. His voice was low but couldn't hide the anger bubbling beneath. The vote had to be unanimous.

Billi took a deep breath. She'd risked not just her life, but Kay's and her dad's too. Her father had tried to warn her in the armory about the possibility of an unexpected attack, but she'd been so angry at him she'd trusted Michael instead. It was only her dad's vigilance that had prevented the archangel from getting his hands on the mirror. No matter how she turned it in her mind, she'd failed. She couldn't allow herself to fail again, not when lives were at stake. "You have my vote, Gwaine. On one condition." She closed her eyes and lowered her head. "I want to leave the Order."

Percy leaned over. "Billi . . ."

"No, Percy. It's for the best." She didn't want to open her eyes. If she did, she might change her mind. The table fell silent. Eventually she looked up and met Gwaine's gaze. He smirked. Victory was his.

"Granted."

17

So Billi was out. Just like that. Dazed, she left the hospital. The doctor had suggested she get some rest; she could visit again after school. She barely noticed the crowded hospital reception, or the rows of sick children lined up in the corridors in wheelchairs, waiting for ambulances to move them to other hospitals because there were no beds left in this one. Billi glimpsed the tired frightened faces of the parents, but she was too empty to feel anything for them. Dimly, she wondered if this was Michael's doing, but he was dead now. It was over.

The house was cold and silent when she entered. Billi dropped her coat on the floor and went straight up into the kitchen, functioning on automatic. She switched on the kettle and tossed two slices into the toaster. She looked around the sparse, ugly room. This is where they'd decided her fate five years ago: that she should be a Templar.

Balin by the sink. Gwaine on the stool opposite, Percy by the cupboard, and her dad here, on this seat. The severed arm in the garbage bag had lain right on this table. Billi stroked its surface with her palm. Dark patches stained the wood. Blood? She wouldn't be at all surprised.

The front door opened and Billi's heart jumped. "Dad?" For a mad moment she thought it was him, somehow recovered and home, and she was up out of her chair and running to the kitchen door.

"Billi?" shouted Percy. He stamped his feet on the mat. "Where are you, sweetheart?"

"Up here." She bent over the banister; maybe he had some news. "How's Dad?"

"He's resting." The steps creaked as Percy came up. "Don't you worry about him."

Billi turned back toward the bubbling kettle. She took out two mugs and some tea bags. A lump of sugar for her, a squirt of honey for him.

Percy paused at the doorway. She knew he was waiting to hear that she wanted to be a Templar again. But she'd quit and wasn't going back. She plunked his mug down at the far end of the table, took hers back to the other end, and sat.

"And how are you?" he asked. He lowered himself onto the stool, looking ridiculous. His knees knocked the underside of the table.

"I know what you're thinking. But it's better this way, Percy. I can't do it." She looked up at him. "I led him there. Because of me, Dad was almost killed."

"Arthur would have faced him eventually, Billi. This is not just your doing. The war against the Unholy takes its toll."

Like she didn't know. Her mum, her dad almost.

"Then the price is too high, Percy." She turned toward her godfather. "And Dad's paid it long enough."

Percy drained his mug. "I've asked Gwaine to keep watches on Art. It does seem that Michael's dead, but something doesn't feel right. It's better to be safe than sorry."

"Think someone might try something?" Billi asked. Arthur had a lot of enemies. A hell of a lot. And even if Michael was gone now, he might have allies that would come knocking. She'd been taught too well to ignore that even the dead could seek revenge.

"That's why I want him guarded," Percy said. "Art's still Templar Master, and we look after our own." He glanced around the kitchen. "I'll base myself here." He grinned at her. "Play babysitter for a while. I'll bring my stuff over tonight. It'll be just like old times, won't it?"

Billi nodded. She didn't want to be here alone. Percy would look after her—he always had. He leaned over and kissed her forehead. "You get some sleep."

* * *

Later, Billi watched people from the study window. The inner temple was busy. She'd never seen so many here, especially at this time of night. Kay peered out over her shoulder, his hair gently brushing her cheek.

"Balin will be pleased," he said. "Don't think the church's ever been so busy."

He was right: they were all headed to Temple Church. Or St. Bride's. Or St. Paul's. Maybe off to Regent's Park Mosque. The stream was steady, dozens of people all making their way through the darkened street. Lots with kids.

"The faithful," said Kay.

"The fearful," replied Billi.

The newspapers were full of stories about mysterious sicknesses. Was it a new superbug? Some new food scare? No one knew. Every kid with even the smallest cough or temperature was being rushed to the hospital. They'd only touched the tip of the iceberg; Michael had managed to infect a dozen places while they'd been watching China Wharf, and not just hospitals. He'd probably been at it just before meeting her at the café—before he'd taken her up the tower. The thought made her sick.

Still she looked down at the people on the streets with some relief, knowing how much worse it would've been if he'd gotten his hands on the mirror. But this hysteria wouldn't last. Now that Michael was gone, the kids he'd infected should recover, according to Father Balin. The panic would pass, and the churches would empty again.

"Billi . . ." Kay stepped into the center of the room. The gloomy table lamp cast his tall shadow against the warrior portraits on the wall.

"Forget it, Kay. I've had this talk with Percy already." She turned from the window. "I've quit."

"But why? We killed Michael. We saved all the firstborn. You did good."

"Did I?" Then why did she feel so hollow inside? It didn't seem like a victory. It had been the same after the Ordeal. "Dad said we have to make hard choices. I did and almost got him killed. I can't make those sorts of decisions."

"So you leave them to be made by people like Gwaine?" There was a bitter edge to the way he said the name.

"He's making your life difficult already?" She smiled wrily. What had he expected?

Kay sighed wearily. "He doesn't trust me. Thinks my time in Jerusalem may have tainted me."

"How?"

"I didn't train just with Christians, did I?" Kay shrugged. Billi watched him as he sat on the windowsill, fingers hooked around his knee. The moonlight on his already white face made him glow. His hair hung like strands of silver thread framing his deep blue eyes.

The study was in the eaves, low-ceilinged with small windows in the pitch of the roof. Densely stacked shelves filled every wall; barely a sheet of wallpaper wasn't covered by bookshelves, old maps, or paintings. The carpet was faded red, and a large black-oak desk dominated the room, its upper surface covered in pale green leather. A bronze inkstand sat in the middle, a plain block with a shallow groove for a pen and two half-filled ink bottles, one black, one red. Her dad's laptop sat to the left, its screen dead black. Thick drapes hung alongside the windows; deep shadows lurked in their folds.

Billi and Kay had spent hours in this room. Here Balin had taught them Latin. They'd read the old Templar diaries and imagined what it was like to be heroes. The stories read like fairy tales and were full of battles, monsters, and heroic deaths. But the tales lied. Battle was stomach-churning terror, and no death was glorious or noble. Death was lonely, frightening, and brutal.

She studied her hands. They were stark-white clean. She'd finally gotten her dad's blood out from under her fingernails.

The war against the Unholy takes its toll, that's what Percy had said.

She looked at Kay and suddenly felt fear creeping into her heart. Who would look out for him now that she had left?

"Quit, Kay. Quit the Templars."

"I can't."

"Why not? Gwaine doesn't want you. Elaine's gone. You

can leave." The more she thought about it the better it sounded. Both of them with her dad, out of the Order. Let Gwaine recruit the Red Knights. Let *them* pay the price of the *Bataille Ténébreuse* from now on.

Kay shook his head. "I've got duties to the Order. With or without Gwaine."

"They're your priorities, are they?" Couldn't he see she was right? The Knights Templar had managed long enough without them; what difference would it make if they left?

"Yes," he said, his lips drawn thin and firm. But his eyes hesitated, darting from her to the wall of old warriors.

"Then why did you come to the tower? That sounded personal."

Kay faltered. He looked up at her, then away quickly, like he was worried she'd see something.

"It doesn't matter," he said.

"What did Michael say in the text?"

"I said it doesn't matter." He shifted uneasily and shoved his hands into his pockets. "It's too hard, Billi. An Oracle can't have emotional attachments. They cloud our judgment. That's why Michael tricked me. I wanted to . . . believe."

"What?" Billi watched Kay intently, her breath catching. He was her only friend. But in the lamplight their eyes met, and it wasn't the way friends looked at one another.

"I can't think clearly with you around." He stood abruptly. His face was inches away from hers—she closed her eyes and felt his warm breath on her eyelashes. He didn't touch her, but their closeness paralyzed her. This was Kay. They'd grown up together. She didn't think of him like . . . this.

Did she?

He stepped away.

"I can't, Billi." The pain was obvious as he spoke. "I can't care about you."

The door opened and Percy entered, carrying a tray. His sleeves were rolled up on his tree-trunk-thick forearms, and he still wore an apron, though it barely covered his stomach. He put the tray down on the desk, then eased himself into one of the armchairs, mug in hand.

Billi sank down in her dad's old leather-bound chair. How could Kay say that? How could he choose the Order over her? Just like her dad.

"Any news on Elaine?" Kay asked Percy, his voice strained. He wouldn't look Billi in the eye.

Percy shrugged. "Nope. Art must have told her to hide, in case he didn't kill Michael." He looked toward Kay. "Couldn't you, y'know, pick her up?"

"No. Elaine's not gifted, but she knows a few tricks. She's off any radar. Since she's got the mirror she's probably in a protected location. There'll be wards and charms all over it."

Percy checked the clock on the wall. Just past midnight. He pointed to the phone on the desk. "Let's give Berrant a call. He's on duty at Crow Street Hospital. We'll find out how your dad's doing."

At least I have Percy. She'd seen her father after school today, and Percy had already been there. The big West African, for all his strength and determination, was soft-hearted when it came to her dad. He was probably the only true friend her father had.

Percy dialed. "Berrant? Everything okay?" He nodded. Then froze. "What d'you mean he moved you? Who's looking after Arthur?" Billi stared at Percy's grim face. He slammed down the phone then rose and ripped off his apron.

"Gwaine's moved the watch on Art. Berrant thought I was meant to replace him."

Billi jumped up. "Where's Berrant, then?"

"Kent. Gwaine's sent him down there tonight to look into some haunting."

"Where are the others?" asked Kay.

"Not bloody near enough," cursed Percy.

There was no one guarding her dad.

18

THEY TOOK ARTHUR'S OLD JAGUAR, BUT WERE FORCED to crawl along. A dense fog had descended over the streets, cutting down visibility to a few yards. Shrouds of ghostly white mist rolled over the windshield as they made their way toward Crow Street Hospital. The parking lot was filled to overflowing, so they went around back to the secluded loading docks and "Permit Only" areas. Percy parked near a fire exit. Kay and Billi clambered out.

Percy reached in and unhooked the hidden latches beneath the rear seat. It tilted out, revealing the weapons cabinet. Tightly packed in foam and plastic to stop them from rattling, the Templars' weapons shone with a recent polishing. He picked out a *wakizashi*, a single-edged Japanese short sword, adjusting the back sheath under his jacket before sliding the blade in. Billi took a pair of hiltless bayonets and a chest holster, shortening the straps in well-practiced moves, then clipped her two daggers into place. She threw on her coat, and by crossing her arms across her chest, drew out her weapons once, twice, three times, so eventually they could pop into her hands in an instant. Next, they divided up a set of holy water vials and crucifixes, then Percy slammed the seat back down.

"What about me?" asked Kay.

Percy laughed. "We get into a fight, Oracle, I want you to run."

"That's not fair! I can fight." He reached out a hand. "C'mon, give me something."

Billi and Percy glanced at each other. Their reply was simultaneous:

"No."

Kay muttered something under his breath, and Percy put his hand on Billi's shoulder.

"Nothing flash, okay? If it all goes pear-shaped, go for the easy kills: chest, throat, stomach, in that order. Understood?"

Billi nodded. She sincerely hoped it wouldn't come to that.

"Maybe we're worrying about nothing. Maybe Gwaine's right and Dad doesn't need protection. Are we just being paranoid?"

"In my experience, you can never be too paranoid." Percy looked at the building ahead. "We'll go in, I'll lead. We grab Art and get out of here. The Canterbury preceptory has medical facilities. We'll look after him there."

"What about Gwaine?" asked Billi.

Percy zipped up his jacket. "I'll worry about Gwaine. Kay, you with us?"

Kay was staring into the fog, which had gotten thicker. The hazy streetlamps barely penetrated the heavy blanket of mist. He shuddered, then looked back at Billi and gave a wan smile.

"Ready," he said. He took a deep breath and smoothed his hair out of his face.

The rear of the hospital block was open twenty-four hours a day with minimal security. There were two large garages, wide open, with a truck backed into each. Bright lights shone out from the loading dock, and two men were pushing bulging carts of soiled laundry into the back of the vehicles. A driver leaned against the cabin, smoking. Percy ducked under the short barrier and walked to one of the rear delivery doors. He waved casually at the guy smoking, then went into the hospital. Billi and Kay were a few steps behind.

More carts lined the hallway, some stuffed with soiled sheets and stained towels, others fresh-smelling and neatly stacked. But the laundry smell gave way to the stinging odor of strong antiseptic.

Even though her dad was on the sixth floor, they didn't take the elevator. Kay groaned as Percy pushed open the doors into the stairwell. Only alternate floors were lit leaving dark shadowy bands on the walls. The steps were two-man wide, wrapped around an open well. Percy took two steps at a time, surprisingly lightly given his size. Billi followed with Kay stumbling behind, cursing. They stopped on the sixth floor, and Percy gave them a minute to catch their breath. He gently turned the handle, which wasn't locked, then faced the two of them.

"You wait here. I'll grab Art." He pointed down the stairs. "Keep the escape route clear. Give me five minutes."

"And if you're late?" asked Billi.

"Wait some more." With that, he pushed the door open, winked at Billi, then left. Billi stared down the dark corridor until the door finally closed.

"Gwaine's done this on purpose," she said. *Just wait until Dad finds out.*

"Maybe he had his reasons," Kay said, but he didn't sound convinced.

"Yeah, like getting Dad killed so he could stay Master."

Billi checked her daggers. She flipped one out and held it over the balcony, trying to catch some light from the bulb on the floor below.

Kay shuffled. He put his hands in his pockets, pulled them out again, then crossed them. Then they went back in his pockets. All in the space of about thirty seconds.

"Relax," Billi said. She was used to this—the waiting. She didn't like it, but she knew there wasn't any other choice. But of course, Kay never went out on Hot Meets. He looked embarrassed.

"Sorry, not used to all this," he said.

He would get used to it, though, sooner rather than later. Billi wondered how he'd be during all those nights, sitting in the dark, no company except his thoughts and the shadows. She wasn't going to miss it.

She checked her watch: three minutes gone. She pressed her ear against the door. She couldn't hear anything. "What d'you reckon, should I—"

Kay jerked up his hand. He took two steps down, moving silent and slow, turning his head, scanning. Suddenly his eyes widened. "They're here."

Billi's heart skipped a beat. She touched Kay's hand; it was stone cold. He pulled away, running to the floor below. She hurried after him and grabbed him just as he reached for the doorknob.

"Wait, Kay! Who?"

Kay closed his eyes, sighed deeply, and pressed his palms over his face.

"I can't tell. There are two of them, but I can't pick up anything except anger . . . rage. And hunger. A terrible hunger." He lowered his hands. "*Ghuls.*"

"They're after Dad?"

Kay nodded, then frowned. "But they've been distracted. Oh God. The children. They're hungry for the children." He went for the door.

Billi pulled Kay away from the door before he did something dumb, like run in and fight. She held him close. "Listen to me: we go and get Percy now." *This is no time for stupid heroics.*

"This is no time for cowardice," he snapped back.

Billi stared into his blue eyes, which blazed with conviction. He was stupid. But right. She pointed up the stairs. "Get Percy." She checked to make sure her crucifix was plainly visible around her neck, then creaked the door open. "I'll look."

"Be careful," he said.

Oh, he cares now, Billi thought.

It was cold, much colder than it should have been. It wasn't like the heating had failed. It felt like someone had left a fridge door open. Frosty mist formed when she breathed. She didn't need to be an Oracle to know something was way wrong. Most of the lights along the corridor were out, so she moved slowly, keeping her stance low and wide. Her skin prickled at the silence. Ahead was a pair of partially opened double doors. The sign above read PICU.

Pediatric Intensive Care Unit.

Where the hell *was* everybody? Shouldn't there be nurses around? She reached the doors and drew her dagger, tightening her fingers around the hilt until they hurt. She pushed the door open with her foot.

A body lay collapsed on the floor: a nurse. A row of deep bite marks along her neck oozed blood, made glossy black in the moonlight. But her chest still rose and sank, so Billi ignored her for the moment and scanned the room.

Three incubators lined each side of the room. Above each was a monitor flickering with glowing patterns and lights connected to the control unit by multitudes of cables, and finally there were the small bodies lying quietly within transparent boxes. The curtains were open, and enough moonlight pushed into the room to make a pearly luminance that left the corners dark. Billi focused into the blackness, staring hard into the inky shadows that surrounded the fragile baby in the farthest incubator.

The darkness around the incubator seemed to tremble. Slowly the shadows peeled back like dripping oil, slick and thick, revealing two women standing in the center of the room. With ivory limbs and curly black hair, they appeared inhumanly perfect, until their red lips parted too wide, almost splitting their faces apart, revealing mouths grotesque with jagged fangs.

"Templar," said the first. She ran her nail along the edge of the incubator. The baby inside began to cry. "Hush now, little one. Soon we'll sing you to sleep." The other giggled.

"Get away from there," Billi said.

Where the hell were Kay and Percy?

Billi watched the two women. They moved strangely, nearly gliding. Each movement was controlled and purposefully small, as though huge energies were barely being held in check.

"Why, Templar? Why deny us the sweetness of their blood?" The woman grinned, and her teeth glistened. "Why deny them our kisses?"

Billi needed to use her wits. She backed out the door; they'd have to come one at a time. Nothing flash. She was intensely aware of the steel in her hand.

"Don't be scared; there's only one of me," she said, goading them.

It worked. There were nine feet between Billi and the two *ghuls*, but they crossed it so fast they seemed to fly. In their eagerness to be first, they collided trying to pass through the door opening. Startled by their speed, Billi stumbled back before instinct took over. Instinct and training.

Nothing flash. Just quick kills.

Billi jabbed with the blade, making one of them back away from the weapon, only to tangle herself with the other *ghul*. Billi slammed the door shut and heard them crash into its heavy steel paneling. Billi jammed her dagger through the door handles and ran toward the staircase, not daring to look over her shoulder. She was so close.

The staircase door flew open. Percy grabbed her and pulled her in, almost ripping her arm off. She just had a chance to glimpse her dad, arm slung over Kay, already half a level below her, when something crashed into her back, hurling her into the steel banisters and smashing the air out of her lungs. She slipped to the ground, and all she could see was a tangle of legs and limbs as Percy grappled with one of the *ghuls*. The woman screamed and clawed and snarled. She looked slight and frail against the giant Ghanaian, but her blows sent Percy reeling. One punch caught him in the temple, and he stumbled down a few steps, legs loose and wobbling. He still held on to the woman's arm, and Billi couldn't believe she didn't fall. Instead she balanced at the top of the stairs, feet braced against Percy's weight.

Billi kicked out, sweeping the woman's legs away. The *ghul* grabbed at the banister rail but missed, screaming as she fell down the five levels of the stairwell. She turned over and over, arms wheeling madly and legs kicking. Billi watched in horror as the woman tumbled like a doll and smashed onto the bare concrete below. She lay there, terribly still, her beautiful limbs bent unnaturally. A black pool of blood spread from her head.

Billi pushed herself away from the edge, from the view.

"Come on!" ordered Percy. He'd caught up with Kay and slung Arthur over his shoulder. Billi got to her feet and followed, still wired from the fight. The others were already well ahead of her.

She heard the door at the bottom of the stairs slam open.

"Billi!" shouted Kay from ahead. Billi dropped to the ground floor to see him run out into the parking lot. She was a few paces behind, but she couldn't help it. She had to look back.

The landing light shone cruelly on the woman's

shattered body. Her torso and limbs were hideously twisted and distorted. Her face was turned away, and her hair was a black sodden mess. Billi covered her mouth to hold down the bile.

Then the woman's hand twitched. There was a sickening sucking as she turned her crushed and blackened face toward Billi. The woman's face twisted into a grin. A few teeth fell out.

Billi screamed and ran.

Outside, Percy dropped her dad into the backseat; then Kay dived in after him. Percy got into the front and waved frantically at her. "Get a move on!"

She shoved the hospital door shut behind her, then saw an abandoned cart nearby. She pulled it over and wedged it against the door handle, then turned.

More *ghuls* came out of the mist. Ripples of fog broke apart and they crept toward the car. Five, six, a couple near the gate, she couldn't tell how many. They didn't rush, didn't shout or yell, just approached with steady confidence, their fierce eyes full of a killer's desire. Just glancing at them, they could have been anyone off the street. Except . . .

Except for their predatory grace and their too-wide hungry smiles. Despite the darkness, they seemed to glow, lit from some unearthly source.

Who were they? Old enemies that had escaped her dad years ago? Or had Mike slowly been creating them over the last ten years? She wasn't going to find out tonight. Billi lowered her head and raced to the car. The engine revved and she dived in through the passenger door. Percy shoved the stick, and the wheels screamed as he slammed the pedal. In the furious glare of the headlights she saw the strange figures scatter as Percy put his palm on the hand brake.

"Let's go." He pressed the release.

The car rocked gently. A pair of bare white feet landed softly on the hood, and a dark coat fanned out, covering the windshield. A sliver of light caught the bright terrible edge of a broadsword; a familiar one with a hacking blade. Then the windshield shattered.

Billi screamed and threw her arms above her head as glass exploded over her. The car shuddered, and she felt something warm splash her face. She kept her eyes shut as the last few shards fell free. The car finally stopped as pressure slipped off the accelerator.

Slowly, she opened her eyes.

Percy sat beside her, arms hanging at his sides. His fingers trembled for a moment, then stopped. His eyes stared empty and wide ahead, and his mouth hung slack. Tiny cubes of broken glass lay sprinkled like diamonds over him, a few embedded in his skin. Billi gazed down and her breath died.

A sword jutted from his chest.

The Templar Sword. His jacket was awash with his blood; it covered the dashboard and it covered her. She could feel it trickling down her face. The sword had been driven straight through him into the car seat, pinning him. A single powerful thrust and he'd died instantly.

Nothing flash. An easy kill.

The person on the hood hopped off, walked around to open the passenger door, and peered in. He smiled at Billi, and her heart froze. He slid his dark locks away from his face with long slim fingers and tilted his head lower, so their faces were close. Close enough for his breath to chill her, close enough for a kiss.

His lips curved in cruel amusement. "Did you miss me?" Michael asked.

19

A YOUNG WOMAN WITH PALE GOLD HAIR AND delicate hands grabbed Billi by the throat and wrenched her out of the car. She didn't even come to Billi's shoulders, but she carried her easily, like a doll, and dumped her on the black tarmac.

"Gently, Eliza," said Michael. "Billi's had a hard day." The woman grinned at him. Michael smiled back. "And I guarantee it's about to get so much worse."

Billi lay in a puddle, staring up at Percy.

He can't be dead. Can't be.

She waited, urged with all her heart, for his eyes to blink. But they gazed far into eternity. Some invisible force squeezed her chest, crushing her lungs until she couldn't breathe.

Percy. She'd never really been alone; she'd always had Percy. When her dad vanished for days on end, she'd had

Percy. He babysat her, cooked, remembered all her birthdays. Billi sank forward until her forehead touched the wet ground.

"What is it they say about Templars?" Michael crouched down, pulling her hair sharply so they were eye to eye. "'You shall keep the company of martyrs.'" He stood up and dragged her alongside him. Arthur and Kay were likewise dropped into the circle of surrounding *ghuls*.

They stood silently, watching their victims, craving the kill. *The hungry dead*—the name suited them so perfectly. Including Michael, there were about eight of them. She stared at the young woman standing over her. What had she sold her soul for? Wealth? Love? To be forever young and beautiful? Had it been worth it? To live forever in the night, to become a blood-drinker? A monster? But the woman just licked her sharklike teeth with her oh-so-red tongue.

Michael walked into the center of the circle and tore off his coat. His T-shirt was gone and his bare upper torso glistened in the drizzle as the black web of tattoos twisted and stretched—spikes and thorns growing over his heart. Down his back were two vertical scars, red, swollen, and poorly healed.

How could he be here? She'd seen his head cut off. Cut off!

Michael caught her staring. He stretched his neck so she could have a better look.

"Can't even see the join, can you?" He laughed.

"Honestly, did you believe I could be killed like a mere *ghul*?"

Billi got to her feet, fighting the fear threatening to drown her. Mike looked at her, amused. Then she slapped him. It wasn't the strongest blow she could muster, but it was the most contemptuous. She felt sick, not just for Percy, but with herself. What had she seen in Michael? Ever? Every molecule in her body recoiled in disgust. He put his hand against his blushing cheek and slapped her back so hard the blow knocked her down.

"*Never* touch me again, mortal." He spat out the last word with venom, then strolled over to the car and reached for the Templar Sword. He gazed at Billi as he jerked the blade from Percy's body. Billi knew she shouldn't succumb, shouldn't show any weakness to the enemy, but she couldn't help it. Tears trickled down her face. Percy's upper body fell forward, his face resting on the steering wheel. His soft brown eyes remained open.

Arthur lay on his back. He'd lost his slippers and looked like a doddering old fool, lying there in his pajamas and bathrobe, wheezing. His top was only partially buttoned, and she could see his chest, white and lined with old scars, the ribs pressed hard against his skin.

"Get away!" Kay was out of the car, brandishing his silver crucifix. He stood in front of Billi and Arthur, a vial of holy water in his hand, a cross thrust out before him.

Michael circled slowly. Then laughed.

He turned to the *ghuls*, and they laughed too, though Billi saw their hesitation. They were soulless; holy symbols were anathema to them. Only Michael's immediate presence gave them the courage to face the Templars. Michael shook his head and held out his palm.

"Kay, give me that." He was laughing so hard he was crying. "I've stood at the right hand of God. I am an angel. An archangel. Do you honestly think *that* little trinket will protect you?" He snatched the crucifix from Kay's hand and tossed it away. "God gave me a duty. Should Man stray, I was to chastise him."

"It's murder," said Billi, painfully aware of Percy's blood splashed over her.

Michael lifted his hands skyward. "It's righteous punishment."

Arthur laughed. It was a rattling croak pulled out of his chest, and it collapsed into a coughing fit. "You abandoned Heaven. Cut off your wings." He pointed at his own back. "That's why those scars never healed. You're a fool, Michael, an arrogant fool. Man hasn't fallen; it's you. Do you honestly think God will ever take you back?"

Michael leaped the short distance and grabbed Arthur's throat, dragging him out of the car and to his feet. His face transformed momentarily into that of a snarling beast, lips peeled back, eyes wild, and face contorted with rage.

"It is not I that have fallen, but you!" He tossed Arthur back to the ground. "Once I have the mirror, and the power of my brothers and sisters, I will sacrifice the firstborn, and God will remember how much I love Him." Michael gazed up into the obscuring mist. "I will send Him a million souls to sing His glory."

Arthur shook his head. "You kill and call it prayer. A sacrifice is done out of love. Everything you do is fueled by hate."

Michael's jaw tensed, and for a second Billi thought he was going to strike her dad's head off, but instead the dark angel approached her.

"You dare criticize me?" He pressed the flat of the red blade against Billi's cheek, smearing it with Percy's blood. "I could threaten you, Arthur. Torture you to reveal where the mirror is, but somehow I think you'd welcome that." He nodded at one of the others. "You don't value your life at all."

Suddenly two of the *ghuls* grabbed Billi's arms and stretched them out on either side of her. Their hold was stone-solid, locking her rigid. Mike rested the sword on her left arm, just above the wrist. He looked over his shoulder at Arthur.

"But what about Billi? Would you sacrifice her?" He looked toward Billi, eyes shining with savage lust. "Sacrifice your beloved child?"

He raised the sword.

Billi tried to pull her arm back, but she couldn't break the *ghuls'* grip. She looked from the blade to her arm, then back to the blade. It would slice through her muscle, through her bone like a razor cutting tissue paper. She of all people knew how deadly it was: she'd spent hundreds of hours sharpening it.

"Well, Arthur?"

Billi tensed. She fought to control her breathing and bound her left hand into a fist. Sweat soaked her back, and her arm trembled wildly. Michael had killed her mother, and now he was going to kill her.

A Templar does not tremble.

But she couldn't stop herself. She wasn't a Templar. She was frightened and weak—not ruthless like she should be. Not the way her dad wanted her to be. She bit her lip and looked at her father, and in that terrible moment she knew. He gazed back at her, blank and cold. It was a simple choice. Save Billi or save the lives of a million innocent children. Arthur turned away

Kay groaned in despair but couldn't help: he was flat on the ground with a *ghul*'s foot pressed down on his head.

Michael sighed in mock sadness. "See, Billi? He cares nothing for you. You're right to hate him." He *tsk*ed. "Last chance, Arthur. The location of the mirror or your daughter loses her arm."

The only noise was Billi's desperate panting. Michael looked at her.

"So be it."

Oh, God.

The blade stung her wrist and Billi screamed. She tore her arm free and collapsed, cradling it in her lap. She stared and saw—

Her wrist. It bore only the slightest cut. Fear gripped her, but she forced her fingers to bend. They did. She opened and closed them. She was okay. Her dad had called Michael's bluff. Tears ran down her face.

Michael laughed and strolled over to Arthur. "That's what I love about you, Arthur: you're an ice-hearted bastard. You remind me of me." He handed the sword over to one of the *ghuls*—a big blond guy beside him. "Take this, Ryan." He flexed his fingers. "There's one guaranteed way to find out the truth."

They ignored Billi. Their attention was focused on Arthur and their leader. Michael put his hands on Arthur's shoulders and forced him to his knees. He ran his hands over Arthur's head, cupping his cheeks and pulling their faces close. Arthur snarled but couldn't break free of the angel's grip.

"Now I'm going to make you open your mind to me." His fingers caressed Arthur's cheeks. "You'll fight; I wouldn't expect anything less. And to tell you the truth, I'm not as subtle as your Oracle. I can't dip softly in and out." His nails dug into Arthur's flesh and drew tiny beads of blood. "I will probably ravage your mind. Tear it to shreds. When I'm done, *I'll* know where the mirror is and *you'll* be a drooling vegetable." He looked over at Billi and winked.

"It might even improve your relationship with your daughter. God knows it couldn't get any worse."

They stared at each other, Michael's fiery eyes glowing with fever, Arthur's, chilly and pale. A feeble groan slipped out of Arthur, then he locked himself rigid. The change was immediate as his eyelids half sank and his blue orbs radiated intense concentration. Sweat bubbled across his forehead, and his breathing slowed as he fell into a trance.

Michael pressed his fingers deeper into Arthur's face. "Open to me," he whispered.

Even Billi, who had no measurable psychic power, felt the tremor of energy ripple between them, angel and Templar Master locked in motionless battle. Waves of quivering emotion washed over her, over them all as the two minds fought for dominance. Arthur's breath hissed through his clenched teeth.

The psychic explosion ripped through her like a supernova. Billi cried as the raw shock wave tore through her mind. Her senses screamed as they burned out, and all that was left was a memory that was both crystal sharp and terrible.

The desert wind at night is cold, but he savors the sharp prickling sensation of it on his flesh. He stretches out his long powerful arms, gazing at his moon shadow upon the sand. Though he has no pride, he knows he is beautiful.

What it is to have mortal form! Mankind is truly blessed with such gifts.

He waits on the hilltop above the city. A man wrapped

against the cold bitter night makes his way slowly up the goat track toward him.

The prophet. Moses.

Below them, the city lies asleep. A few torches blaze along the palace battlements and among the patrols of soldiers making their way through the narrow streets between the mud-brick huts and houses. The city has been disturbed by dark omens and supernatural signs.

But they think the worst is over.

They are wrong.

The prophet stops some yards away. He's dressed in simple heavy cotton and carries a tall stick, a branch of a cedar. Once he would have worn the softest white linen and carried a golden scepter. Like his brother.

The pharaoh.

"Is it done?" asks the prophet. "Are they . . . dead?"

Michael gazes at his companion. It is a foolish thing to ask, and almost worth his silence. But he sees the man tremble, though he fights it. He should *be afraid, the archangel thinks. Moses is merely a man, while he is . . . Michael.*

"Yes. They are dead. The firstborn of every Egyptian family."

"And what of my people?" Moses's voice quivers as he asks.

"They did as they were told and marked their doors with blood." Michael motions across the sky. "And I did pass over."

The prophet covers his face. Perhaps the deed, now done, weighs more heavily on his soul than he had expected.

"And now?" he asks.

Michael crosses his arms and sees lights appear in the windows and doorways beneath them. "And now they know to fear the Lord God of Israel."

The Angel of Death smiles.

Somewhere in the city, a cock crows at the rising light.

And the screaming starts.

The screaming got louder, and Billi shifted her head toward its source and saw Michael stumble away from her father, bewildered by this noise. Kay remained held down, but even the *ghuls* groped around, dazed by the psychic assault. Billi was on her knees, her head pounding with the worst migraine she'd ever had. It felt as though someone were hammering nails into her eyes, each blow driving a brutal shaft of agony through her skull. And the screaming . . .

Two fierce white eyes stared at her out of the mist, perhaps some demon awoken by Michael's awful memory, roaring at her. The others gazed about, bewildered and confused by the onslaught. The eyes grew larger and brighter, and the screams rose to an ear-splitting level.

A van burst out of the fog, its headlights on full beam, blinding Billi. The horn was being held down as the van accelerated into the crowd.

Billi leaped to her feet. She had to get her dad.

"Kay!" she shouted, her voice barely audible over the horn. She shot a look at him, and he used the distraction of the oncoming van to break free from his stunned captors.

Billi ran up and kicked Michael squarely in the chest. Michael stumbled back a foot, and that was enough. The van smashed into him and jerked up once, twice, as it drove over him.

Billi grabbed her dad. The Templars! It had to be them! They'd come to the rescue. The driver pulled a savagely sharp turn. Any second now the doors would crash open and the other knights would storm out.

The door did crash open, but the other knights did not appear. Instead a crazed figure waved frantically from the driver's seat, her iron-gray hair loose and wild like some ragged old lion's mane.

"C'mon!" cried Elaine. The wheels steamed, and the smell of burned rubber saturated the air as she revved the van, ready to flee the instant she released the brake. Kay took hold of Arthur's other arm, and they got him to the vehicle. Billi slid the side doors open and threw him in.

"Billi!"

She turned and ducked fast when she heard Kay's warning. The Templar Sword hissed over her head, tearing the side of the van. The blond guy raised the weapon up, but Kay charged before Billi could respond. He knocked the *ghul* over and delivered two big kicks into his ribs. The Templar Sword clattered away. Kay went for it, but Billi grabbed his collar.

"Leave it!" she cried, pulling him back. The other *ghuls* were almost upon them. But where was Michael?

She glanced over to where he'd been hit.

He was slowly lifting himself off the tarmac; she could see that his chest was obscenely crushed, and white bone jutted out of his black blood-soaked flesh. His face was one big bruise, and his head was deformed. It seemed impossible.

He can't be stopped.

She jumped into the van, and Kay slammed the door shut.

The van shook as Elaine burst off. One *ghul* jumped at the windshield, but a sharp turn of the steering wheel threw him off. Visibility was practically nothing, but that didn't stop Elaine. They roared away from the bloody scene.

20

THEY MADE THEIR WAY NORTH. ONCE OUT OF immediate danger, Elaine slowed down. Billi clambered into the passenger seat. Elaine's eyes were red with tears as she wove the old van through the streets. Billi glanced at the signs.

"We're heading to Stoke Newington?" she asked.

"Safe house. No one knows about it but me." Elaine shook her head. "I ran him over. And he got up. Bloody hell."

"Where are the others?" Something like this needed the other knights. She couldn't believe they hadn't come. Where were they? Especially now that Percy was dead.

The thought made her shiver. "Elaine, you know that Percy's . . ."

"Yes, I saw." Elaine sniffed and wiped her face on her sleeve. "How's your dad?"

How was he? Billi shook her head in despair, wishing this were a bad bad dream. But they were all trapped in it. She looked over, hoping her dad could think of a way out.

He sat in the corner, a blanket over his shoulders. His head was sunk in his hands, and Billi noticed how small he looked.

And how . . . defeated.

He raised his head and wiped his hand over his face. He gazed despairingly out the rear window and sighed deeply. Billi watched the way his chest rose and sank; his body seemed to shrivel as the air went out, like he was empty. He turned, and their eyes met.

Billi almost lowered her eyes, tried to pretend she hadn't seen him weak. This was a part of Arthur she hadn't known existed. The human part. However, as she gazed at him, the mask fell back. His face hardened, the small glimmer of frailty vanished, and an impervious steel face replaced the human one. Father and daughter looked at each other for a moment longer. Then Arthur's gaze shifted to Kay.

"Well?" he asked.

Kay was texting as he spoke. "Michael wanted to deal with us first, then hunt down the others." He sank into the seat, exhausted. "Now he won't have the chance."

"You know that for sure?" asked Elaine.

"Yes, I do." He threw the mobile out the window. "It's done. I've sent the 1310 code to everyone."

Of course, thought Billi. *Silent Running.* Arthur had

established this new rule after the Nights of Iron. If ever the Templars were threatened again, an alarm code would be sent out, 1310, symbolizing Friday, October 13, the day the Templars had been captured by the Inquisition. Every Templar was to immediately abandon his position and retreat to a safe house. Each safe house would be comprised of three knights, called a lance. Billi and Kay were meant to have gone with Percy to an apartment in the East End. From there, safe communication would be reestablished.

But not with mobiles. If any lance was compromised, it had to be assumed the enemy might use their mobiles against them—the way Michael had when he'd texted Kay. Instead they'd meet at prearranged rendezvous points. Places that were open, crowded, and very public. Almost impossible to be spied upon or trapped in.

Billi rubbed her temples. The drumming pain continued to kick away behind her eyes. She could still smell the dry desert air from the vision. She glanced up at her dad. Had Michael penetrated his mind?

"You okay, Dad?"

His eyes opened a slice. "If you mean have I turned into a drooling vegetable—I haven't." His eyes closed again. "Michael got nothing from me."

"But that vision, the man on the hill." Billi remembered those awful screams rising from the ancient city. "What was it?"

"Michael's own memories. Of the last time he unleashed

the Tenth Plague," said Kay. He looked gray. The psychic attack must have hurt him badly. "He hoped to smash through your father's defenses with a tidal wave of his own memories, drowning Arthur's mind beneath it."

Billi looked at her slumped-shouldered father again. She had to admit it, the old man was tough.

Elaine brought them to a row of garages near Abney Park Cemetery. The huge graveyard was a Victorian necropolis designed to absorb the sudden boom in London's population in the nineteenth century. Now it was derelict and overgrown due to decades of neglect. The rusty iron railings surrounding it were wrapped in ivy, and beyond was a black labyrinth of broken gravestones, graffiti-covered mausoleums, and a wild mass of out-of-control bushes, trees, and long grass.

"Home sweet home," said Elaine. "Do open up those doors, would you?"

The rear of the garage was cluttered with old furniture, overspill from Elaine's pawn shop, no doubt. The safe house was upstairs, and they entered through a side door next to the garage. As Billi helped Kay with her dad, she noticed a small alcove in the right doorpost. It contained a black box. A mezuzah. Elaine touched the box and kissed her fingertips, then went in. Billi inspected the box. She knew that a scroll bearing a Jewish prayer, *Sh'ma Yisrael*, was inside. A ward against evil spirits. But would it protect them against Michael and his *ghuls*? Billi wondered.

A steep narrow staircase rose from the front door to the floor above. The wall was lined with old photographs, but Billi concentrated on getting her dad up, not easy, given the space, but they managed after almost ten minutes. They turned right and entered a small, spartanly furnished living room. Against the far wall was a kitchenette with a stove and a compact fridge that hummed loudly.

"Drop Art in the main bedroom," Elaine said, pointing at a door in the corner. "I'll check his stitches in a minute." Billi nodded to Kay, and they hauled Arthur the last few feet. The bedroom had a cupboard, desk, and a futon covered in gray army blankets.

"Dad'll feel right at home," Billi said as they lowered him down. He lay there coughing.

"Water," he said. Kay went out to get it. Billi lifted her dad's legs onto the bed and then looked around the room.

So this was Elaine's little getaway. A Tibetan mandala hung over the bed, and several North American spirit traps dangled from the ceiling. It looked like the bedroom of an old hippie. Billi inspected the photographs and suddenly stopped.

It was her mum. She had her arm over Elaine's shoulders and was leaning back, her belly pregnant and huge. Elaine grinned at the camera, and her mum was caught mid-laugh.

"Who took this?" asked Billi.

The bed frame creaked as Arthur looked over. "I did," he sighed. "Ages ago."

Billi stared at the photo. She'd thought about it since seeing the calligraphy back at Elaine's Bazaar, how Elaine and her mum had been friends. They'd both been outsiders. Elaine looked centuries younger; her hair was black and the wrinkles shallow. But Billi couldn't stop looking at her mother. The laugh was big, but it didn't spread to her eyes. They were clear and locked on the photographer: her dad. Jamila cradling her bulging belly. Billi's mouth went dry. That was her in there, about to be born. What had her mum been thinking? Could she have imagined the events that were to unfold—what would happen to her and her child? But those black eyes—the eyes Billi had inherited—didn't reveal anything.

Kay entered and Billi stiffened. He passed Arthur a tall glass of water, then he left. Arthur drained the glass in one gulp, then put it down and looked as if he wanted to speak. Instead he sank into the pillows and closed his eyes.

What were they going to do? They had no plan and no support. For all she knew, Michael could be hunting down the others right now.

It looked hopeless. Billi gazed at her sleeping father and wished he could give her the answers. But she wasn't sure he even had them. She closed the door quietly as she went out.

Kay was slumped on the sofa. Billi thought he looked paler than usual. She kicked his heels and he shifted over.

"Thanks for that," she said. "taking out that *ghul.*"

"Told you I could fight." He flexed his biceps in a mocking pose.

"Let's not get too carried away. Tripping someone does not make you Bruce Lee." Still, it had taken some guts. Billi sighed, and for the first time in ages, relaxed. Maybe Kay would be a hero after all.

Elaine came back from outside and tossed a stuffed garbage bag into the center of the room. "There are a few spare sleeping bags and sheets in there. Make yourselves comfortable."

"Where are we sleeping?" asked Kay. Elaine pointed at the sofa, then the floor.

"Take your pick."

The acrid sting of cigarette smoke woke her. Billi shifted onto her side, careful not to fall off the sofa. It was lumpy and uneven; half the springs were missing, and it sagged in the middle. Now that she was awake, Billi felt twinges and aches along her back. She rose slowly and stretched.

Soft moonlight filtered through the thin cotton sheets that served as curtains. Kay lay sprawled on the floor, his pale foot sticking out from the unzipped sleeping bag. His black T-shirt made the whiteness of his face all the more stark and icy.

He sleeps with his eyes open.

Just a sliver of blue peeked through Kay's parted eyelids,

sparkling. His chest rose and dipped, his breath a soft whisper.

Her dad's door was ajar. She saw his silhouette beside the desk, and a red tip burning along his fingers.

He's smoking. He's just had a lung punctured, and he's having a fag.

She went to the door and pushed it open.

"It's not like you have a lung to spare," she said. "You should quit."

Arthur raised the cigarette to his lips, stopped, then put it back in the ashtray. "Like you?"

If this was his attempt to make her feel guilty, after everything that had just happened, well, he was going to be disappointed. Billi took the smoldering stub and squashed it out.

"So why did you quit?" he asked.

"I'm not a Templar."

"You sure? Not doing too badly." He smiled, the corners of his lips turned up slightly. But it seemed wrong, his face straining like that. The corners turned back down.

Billi laughed. "Except for hurling my guts during the Ordeal. Except for bringing the Angel of Death to our home. Except for almost getting you killed. "

"We all make mistakes."

"Yeah, but one day mine will be fatal." Billi looked at her father's gaunt face. "I can't take it, Dad. I don't want this life. This responsibility. We're in this mess because of me." She sank her face into her hands.

"No. We're in this because of Michael." The bed creaked as he twisted himself out of it. His bare feet cautiously touched the floor, and a weak hiss slipped from his clamped teeth. "It's not a duty you can just abandon. For better or for worse, it's the life you lead."

"No." She raised her head so they were eye to eye. "It's the life *you* lead." She stood up. "I'm not going to become like you." As she said it, her breath caught in her throat. He didn't feel anything for anyone. She looked down at the tiny cut on her wrist. He didn't care about her, so why should she care about him?

"One day you'll understand, Billi. You'll make hard choices, and you'll need this life to make them."

"No, I won't." Billi went to the door. She looked back at him, battered, scarred, his chest wrapped in fresh white bandages. Arthur should have died a hundred times over. Maybe deep down that's what he wanted. He wanted to destroy himself. She wasn't going to let him destroy her.

"Billi, I know you're angry at me. I wish there was another way."

Billi turned the handle. "It's not anger I feel." She opened the door, and her eyes went to the picture of her mother. "It's pity."

21

SHE IS DREAMING—SHE KNOWS IT BUT CAN'T DO anything *but be carried along by the ancient phantoms lingering just on the other side of life. These streets she walks are long vanished under the sands and the hot white sun. The Eye of Ra has sunk and risen across the horizon countless times since. But the heat of it burns her face, and the coarse grittiness under her bare soles feels real and immediate. She scrunches her toes in the bleached white sand and lets the particles tickle her feet.*

They come out onto the streets bearing their terrible loads. The poor wear simple tunics of tan-colored cotton, while the rich and powerful are wrapped in sparkling white linen.

But whitest of all are the burial shrouds.

Somewhere in the palace the pharaoh lays out his dead first-born child at the foot of the black marble statue of Anubis. These gods, once so mighty, will fade like this city into legend as a new, greater, and more terrible deity takes their place. But religion requires sacrifice. Billi knows this to be true, and somewhere deep inside, fears the price yet to be paid.

The dead line the streets. Rich and poor, slave and noble made equal. The rows of white bundles seem to go on forever.

But one draws Billi closer. She drifts through the mourning Egyptians like a ghost, pulled toward this one single shrouded figure. Her hand acts of its own accord as it reaches out to touch the familiar face, covered by the thin cotton. Her fingers trace over the cheeks, cold despite the desert heat. Thumb and forefinger pinch the corner of the cloth, and she pulls it back—

Kay held Billi tightly to him as she screamed. Her skin dripped with sweat, and her chest ran hard and rapid with fear. She grabbed hold of him, and they hung on to each other as she fought down the nightmare.

A dream, just a dream. It's just a dream.

Eyes squeezed shut, she pressed her forehead against Kay's chest as he knelt beside her on the sofa bed. She wasn't an Oracle; her dreams didn't mean anything. Anything. She tried to focus on the back of her eyelids, but couldn't. Kay's scent sparked off old memories, back to when they were little, sneaking into bed together while the Templars talked downstairs. It was the closest she'd felt to being part of a family. Touching him, being this close to him, she picked up the warm, slightly oily scent of his skin, not dry and cold as she'd imagined, but strangely earthy, moist. She felt how his chest slowly rose and settled back, and realized he wasn't quite as skinny as she'd always thought. He didn't have the inhuman physique of Michael, the shape of a marble statue brought to life, but there was hidden strength under his skin, and maybe more than bone and sinew. His arms were wrapped around her, and his hands were soft. Maybe she could rest here for just another minute.

Kay coughed and pulled back. "You okay?" He was blushing. On a near-albino it looked pretty extreme.

Oh God, he was reading my mind. What had she been thinking? Billi nodded and looked around, anywhere but at him. Dawn filtered in through the small windows, filling the living room with a soft golden glow. Billi slowly stretched, from the toes, legs, torso, shoulders, arms, and fingertips, reaching upward as far as she'd go, letting the kinks and knots in her muscles slip out. Kay sat there watching.

"Why don't you stop gawking and get me some breakfast?" Billi was wearing an old T-shirt and a pair of sweatpants. She grabbed a sweater and put it on, uncomfortably aware of his presence. She slipped her feet into her trainers and sat down at the table while Kay crossed the room to the kitchenette. He fumbled around in a cupboard and began putting out butter and plates. He was all fingers and thumbs, spilling the milk and burning the toast.

"Dad and Elaine?" she asked.

"Still in bed." Kay almost dropped the bowl. "Separately. Obviously."

She took a plate from him. "Obviously."

Kay mixed a bowl of muesli with a thick spoonful of honey, then pushed it over to her.

"My favorite. Now how on earth did you know?"

Kay ignored her taunt. "What's next?"

Billi took a mouthful. If nothing else, Kay mixed a mean muesli. "No idea. But I'm sure Dad'll have a plan. And knowing him it'll probably be insanely dangerous."

Billi glanced at her dad's door. "Why didn't he give me the plague when he met me? I'm a firstborn."

"Michael wouldn't have wanted to give the game away by infecting you. We would have known he was behind it." Kay's fingers curled into a fist. "But I marked him, Billi. I've seen his aura now, and I know the color of it, the shape of it, everything. I know what he's made of."

"What's for breakfast?" asked Elaine as she came out of the spare room. She held a cigarette between her fingers and switched on the gas stove. She slowly rotated the end of the cigarette until it caught fire, then took a deep drag. "Better."

Arthur's door creaked open.

"Morning." He shuffled to the table and sat. He looked better, but not by much. There was a tinge of color in his cheeks, and though his eyes didn't look as sunken as they had been, his jeans and tatty green sweater seemed two sizes too big and hung loose over his frame.

He looks so feeble, Billi thought. A strong breeze would knock him down. But Elaine had checked him over, and

Billi hoped the worst had passed. All her dad needed was serious rest. Somehow, though, she knew he wasn't going to get it.

Eggs came out of the fridge and were soon frying with mushrooms, onions, and a spoonful of chili. Elaine cleared her throat as she poured the teas.

"What's the plan, boss?" she asked.

"Simple. We regroup and take the fight to Michael."

Billi rolled her eyes. What a bloody surprise. She looked around the table. Didn't they get it? There was no way to defeat Michael. This was suicide.

She had to make them understand. "I think—"

"We know what you think," snapped her father.

"Have some sense, Dad!" Billi bolted to her feet. "Look at you. You can barely lift that mug, let alone a sword. We can't fight Michael!"

"There has to be a way. We just need to find it," said Kay. Everyone turned to him. He wore a mask of determination that worried Billi. "I'll rally the others."

"Thank you, Kay." Arthur slapped his palm on the table, his old strength suddenly returning as he sensed the battle turning in his favor. "I'm proud of you."

He might as well have kicked Billi in the guts.

I'm proud of you.

Of you.

Her dad never spoke to her like that.

Hadn't she done anything he'd been proud of? No. As

far as Arthur was concerned, if she wasn't a Templar, she wasn't anything.

I'm proud of you.

Billi reached the door and opened it. Her heart shriveled with misery, but she quashed that. She wasn't going to go to pieces. Instead, blackness swelled, and that filled her heart now.

I'm proud of you.

He'd asked her if she hated him, back in the armory. Why?

Because it would be easier if she did. Easier for him.

She meant nothing to him. Michael was right.

"Billi?" started Kay.

She slammed the door behind her.

22

BILLI RAN. SHE RAN DOWN STOKE NEWINGTON Church Street. Past the garbagemen loading up their truck, past the old Sikh arranging fruit outside his grocer's shop, past the office workers at the bus stop. Billi's feet hardly touched the ground, and her rage wouldn't let her stop. The gates of Clissold Park stood open, and the park beyond was carpeted in a low white mist, which Billi ran into. She didn't care where, just away.

I'm proud of you.

She couldn't get it out of her mind; the way her dad had smiled. At Kay.

Oh, yes. She should have known: Kay was the Oracle, after all. He was important. And she? What was she?

She wasn't even a Templar.

Billi barged past two joggers in Day-Glo lycra outfits and overtook a trio of nannies with designer prams and designer babies. The west exit onto Green Lanes suddenly appeared ahead out of the mist, mere feet away.

As did Kay.

Billi was almost on top of him when she realized he was there. He raised his hand and smiled—and found himself lying on the dewy grass, groaning and clutching his face. Billi stood over him, the knuckles on her right fist hot and bruised.

"What the hell d'you do that for?" he cried.

Would Arthur be so proud of him now? She wanted Kay to be angry, to get up and fight. Just so she could smash him in the other eye.

Some Templar.

She nudged him with her foot. "Get up." He didn't respond. She kicked him.

"Ow!"

"Just get up."

The three nannies passed by, giving Billi long sideways glances, no doubt memorizing her face in case of a police lineup later.

"What the hell are you looking at?" she shouted. Billi slumped down on a bench, struggling to get her rage under control. But all she could see was everyone praising and adoring Kay. Marvelous Kay.

But it wasn't his fault. Not really. She tried hard to believe it, but the urge to punch in his pasty white face remained incredibly strong. She lowered her hands and stared at the scattered leaves on the ground.

"Why?"

He shuffled, perhaps watching out for a second attack. "Why what?"

"Why did you come after me? You always do. Like some . . ."

"Guardian angel?" Kay suggested.

"Like some stalker." She rolled her eyes at him, showing it was okay for him to approach. She could never stay mad at Kay for long.

Kay laughed, and the bench creaked as he sat beside her. He'd lowered his hands and Billi could see the swelling around his left eye. It was going to be a big, fat, ugly bruise.

Really big. "Sorry," she said.

Kay sat very close to her, but for some reason she didn't feel like moving away. She looked at him sideways. He was actually quite good-looking, in that malnourished indie pop star kind of way. He watched the magpies flutter from the bare branches to peck at the damp soil. Kay's bright eyes took in everything; he seemed to be amazed by it all. There was that secret smile again, the one that came from seeing things Billi wished she could see, just once.

"Looks like it's clearing," said Kay. The mist had evaporated except for wispy tendrils that clung stubbornly to the ground. The morning sun was bright in the sharp blue sky.

"Why do you think my dad's like that?" She couldn't bring herself to ask what she really wanted.

Why doesn't he love me?

"You're wrong about your father."

"You know that? For certain?"

He moved closer. His voice was quiet, and Billi could feel his breath move in and out, gently caressing her cheek. His hand touched the side of hers, and she sat very still. She waited, heart pounding, part of her telling herself this was just Kay, the boy she'd grown up with.

But it wasn't. This Kay was very different. She turned her head slightly so his breath was on her lips. She lowered her eyes, looking at the curve of his throat down into his T-shirt and the way his chest moved as he breathed.

Kay turned his face away and stood up.

Billi sat there, stunned. What had just happened?

He pushed his hand through his hair, not knowing which way to look, so he focused on his boots.

"Just know that you're wrong about your father."

No one commented on Kay's swollen eye when they came back. Arthur and Elaine were still at the table, but breakfast had been cleared away and replaced with a pristine white linen cloth. On it sat a large round biscuit tin and a leather-bound book, small, wrinkled, old.

"There's a packet of peas in the freezer," said Elaine. It took a second for Billi to realize she was talking about Kay's eye. Kay found it and pressed the bag against his bruised face.

Billi moved to the other side of the table, putting as much distance between her and Kay as possible. They hadn't said a word to each other on the way back from the park.

The biscuit tin had a copperish tinge, and the lid was engraved with a profile of Queen Victoria and Albert. Billi didn't think there were biscuits within. The book she didn't recognize.

"A diary?" The binding was similar to others she'd seen in the Templar library, though this one looked far older. It bore small bronze clasps, and the title was in gold leaf. Billi leaned over to read it. But as her eyes passed over the tiny letters, a cold dread crawled into her.

"The *Goetia*," she said, looking up at her dad. "It's not possible."

The Lesser Key of Solomon. King Solomon's occult writings on how to summon and bind Ethereals: devils, *Malakhim*, and watchers. She didn't know the book still existed. It was a book of necromancy, the darkest *maleficia*.

"Where d'you get it?" She stared at it warily, as if it were some deadly dormant creature.

"Off some fool who thought he could summon the devil," said Arthur.

"You're joking, of course."

Arthur looked at her. It wasn't his joking face.

"What happened to him?"

"Something bad," said her dad in the tone that

meant the conversation was over.

He peeled off the lid of the tin. Inside, covered in Bubble Wrap, was the Cursed Mirror. Its surface rippled like oily water.

This was what it was all about, this small copper disk. How much pain, torment, and slaughter was bound in its surface? Billi thought about the trapped watchers, about the Nights of Iron, and Percy sitting there with his life blood dribbling down his chest. How many had already died because of it? And how many were still to die?

"This is the only way," said Arthur. "We can't kill Michael. But we can bind him. With this." He touched the book's cover softly; even he was afraid of it. "We can draw him into the mirror and trap him in Limbo with the other watchers, forever."

"You can't. Even Solomon never managed that. Michael's an archangel," Billi said.

"Solomon faced Michael at the height of his powers. He's not the archangel he used to be," replied Arthur.

Billi shook her head. "There's no one that powerful."

Arthur stood up. "Yes there is," he said, and slid the small deadly book across the white tablecloth.

To Kay.

23

ELAINE SUMMONED UP A PROGRAM ON HER LAPTOP. Billi stood behind her while Arthur and Kay sat on either side, watching a star chart appear on the screen. Elaine put on her spectacles and began clicking through the time icon in the corner.

"What are you looking for?" Billi asked.

"We need to optimize Kay's chance of success, so this"—she tapped the screen—"is a program mapping the movement of the planets over the year, for the Northern hemisphere." She clicked open another folder, and Billi saw a list of files, one for each of the Templars. Elaine double-clicked Kay's. A spreadsheet appeared, annotated in Hindi.

"And these?" Billi squinted, but the symbols' meaning didn't become any more clear.

"Vedic astrological charts based on the date and place of

birth." Elaine highlighted a row of numbers. "A Brahman mate of mine calculated one for each of you."

"What religion don't you dabble in?" asked Arthur. "Lot made do with just Christianity."

"Which was why, as you know, he was crap and always needed my help," said Elaine. She went back to the map of the heavens and opened up a scroll, which she pasted the numbers into. She hit RETURN and leaned back. "Give it a minute." She waved at the kitchenette. "Someone put the kettle on."

Kay got up, and Billi took his chair. "Why are you doing this?" Elaine wasn't a Templar, yet here she was, in charge of its most precious treasure. She wasn't even the right religion, but they were depending on her to beat their greatest enemy. They always depended on her.

Elaine tapped out a fresh cigarette. She offered one to Arthur, but he declined.

"Oh, that's easy: somebody has to." Elaine smiled to herself. "You knights are obsessed with dogma, doing things one way and one way only. If it's not in the Templar Rules, you're not interested. That's why you end up in such deep trouble. Your approach is blinkered." She pointed at Arthur. "Art, on the other hand, just wants to win, don't you, Art? So you hire the best—me."

"But you're not an Oracle," said Billi.

"Thank God. I sleep badly enough without being disturbed by mad dreams. I've a tiny bit of psychic ability"—

she turned her head toward Kay—"but not like golden boy there. Nothing flash like aura-reading or telekinesis. But enough to know what's right and what works. The rest is keeping an open mind."

It was just like Billi's combat training. Arthur and the others hadn't taught her karate, judo, kung fu, or anything that could be labeled. She'd been taught how to punch hard, kick harder, grapple, lock, and hundreds of other moves taken from all styles, all disciplines.

"That's why we sent Kay east." Elaine sighed. "Once he's trained, he'll take over."

"So you're training your replacement," said Billi.

Elaine glanced at Arthur. "Aren't we all?"

Arthur put his hand on Elaine's shoulder. Billi watched the two of them. A lot of unknown history was there, and she knew she'd never get to the bottom of it. Despite the casual way Elaine had said it, leaving a Jew in charge of the reliquary must have created a major scandal within the Order. Even as Master, Arthur would have fought hard to get the others to agree. Her dad cleared his throat as Kay came over with the teas.

"We need to make contact with the other knights," he said. "Even if Kay succeeds in finding Michael, there will still be *ghuls* doing his bidding. They're serving him right now, but once he's gone they'll splinter. Then it'll take us years to find them."

He was right. *Ghuls* weren't brainless undead; they

retained a lot of independence despite the fact they'd given their souls away. They'd hope by serving Michael he might donate more of his own supernatural powers, thereby granting them greater strength. She'd read that the most powerful *ghuls* could change shape, their unholy energies metamorphosing their flesh. If they could do that, hunting them down would be impossible.

"We'll need to strike them the moment Michael's been bound into the mirror," said Arthur.

"How?" asked Billi.

"When I know who's survived, I'll be able to tell you." Arthur pointed out the window. "Trafalgar Square is the rendezvous point."

It made sense. Lots of people, lots of ways in, lots of ways out. Michael would need hundreds to cover all the possible escape routes.

Arthur continued. "We agreed that any surviving parties would meet at six p.m.—rush hour. I want you to touch base with the others and tell them what we're planning—gather what news they might have. Report back to me, and I'll formulate a strategy."

"Gwaine's in charge now, Dad."

"No he's not." He scowled and turned to Kay. Despite her father's frailty, Billi saw the fire in his eyes. This was Arthur doing what Arthur did best. "You'll need to be careful."

Kay spoke slowly, but Billi caught the nervous

excitement in his voice. "I've marked Michael's aura now. I'll spot him before he spots me."

"Good man."

"I'm coming," said Billi.

Arthur's eyes narrowed. "This is Templar business; it's not your problem now."

"I'm not doing it for the Templars."

"Surely not for me?"

"You're right. Surely not."

For herself. For revenge. For what Michael would do if she did nothing. And maybe . . . maybe for Kay. He'd need her if things turned violent. Which, given the situation, was exceedingly likely.

Kay smiled slyly. "You're not turning hero on us, are you?"

She shook her head; that wasn't it at all. "Have you noticed how the Templar graveyards are full of heroes?" She looked up at him. "So don't you be getting any ideas yourself. We do the job, no more, no less." She turned to her dad. "Right?" He nodded in agreement.

The laptop chimed.

"What have you got?" Kay asked. He looked both eager and apprehensive. Trapping Michael would be his Ordeal—the test Oracles were never given. Billi could see that Kay wanted this too much, and it made her nervous.

They all stared at the map. Lines were drawn from star to star, marking out astrological patterns, but to Billi it just looked like random shapes. Elaine took a deep breath and highlighted a series of points. These nodes lit up red, and a date appeared at the bottom of the screen.

"Seven days," said Elaine. She put her hand on Kay's. "We bind Michael in seven days."

A dull, low, gray sky hung over a packed Trafalgar Square. Billi was glad to be off the bus; she'd been feeling sick all the way, trapped under some bloke's stinking armpit in the crowded, juddering vehicle. Drizzle spat on her cheeks, and she pulled up her hood, then walked through a band of tourists, with Kay right behind her, weaving through backpacks and avoiding the cameras.

"Sense anything?"

Kay shook his head. "All clear."

In the center rose Nelson's Column, 165 feet high and guarded by four immense bronze lions. In each corner of the square was a pedestal. Three bore statues of the great and good, but one was empty. An elevated boulevard ran along the northern side of the square, in front of the National Portrait Gallery. Billi and Kay stopped beside the low wall on the balcony edge of the wide walkway. From here they could watch over the entire area. Street entertainers gathered small crowds to watch their performances. One guy was dressed as Charlie Chaplin, playing out a routine almost a hundred years old. A couple of Rollerbladers wove in and out of a row of upturned cups. A

Roman soldier painted silver stood statue-still with a bucket for change at his feet while children made faces at him. Billi watched them laughing as their parents tried to get them in order and into the gallery.

There were children everywhere. She watched a small boy in blue chase a cloud of pigeons off the ground. The air filled with flapping gray-and-black feathers, but the birds were too canny and experienced to collide with anyone. The flock took off, circled widely, then landed not a dozen feet away. The boy set off after them again.

She watched the happy crowds and shivered. It was cold here, alone.

No, not alone anymore. Kay stood beside her.

"It'll be okay," he said. She wasn't sure if he was talking to her or himself.

"Kay, the eternal optimist." Billi laughed.

"True, very true." He gestured at the people below them. "If you could only see, just for a minute. Really see. Then you'd never give up."

She watched him. Kay's face held a gentle calmness, a certainty of purpose. He never doubted. It wasn't the vicious fanaticism of her dad's—just an unshakable faith in what he did.

"Why d'you think He lets this happen? God, I mean."

Kay locked his fingers together. "You mean is this all part of His plan?"

"I suppose. You're the one that's spent the last year in

Jerusalem. Someone out there must have an idea."

"Y'know what the imam of Al Aqsa mosque told me?" He looked at her, eyes attentive. "Rabbi Levison said the same thing, so did the abbot of the Nestorians. Strange, isn't it? They couldn't agree on religion, but they could all agree on God's plan."

"Well, what did they say? About knowing the will of God?"

"They said, and I quote"—Kay shrugged—"'I know nothing.'"

Billi wanted to kick him for making a joke, but realized he was serious.

"What?"

"If someone says he knows God's will, he's either lying or insane." Kay straightened up. "The best we can do is follow our hearts."

"But Michael thinks he *is* doing right. He's following his heart."

"One made black with bitterness." Kay shook his head. "The heart needs to be about compassion, Billi."

Billi looked at Kay's long fingers, his delicate white hands. They were not the hands of a warrior. "Dad says it's our job to be ruthless."

"Your dad's not as ruthless as he likes to pretend. Believe me."

Her dad not ruthless? Maybe Kay wasn't that gifted after all. Billi gazed back out across the square. She thought of her dream, of all those white shrouds. They had to stop Michael. Compassion wasn't going to come into it.

"Do you think you can do it? The binding, I mean."

"I have to try."

"Kay, if you're not ready, then you've got to say so. Getting killed isn't heroic."

"Billi, aren't you afraid? When you go out on a Hot Meet? During the Ordeal?"

What sort of stupid question was that? She'd spent half her life scared out of her wits.

Kay frowned, then turned to look at her. "Do you know how I feel when I see you go out?" He lowered his head. "Unworthy."

"So it's just about heroics?"

"Some things are worth fighting for."

"What things?"

Kay pulled off his cap and twisted it. "That dream of yours."

"But I didn't tell you— Oh."

"All those bodies in the streets, all that grief." He took hold of her hand. She tried to ignore how good it felt. "Can you imagine what it'll be like here? How many dead? If we don't stop Michael, who will?"

"You'll risk dying to stop him?"

"Could you live with yourself if you didn't?"

Billi opened her mouth, but no answer came. She wanted to shake her shoulders, to throw the weight off her, but she couldn't. Kay was right. Someone had to stop Michael. Knowing what she knew, how could she pass by and let others take the burden? This had nothing to do with the Templars, and everything to do with doing right. But it didn't make the weight of it any less.

A couple walked past. They held hands, and the young man had a balloon, though he looked to be in his twenties.

"What do you see, Billi?" He reached over and touched her arm lightly. "He's just proposed to her. She said yes. You can see it by the light. He's thrilled but scared. They'll love, they'll live, and they'll die. Like all things." He seemed lost in thought. "But isn't that enough? Isn't that worth dying for?"

"Don't talk like that."

"Billi, you need to be—"

Billi kissed him. She didn't want to hear any more.

She did it without thinking, because if she thought, her courage might have failed. He was warm, and that heat flooded through her, a tingling sensation that sank into her bones. Her fingers tightened around the balcony edge, so Kay was trapped between her and the low wall, their bodies squashed together. He cupped his hands around her face, and Billi felt his eyelashes flutter against hers. Then, with a slight sigh, he drew away. Away, but not far. Not far at all.

His azure eyes were huge, clear, and flawless. Billi could see her own dark orbs floating in them. Kay's palms were hot against her cheeks. She gently leaned back and touched her tongue over her lips. Kay tasted nice.

"Not interrupting anything, am I?"

They broke apart, and Billi saw Bors standing in front of them, hot dog in his hand.

Doesn't he ever stop eating?

Bors leered and ran his tongue over his ketchup-smeared mouth. "Because if I am, I could come back later."

"We'd finished," said Kay, acting unfazed and leaving all the blushing to Billi. "You the only one?"

Bors shook his head. "Master Gwaine and Gareth are with me."

"Seneschal Gwaine, you mean," said Billi.

Bors pushed the last of his snack into his mouth. He talked as he chewed, spitting out gobs of pink meat and onion.

"Was it Arthur who gave the 1310? Needed his bedpan changed, did he?"

How dare he say that about her dad? Bors's piggy face broke into a grin as he saw her fingers curl into fists.

"Try it, little girl."

She stepped forward, but Kay raised his hand.

"This is pointless. Arthur's in charge and it's as simple as that. Gwaine will toe the line if he knows what's good for him."

Bors wiped his mouth with his jacket sleeve. "Think I'm scared of Arthur?"

"Of course you are," said Gareth, emerging from the

crowd. "The Devil himself is scared of Art." He signaled to Pelleas, who was leaning against a wall, on guard.

They'd made it, thank God. There were smiles and hugs all around. Even Bors, despite himself, looked relieved.

Kay explained Arthur's plan, and they all listened silently. Billi stood beside him, amazed at how confident and sure of himself he was. He told them about the binding, and she could tell they were impressed.

"Why not now? Why in seven days?" asked Bors.

"The alignment of planets. Technical stuff," said Billi. "You wouldn't understand."

Kay interrupted before Bors could reply. "We need to optimize my chances of success."

Pelleas and Gareth looked at each other. Billi noticed Gareth shaking his head.

"What? What's wrong?" she asked. "Hold on. Isn't Berrant meant to be in your lance? Where is he?"

Pelleas looked at her, stuck in indecision. Then he frowned. "Berrant's dead, Billi."

She stared at him. "Dead?" The words took a long time to register. "You weren't going to tell us, were you?"

"It shouldn't change our plans," Pelleas said, his eyes downcast.

"Bloody hell, Pelleas, it changes everything!" Berrant had been a knight for what, only two years? She couldn't believe it. They'd had an easy friendship; he'd trained under Arthur as a squire before she had, and the two of them had swapped stories about how terrible her dad was. And now he was gone.

"But how?" asked Kay.

"Michael found our safe house." Pelleas glanced over at Gareth, who nodded wearily. "After we got the 1310 code, we dropped everything and ran. Sat tight until we could come here. But it was just before dawn when we spotted *ghuls* outside the house. Two came through the front, more through the back. Berrant killed a few, but then Michael joined in."

"We didn't have a chance," said Gareth. The pain in his eyes was hard and deep. Billi knew he and Berrant had shared a long history. "Berrant held back to give us a chance to escape."

"But the wards, aren't they meant to hide you from magical detection?" asked Billi.

Bors butted in. "The wards on our safe houses aren't strong enough. We might as well have a neon sign on our roof saying 'Templars Here.'"

"Are you sure it's because of the wards? Maybe one of his *ghuls* spotted you, followed you?" asked Kay.

"Your wards didn't stop him in the reliquary, did they? What makes you think they'll stop him now?" asked Bors. He spat some gristle at Kay's feet. "You may want to take your own sweet time performing your mumbo jumbo, but Michael's picking us off. In a week there won't be any of us left."

Bors was right, though Billi hated to admit it. She looked at Kay, knowing the question was one only he could answer.

Kay's face was grim. The survival of the Knights Templar depended on him.

"Then we can't afford to wait seven days to do the binding, can we?" He turned to Billi. "We'll do it tonight."

24

"NO, I FORBID IT," SAID ARTHUR. THE MOMENT THEY'D returned, Kay had explained the danger they were in. Arthur was completely unmoved.

"But Dad, Berrant's dead. The others—"

"Knew the risks when they joined. We all do." He looked around at Kay, Elaine, and finally at Billi. "Have you thought about what might happen if we rush this and get it wrong? What might happen to you." He gave a derisive snort. "You cast your soul out into the Ethereal Realm when you're not ready, and it'll be torn to pieces by the spirits out there, if you're lucky. Worst case they'll use you as a bridge to get here." He shook his head. "Might as well chuck you bleeding into a shark tank."

"I'm willing to take the risk," said Kay.

"Are you?" Arthur's eyes narrowed. "Are you willing to take responsibility for all the dead firstborn if you foul it up?" He shook his head. "No, we wait."

Billi peered out the window. Fat dark clouds hung over the city, swollen with rain.

"Then that's it. The Knights Templar will be wiped out," she said.

"Better we lose a handful of men than all the firstborn children of Britain."

Elaine tossed a newspaper across the table. "But they're dying already. Michael's been busy while we've been sitting here on our arses."

It was tonight's *Evening Standard*. The headline was bold white on a black page.

WHAT KILLED THEM?

There was row upon row of photos. Some taken from holiday snaps, others were school pictures, kids in their uniforms self-consciously grinning at the camera. Billi scanned the article and stopped at a name she knew.

"Rebecca Williamson." She barely recognized her in the photo. The face looking up at her was a cheery blond girl with plump cheeks and dimples. Nothing like the skeletal child she'd spoken to in the hospital.

"He's killed them all. There must be fifty or more of them."

"So it's out." Arthur frowned. "It'll be fast now."

Billi looked up from the pictures of the dead. "What will?"

"Panic. Hysteria," said Elaine. "If people can't explain it, they get afraid; you just watch. By tomorrow you'll have parents stopping their kids from going to school. If little Jimmy gets a sneeze he'll be down to the hospital before he's wiped his nose."

"That's what he wants, don't you see?" Arthur took the paper from Billi. "He'll force us to confront him, play our hand too early, just because of these deaths."

"Jesus Christ, Dad, we have to do something." Billi stood up in front of him. "Michael's searching for us right now. D'you honestly think he'll kindly delay his hunt for the next seven days just for us?"

Elaine gently pulled Kay around to face her. "Can you do it?" she asked.

"I have to," he said, swallowing hard.

Arthur sat down and turned the ring on his finger. The other three stood around him, waiting. Eventually, with a sigh, he nodded.

"Fine. Tonight."

The only illumination in the loft was a single lightbulb suspended from the underside of the roof. The air smelled of dust and fresh paint. Billi tucked herself into an alcove beside her father.

The loft had been swept clean and the dormer windows painted in. Elaine and Kay were on their hands and knees putting the finishing touches on a six-foot-circle, the binding seal. Inside it was the six-pointed triangle with the Cursed

Mirror lying, polished and gleaming, on a black velvet pillow in its center. Despite the cold, Kay was bare-chested and sweating. Across his forehead, around his neck, arms, and chest were small silver talismans, *maqlu*, tied into place with thin leather straps. He copied cuneiform wards off the *Goetia* beside him, a pot of white paint in his right hand, a delicate pointed brush in his left. He looked up at Billi briefly, winked.

He looks shattered. He was constantly wiping sweat off his forehead; the concentration was intense.

It had to be. A mistake now would be worse than fatal.

He blew on the finished calligraphy, then inspected the scroll, checking each line for mistakes. Elaine, bent double beneath the low ceiling, peered over his shoulder. Satisfied, she tapped him on the shoulder and nodded.

The ladder clanged noisily into place and Arthur pulled up the hatch, sealing them in the loft. Elaine joined Arthur and Billi, just outside the seal. All three knelt there, watching Kay.

But was he ready? Billi had read enough about necromancy to know what might happen if things went wrong. The theory was dangerously simple. Kay would use the *Goetia* to open a portal into the Ethereal Realm, trying to locate the path to Limbo. Once the portal was fully open, he would cast his own soul free of his body to seek out Michael's presence in the ether. Kay had explained that every creature had two components. The first was a physical aspect, the body in the mortal realm. The other was its soul, its aspect in the Ethereal Realm. And each soul glowed with a color and brightness unique to the individual. Michael would be easy to spot. An angel's soul, a being of light, burned brighter than most. Once found, Kay would then draw the dark angel's soul through the portal and shut the door. But in the dim loft space with the dense shadows around them, Billi was scared for Kay. What if it did go wrong? His soul could be lost in the endless ether, prey to the spirits that dwelled there. They could tear his soul to shreds.

Or worse. They might use Kay to come through. There were countless spirits out there, some like the one who had become Alex Weeks. Devils most of all envied and hungered for what was denied them: physical existence. To be able to taste, to eat, to feel . . . If a mortal soul strayed too far into their domain, they'd try to place themselves in the body left behind. A permanent possession. She looked across at Kay, her heart in her throat. She couldn't lose him too. Maybe this was a mistake. Maybe they should wait another seven days. Maybe . . .

Kay glanced up. He smiled at her, and, exhausted as he was, there was that lightness in his face, in his smile that seemed to brighten the room and push the shadows away. He gave her a wink and turned to Elaine.

"I'm ready," he said.

With Elaine's help, he tightened the straps and lashes, adjusting the plate on his forehead. Three small silver talismans hung around his neck. He unhooked one and clenched it between his teeth. His breath hissed fiercely through his nostrils.

Then he sat in lotus position, the mirror on his lap. The bulb, directly overhead, threw weird shadows and reflections against the sloping inner walls of the loft. Kay tilted his head back, eyes unfocused, and let his breath drop to the slightest breeze.

This was it.

The bulb hummed and dimmed away to nothing, sinking the loft into utter blackness. Billi felt her dad shift, and goose bumps rose along her skin as though someone had stroked her with ice.

Kay moaned.

The mirror began to glow. First it was just a dim pulsing hue of orange, red, and gold, fading and rising over long intervals. It was barely bright enough to light Kay; just an eerie sheen that rippled over his glossy white torso. His teeth bit hard into the silver, and his lips were drawn back into a silent, feral snarl. His breathing was coming in and out in sharp desperate pants.

A chill breeze rose from nowhere, and frost crept along the ground. The floorboards turned white as icy ribbons formed on their surface. In the increasing brightness Billi watched her breath form white clouds.

Intense light poured from the mirror. The blaze was steady and multihued. Patterns thrown against Kay's flesh showed shapes moving against the light source, and Billi almost jerked forward in surprise. Kay's chest rose and dropped like a marathon runner's, and the sweat glistening on his body had turned to tiny ice droplets that clung to his skin.

Voices whispered in the air, a distant babble of tongues that swam and flickered in Billi's ears, incoherent but urgent and urging.

Kay's body jerked like it had been hit with electricity, and the talisman flew from his mouth.

Tendrils of black smoke seeped out of the mirror, creeping cautiously along his quivering muscles, wrapping themselves about his arms and neck, probing at his eyes, his ears, his mouth. . . .

Kay screamed, and in that moment the smoke was sucked into him. His eyes stared out in horror, and their blueness faded as the dark filled his body. He shook as thick mists funneled into his mouth, choking him.

"You can do it, boy," whispered Arthur. He gripped Billi's wrist, guessing rightly that she wanted to jump in and help Kay.

Elaine began reciting in Hebrew, *"Adonai Eloheynu Adonai Echad . . ."*

Kay's body pulsed, and gross swellings bubbled and rippled under his white skin; shapes seemed to swim along his veins, and black tears dribbled from his ebony eyes.

It's too much. He can't do it, thought Billi. She

tugged, but her dad's grip just tightened.

The roof tiles creaked and cracked; tiny ceramic shivers sheared off due to the intense cold. The wooden joists were brittle with icicles, and the floorboards moaned as they twisted under the terrible chill.

"No," murmured Arthur. He looked around at the growing ice.

Something was wrong. This wasn't the multitude of colors Billi had seen when Kay had inadvertently opened the portal to Limbo, and this certainly didn't feel like a path into Heaven. . . .

Oh no. They were trying to come through.

From Hell.

Kay's eyes rolled sightlessly—they were black marbles—and oily tears streaked his cheeks. A face, twisted and grinning, pushed against his chest from the inside, then sank away, leaving red welts where its teeth had pressed his flesh. Large tumors rose over his body, and Kay arched his back, unable to scream. The devils were trying to use him as a bridge into Earth, the Material Realm.

Billi leaped across the seal. It was like she'd jumped naked into the freezer; the coldness seized her lungs and made her gasp. The black smoke, now a solid tentacled mass, sensed her presence and twisted toward her. Instinctively, Billi pushed her silver crucifix into her mouth and bit hard, then grabbed Kay. She tried to lift him, but invisible forces held him down. The tentacles began to crawl up her legs, and she felt their freezing touch sink through her skin into her bones.

Oh God, I can't—

Arthur grabbed the mirror and tossed it out of the seal. The voices screamed, but only for an instant.

Billi collapsed in the dark. She felt Kay's body go limp beneath her. He was ice cold. She wrapped her arms around him, pressing her body against his back, shivering but gripping him tightly.

C'mon.

Kay coughed and jerked. He let out a long aching groan. Billi felt his hands squeeze hers.

"Billi," he whispered. His voice was dry and cracked.

There was a gentle humming in the air. The bulb came back to life.

Arthur knelt beside her. His face was white with fear.

Elaine turned Kay over and stared into his eyes. She touched the silver plaque against his forehead. Then she rocked back onto her haunches and let out a long sigh of relief.

"Well, bollocks to that idea," she said.

25

"PUT HIM IN MY BED," SAID ELAINE. KAY WAS slumped between Billi and Arthur. He was heavier than he looked, and Billi grunted as she finally dropped him onto the mattress. Arthur was sweating heavily, and favored his left side.

"How are those stitches holding up?" Elaine asked. Arthur waved her off, so she checked Kay instead, inspecting his eyes, his mouth, and ears. She'd removed most of the talismans from his body and arranged them around the bed.

"Is he okay?" asked Billi. "He's not, y'know, possessed or anything?"

"If you're wondering if his head's going to rotate around his neck"—Elaine stepped away from the bed—"no, it's not. Some rest and he'll be fine. Have bad dreams, though, I wouldn't wonder."

They retreated into the living room. Billi collapsed onto

the sofa, sick and exhausted. She'd been so sure Kay would be able to do it—they all had been—but it had been too soon. She knew he'd feel that he'd failed his Ordeal. It had been so important to him, wanting to measure up to the other knights, to her, even. Kay would want to try to make up for it—to try again. But would he be strong enough to try again in seven days' time? She didn't know. That's assuming they had seven days.

What were they going to do? Spend the rest of their lives running? Hiding in different holes every night? Always looking over their shoulders for the Angel of Death? They had only their lives. Michael had all of eternity.

"That's it, then," said Arthur. "My own stupid fault."

"It's not, Dad. You were right, we were wrong. We forced you into it."

He laughed—not for long, because he went pale and bent over, cramped. He hissed through gritted teeth as he straightened.

"Forced me, did you? I just . . . hoped." He almost laughed again, and Billi watched his face brighten. Arthur finding something funny, now that was a first. "Foolish. To have hope."

Elaine touched Arthur's arm. Billi caught her look, one of deep concern.

At least it can't get any worse, she thought.

Elaine pointed at Arthur's chest. "Don't be shy. Let's have a look, then."

"It's nothing." He grinned, but it wasn't pleasant. "Had worse."

But Elaine wasn't having any of it. She got him to take off the dressing gown and lift his sweatshirt.

Blood caked his stomach. The bandages were brown with encrusted blood, and fresh scarlet wept through them, thin trails dribbling along his abdomen.

"You stupid, stupid idiot," Elaine said. She jerked her thumb at the cupboard. "Billi, get my kit. It's at the bottom."

The first-aid kit was military issue: full of gauze, morphine, and needles. Elaine began cutting off the useless old bandages.

Billi winced when Elaine tore off the dressing.

Arthur scowled at Elaine as she popped the plastic sheath off a syringe. "No drugs."

"Martyr till the last," replied Elaine. "Shut up and lie down."

Arthur ignored her, lifting himself onto his elbows and summoning Billi nearer. "The others will be waiting. They've got to know the binding's failed. Don't want them going off half-cocked thinking we've taken care of Michael."

"Leave her be, Art. The girl's done enough."

That's right, I have.

But Arthur looked up at her, face feverish. He demanded her obedience and she wouldn't give it. She wasn't a Templar anymore. He couldn't order her around. But . . .

If this wasn't her problem, whose was it? If she'd dealt

with it, she promised herself, she and her dad would talk about the Templars again. She nodded once.

"Waiting where, Dad?"

"Southwark. At the cathedral." His voice was urgent. "They'll be there for matins."

Then the needle went into his leg, and he sank back into the sofa. Elaine spared a moment's glance at Billi. She wanted to say something, Billi was sure of it. Instead she bit her lip and set to work.

Five in the morning. It was five in the morning and matins was in an hour. The world was asleep, and here she was again. Billi stared empty-eyed at the fog outside the window, willing herself to get up, get her coat on, and get out.

She found an old racing bike in the back of the garage. The rust on the chain wasn't too bad, and she dug up some spare batteries for the lights from a toolbox on the shelf. She zipped up her jacket and pulled the hood down so only her eyes peered out.

The icy fog broke over her in ghostly waves, and the night was silent but for the creaking pedals. Billi fell into a semiconscious, mechanical state of mind, just letting her legs turn the wheels, focusing on the spot of hazy lamplight ahead of her. The black tarmac ran under her wheels as she made her way into the heart of the city.

Killing Time, that's what the other Templars called the misty gap between the night and dawn. How many times had she lain half asleep in bed, listening for the front door and the clatter of her dad's weapons on the kitchen table? Then the prayers and the muttered discussions of murder?

The chain rattled off the gears and shook Billi out of her dreamy memories. The loose chain dangled on the ground. She stopped by the roadside and inspected the bike.

Bugger, bugger, bugger.

It had broken. No way to fix it. She looked around. Fleet Street. Southwark was still a couple of miles on.

She'd dump the broken bike and get the night bus. Billi patted her pocket, relieved she'd remembered to bring money.

Laughter drifted out of the darkness, and Billi's blood froze. It was harsh, cruel, and laced with malice. It echoed between the walls and through the gray mist.

"Welcome home, Templar." The voice, a woman's, seemed to come from behind Billi's shoulder. She spun around; there was nothing. Another laugh, just as vicious.

They glided out of the darkness, first indistinct and hazy, then forming into the shape of two women, the same ones she'd first seen in the hospital. They stood just within the glow of the orange streetlight, each moving with a predator's patience, eyes glowing with eagerness. The one who had broken herself on the bottom of the stairwell walked clickety-click on her imperfectly healed body, her left leg and part of her hip at right angles to the rest of her, her face swollen and black. The mist hung white tendrils around her long slim limbs: a ghostly embrace.

Billi took off through the side alleys off Fleet Street, her feet guiding her south along bare, slippery cobblestones that echoed hard with her steps.

She looked around just for a moment.

Nothing.

She turned into Pump Court, and somehow there they were, in front of her. The blank glass windows looked down at her like faceless spectators, and she saw the women part, one move behind to stop her from backtracking, the other ahead of her.

Perfect hunters, forcing the prey to them.

Billi dodged left, then immediately spun right. She dived past the *ghul*, and sharp nails slashed through her sleeve, but she was too buzzed with adrenaline to feel pain. She ran through the cloisters, with its low ceiling and white-painted rows of columns. She had only one driving thought.

Sanctuary.

She saw it suddenly looming over her. A pale stone building with tall stained-glass windows and massive black doors that seemed to hold the fog and darkness at bay. Temple Church. No hungry dead could profane a house of God. If she could reach it, she would be safe.

Billi ran across the flagstone courtyard sprinkled with predawn frost. The two *ghuls* screamed, and she saw a blur of movement head.

Billi fell down the steps to the entrance. Iron-stiff fingers dug into her shoulders, but somehow she wrenched free.

Sanctuary! She stretched out to touch the arched west door—her only hope. Suddenly she was jerked backward. One of the *ghuls* locked her fingers around Billi's throat and hoisted her off the ground, making her head pound with trapped blood.

"Sanctuary," Billi whispered, hands straining out, fingers fully stretched, their tips so tantalizingly close.

The church doors exploded outward, hurled apart by a hurricane. Devastating white light consumed them, and the sisters let out hellish banshee-high screams before being swept away by the roaring wave.

Billi crashed to the ground, paralyzed by the brightness. The light wiped out everything around her, and it carried thousands of voices, a deafening cry of rage. She curled into a ball, eyelids squeezed tight, fists covering her face, but she could not escape the light. It burned through her eyelids, searing her retinas.

And then it was gone.

She lay there, too terrified to move. Her head echoed with the sudden absence of noise, and it was a minute or two before she dared to lower her hands and, slowly, open her eyes.

A door creaked on one hinge. The wood was warped and its surface coated with ash. Behind her, jagged splinters had embedded themselves into the wall. There was nothing left of the *ghuls* except dirty black smears where they had stood.

Inside, the church walls were streaked with soot, and the flagstones were cracked and polished black, as though exposed to immense heat. Thousands of tiny pieces of paper torn from the hymn books floated in the air, burning like sprites at a ball. Glass tinkled onto the stone. Every single window had been shattered, leaving jagged glass teeth sticking out of the frames. Thin columns of smoke spiraled off the smoldering remains of the pews, each now a deformed ash skeleton.

But within this devastated burned-out shell, Billi saw someone.

Standing in the center of the choir, alone and bright in the darkness, lit as though glowing from within, was a man. Billi squinted, narrowing her eyes because he shone so brightly—as though he were a star made human. But slowly he dimmed, and she gasped.

He could have been Michael's twin. They had the same flawless marble-chiseled features and thick sensual lips. She couldn't see his eyes, though, they were hidden behind black glasses. The smoke coalesced around him into a suit of dull black. He walked toward her, the floor hissing as his bare feet trod the glasslike stone.

"Hello," he said.

He had shone so bright, the brightest star.

The Morning Star.

"Bloody hell," said Billi, still curled up on the floor.

He smiled. "Exactly."

Then the Devil reached out his hand and helped Billi up.

26

BILLI EXPECTED TO FEEL PAIN OR INTENSE HEAT WHEN he touched her. But no, it was just a simple lukewarm palm. Nothing special about it.

"Well, SanGreal?" He watched her. He stood in the center of the molten holocaust, and the vapors of steam and smoke raveled around his limbs like serpents.

Billi stepped into the center of the round. It was the oldest part of the church, and was where she'd been initiated into the Poor Fellow-Soldiers of Jesus Christ, the Knights Templar. She remembered the candles, the nine empty chairs, and the knights standing among the stone effigies of former and ancient patrons of the Order.

They were still there. On the floor around her were eight carved stone knights. William Marshall. Geoffrey de Manderville. Gilbert Marshall, among others. But now their features had buckled and melted into wormlike shapes, all nobility deformed and destroyed.

Satan drummed his long nails against a smoldering marble column.

"You tried to come through during the ritual. But we closed it down. How?"

He drew a circle in the air. "I need no trinkets to come to Earth." He pressed his foot on one of the melted effigies. "I can come and go as I please. I still retain all my powers as an archangel. Unlike my brother."

"You're not trapped in Hell?"

"What is Hell, SanGreal?" He spread out his arms. "Hell is the cry of a starving infant. Hell is the begging for mercy then denied. Hell is the betrayals between man and wife." He pressed his hands together, and the smile stretched. "The lies between father and child." He tapped his chest. "Hell is where the heart is." The Devil looked around the ruined church. "If God hears every prayer, who hears the curses? The cries of pain? The bitter lies? We do. Eventually the torment is so great the ether tears open and a devil enters the Material Realm."

"You're lying. If that were true, the streets would be full of devils."

"How do you know they're not?" His eyebrows arched.

Billi backed away, but she had nowhere to run. As she retreated into the church, into the chancel, Satan stepped closer. Suddenly Billi felt her back against the altar. He stopped.

"I am here to help you," he said.

"How?"

He pointed at the altar behind her.

A sword had been driven into the large marble block. It stood proud, bright, and high. Three feet long, the blade was only thumb-wide. It seemed likely to snap with the slightest impact. The hilt was neatly wrapped in silver wire and long enough for two hands, the pommel a plain walnut shape. Light slipped over its cutting edge like quicksilver.

"What is it?" she said, unable to take her eyes off it.

"The Silver Sword."

"Who made it?" Billi stepped closer, awed by its beauty.

"I did. During the Rebellion."

The Rebellion.

The war in Heaven.

"That sword will kill Ethereals. I guarantee it," said Satan.

Billi climbed onto the altar. The sword was plain, elegant, and without adornment. No jewels, engravings, or runes of power. But it radiated a purity of purpose that all other swords merely hinted at.

"Jesus Christ," she said.

"Him too."

She touched the hilt, and a wave of energy ran up her arm, electrifying her body. She shook once as the fire burst through her heart, and then the pain evaporated and she felt swollen with power. Her fingers wrapped themselves around it, and she pulled gently. Effortlessly, she drew the blade from the stone. She'd expected it to be unwieldy, given its odd proportions. Instead, it sat in her palm with the lightness of a paintbrush. She carved her name in the air, and it responded to the merest suggestion of wrist movement.

"That sword will make you invulnerable to Michael's powers."

"You're giving me this?"

"No, exchanging it. A deal."

"For my soul?"

The Devil grinned. He was close, and the faint odor of putrid meat wafted from his mouth. He walked out the ruined west door. "Come with me."

Out of the fog crept a rusty old car. It could have been black but was so covered in grime it was impossible to tell. The paint was peeling off the body, and the engine rumbled deeply like a snoring giant. Billi felt the vibrations travel through the ground and into her bones. The driver wore rags and was little more that a flesh-covered skeleton. His eyes, mouth, and even his ears had been stitched shut. Dried blood encrusted the torn skin.

Billi's hand tightened around the Silver Sword.

The Devil stepped in and settled himself in the patched-up leather seat.

"I won't hurt you, SanGreal."

That's what Elaine had said. Devils couldn't directly hurt humanity. But Billi knew she was in terrible danger.

The low lamps of the car's interior shone warm gold, the engine rumbled softly, and the cold outside prickled her.

She stepped in. The Devil sighed and shut the door.

She watched the city glide by, lit by the orange sodium glare of the streetlights, lost and diffused in the fog. The darkness surrounded these hazy spots, deepening in the crevices of the architecture. Blackness gathered under the bridges, in the empty doorways, and the many side streets that ran through the city. Billi saw a young girl, not much older than she was, curl up with a patchy sleeping bag in the dark open mouth of an alleyway. Billi wondered if she would still be there in the morning, or if the shadows would claim her. Maybe the Devil was right and Hell was here, just the other side of the windowpane.

The car drove the empty streets, and it seemed as though light shrank from it. The darkness crept alongside the wheels, and Billi sensed the chill of other things just out of sight—perhaps the devils that prowled the dark, answering cursed prayers and promising damnation. If they were there, they lurked invisible, beside her and in the presence of their master. The city beyond the window seemed to fade until all was mist.

Then the car stopped and the door opened. The driver bent low as the Devil stepped out. Billi went next and looked around.

They were outside Elaine's safehouse.

"Why are we here?" The upstairs windows were dark. Everyone must be asleep.

"So you can fulfill your part of the bargain. You want the Silver Sword, don't you?" He waited, the sword resting casually against his shoulder.

"You want my soul?" Billi gazed up at the windows, wishing someone would look out and see them.

The Devil laughed but shook his head. He touched the lock, and the apartment door swung open. He pointed up the stairs.

"I want you to kill your father," he said.

27

"No!"

What else could she say?

"Are you sure? Don't you want to save the first born?" The Devil raised an eyebrow. "Or Kay? Doesn't he deserve to be saved? You can do all of it"—he wrapped his hand around hers and tightened his grip—"with this."

Billi grimaced as he squeezed her fingers against the sword hilt. "No."

Suddenly he released her. Satan steped back, his attention on the streetlight sparkling along the sword's edge. "If positions were reversed, do you think Arthur would hesitate?"

She wanted to say yes, that her dad wouldn't choose duty over his daughter, but the words refused to come out. She remembered what Michael said—and him bringing the

Templar Sword down on her arm. Arthur had done nothing.

Her life, or the life of every firstborn.

That would be no choice at all for him.

"That's right." The Devil lifted her hand, raising the blade. Billi pushed with all her strength, but she couldn't fight him. The weapon's edge brushed her neck. The slightest pressure and it would open her throat wide. "He wouldn't pause for a moment, would he?" He released her.

Billi stood at the doorway looking up at the bare bulb at the top of the narrow flight of steps. The fog around her rolled in, eddies of mist turning slowly in the entrance.

"No." She couldn't. Maybe her dad would choose duty over her, but she wasn't like him. She might hate him, but even if she wasn't a Templar, she certainly wasn't an assassin. "Why do you want him dead?"

"They say that I am afraid of Arthur SanGreal. They are right." The Devil took off his glasses. His eyes . . .

He had none. Blood rimmed the edge of his sockets. The lids were wrinkled and curled back, revealing two empty holes. He gripped her cheeks and pulled her so that their faces were a few inches apart. "That's because I've finally met a mortal more ruthless than I." He gestured at the empty sockets. "Your father's work."

She wanted to look away, but she couldn't help herself. Staring into them she saw endless darkness, an abyss. The more Billi gazed into them, the more she felt she'd fall, fall forever.

"I was summoned years ago by a bishop who thought he could command me using Solomon's book. But as I appeared, the Templars intervened." He put his fingers in the two holes. "Coming out of the Ethereal Realm into this world of clay isn't easy. Tearing through the caul of reality takes immense effort, and we arrive weak, disoriented. Otherwise your father could not have done what he did."

That was how the Templars had got the copy of the *Goetia*. From this bishop. "So you killed the priest?"

"I? Not I, SanGreal." He pushed the glasses back. "It was Arthur that punished the poor man." Billi's reflection shone in the dark lenses. "His passing was not gentle."

Billi dropped the Silver Sword, and it clattered onto the cold stone. "Kill him yourself," she said.

The two of them held fast, Billi against the wall with the Devil pressed against her. He slowly released her, leaving a row of bloody nail marks along her cheeks. He dipped his forefinger into his mouth. "Do you know what went through your mother's mind as she lay bleeding to death in the hallway? Alone and abandoned?" He looked at her with his void-filled eyes. "She realized, sooner or later, that *you* would turn into *her*." He smiled cruelly. "*You shall keep the company of martyrs.* Isn't that the fate of all Templars?"

"I'm not a Templar." But even as she said it, the words tasted like ash.

The Devil laughed. "Do you really believe you have any choice?"

Was he right? How else could she stop Michael? She thought about what her father had told her—how one day she'd have to make a hard choice and be ruthless. This was it.

She reached for the sword.

"No, not with that. You must find your own way to do this. Leave it here until it's done."

Billi went up the stairs.

She unlocked the door and entered the living room. She thought they would have stayed up, but Elaine was slouched on the sofa, snoring. The side light was on, and a copy of a book, *The Talisman*, lay open on her lap. Billi inched past her and took a knife from the kitchen drawer. It was a narrow-bladed skinning knife, hard and softly curved. It would slip between ribs easily.

An assassin's weapon, that's what Percy would have called it. He'd hated knives because they could be hidden in a smile. He'd said that assassins killed as they embraced their victims.

Billi entered the bedroom.

The curtains fluttered in the breeze; her dad never completely closed his window, not even when it was snowing outside. Just enough light slipped through the gap for her to see that he was asleep. He was lying on his back with the blankets half hanging off the bed, his upper torso covered in fresh white bandages. He'd been fighting his entire life; first in the Royal Marines, and then as a Templar. He'd survived all those battles, all those midnight Ordeals with *ghuls*, werewolves, ghosts, demons.

The Unholy were right to fear him.

Moonlight caught the sharp edge of her knife. Any chest wound deeper than seven inches was fatal; Billi had ten.

"Jamila?"

She froze as he whispered her mum's name. Arthur's head shifted as he rose and leaned against the wooden headboard, and his face fell into a shaft of moonlight. His eyes were red-rimmed, still dilated from the morphine, but they came into focus. "Billi," he grunted. "I thought it was . . . never mind."

Then he saw the knife.

His eyes stayed on the weapon, like his brain just couldn't register it.

Assassin.

The best assassins were trusted—loved, even—by their victims, until it was too late. How could you get close to your target unless they trusted you?

How else could you kill Arthur SanGreal?

One life against thousands. It was one life against hundreds of thousands. The devil was right: if their positions were reversed, Arthur wouldn't hesitate.

Slowly he raised his gaze until those blue eyes of his met her black orbs. Did he know why she was there? There to kill him? He didn't try to stop her; he didn't shout for help. He just sat there, his cheeks creased ever so slightly, and those wrinkles around his eyes bunched up. He smiled at her. "I understand," he said. He looked down at his chest, then turned his face toward the light through the window. And waited.

Billi stood beside the bed, her heart pounding so hard she could hear it. Sweat coated her back. She'd barely walked a few steps, but her legs quivered with effort. Only her hand was steady. She closed her eyes. She thought about Rebecca Williamson dying alone and afraid. Like her own mother. Like he would, one day, let her die.

One life against all the firstborn.

Her dad's life.

She slammed the knife forward.

28

THE KNIFE STOOD JAMMED IN THE HEADBOARD.

Arthur looked up at her. Tears lined his weather-beaten cheeks.

The door crashed open and the light came on. Billi blinked in the sudden brightness. Elaine stood braced against the door frame. Her hair was as wild as a witch's, and she stared at them, then at the knife a few inches beside Arthur. Her mouth hung open, then clamped into a furious grimace. "Tell her, Arthur! Tell her!" she hissed through her gritted yellow teeth. She then straightened her baggy pajamas and slammed the door shut as she stormed off.

"Oh God." Billi stepped away from the bed, her entire body trembling. She stared at the bright blade quivering in the wood. "What? What, Dad?"

Arthur straightened up. "I'm sorry, Billi. I'm sorry

about all of this. I just wish there'd been another way. But you couldn't know. It was Kay."

Suddenly it seemed so hard to breathe. Arthur took a deep breath, then spoke. "Kay said this night would come." He took hold of her hand; it was the only way to stop it shaking. "He prophesied you would kill me."

Billi shook her head wildly. "No, Kay doesn't have that power. He said so himself." Telekinesis, telepathy, aura-reading, all the extrasensory perceptions, but not this; he couldn't see into the future.

"'*She will sacrifice the one she loves to save the children.*' That was what Kay said, back when we first found him." His voice was just above a whisper. "Those fits he used to have, they were visions. We didn't understand at first. But this one kept coming back again and again." Arthur faced her. "Young psychics have an extraordinary potential. But it's wild and will drive them insane. Kay was already in a bad way when we found him." Billi gazed at him, bewildered. Did Kay know any of this? Arthur continued, "He'd been moved from foster home to foster home until eventually Father Balin made him a ward of the Temple, and that's when Elaine began looking after him."

"So Elaine's known about this all along? And she kept it from Kay?" It was bad enough that her father had betrayed her, but now she knew Elaine had been deceiving Kay too.

Arthur's hand went to the side table, touching the pack of cigarettes lying there. He almost pulled one out, but stopped. "Something deadly and terrible was coming, and Kay said, 'She will sacrifice the one she loves to save the children.'" He motioned to the door. "Elaine and I argued about what it meant. Prophecies, especially ones looking well into the future, are dangerously ambiguous."

"And you thought it meant you?" asked Billi.

"Who else could it mean?" he asked.

Billi closed her eyes. She wanted to shut everything off. It was too much. Because of a boy's vague prediction, she'd spent the last five years being beaten, tested, trained, and taught how to do terrible things. All so she'd be ready to kill her father. She struggled with her breathing; it was as though an invisible vise were crushing her from all directions.

"Why didn't you tell me?"

"I couldn't, sweetheart. I couldn't." He covered his face with his hands and sank down. He looked as if he were collapsing into himself.

Sweetheart? The word seemed so wrong coming from him. Arthur looked up at her, imploring, his face pale and bloodless in the moon glow. It looked like the face of a dead man.

"Kay knew something was coming. And he knew that only you could stop it." He struggled out of bed and leaned heavily against the bedpost. "But I would have to die."

Oh my God. Of course. All to stop the Tenth Plague.

"That's why I've trained you the way I have, Billi. I had

to. D'you think I'd wish this life on anyone, most of all you?"

Kay had tried to tell her. *You're wrong about your father.* He knew, he could see, Arthur did love her.

"But I couldn't let it show, how much it hurt being . . . cruel. I had to harden your heart. Toward me. Make you ruthless enough to do what was necessary."

It was sick.

"So I'd kill you when I had to." Billi closed her eyes; her head spun with all this. Her dad had brought her up to kill him. And the other Templars, even Percy, they must have known. She'd been lied to by everybody all her life. They'd ruined her life for a prophecy. A prophecy that was wrong. Ruined for nothing.

"Say something, Billi," said Arthur.

"Jesus. I never knew how completely insane you were until now." She backed toward the door. "You sick, sick bastard! You brought me up to be your killer?" Billi turned away in disgust. They'd all known and stood by and let it happen. All the other knights and Elaine. She wasn't even a Templar. She was merely their weapon.

Kay opened the door. His hair was tangled and half covering his face, and he looked worse than her dad. He tried to say something, but instead just stared at the pair of them with bewildered fear. Billi turned on him.

"And Kay? Did Kay know?"

Arthur shook his head. "No. Those visions were driving him beyond madness. Elaine worked endlessly to draw him back, to rebuild his sanity. He kept his sanity, but the power of prophecy was lost."

Billi covered her face, not able to cry, not able to scream—trapped between hate and pity. Arthur went to wrap his arms around her.

"Don't you touch me," Billi snarled.

He lowered his hands and backed away.

Lies, lies, lies.

The Knights Templar.

Bastards.

They migrated into the living room. Elaine had pulled back the curtains to let in the gray predawn light. Arthur shuffled in behind her, and Kay just stared.

She should be exhausted, but the trembling energies from the Silver Sword still surged through her, settling deep in the marrow of her bones.

"Tell me, Billi, from the beginning," said Arthur.

She stared at them. There was a subtle change in Arthur's face. The burden of his secret gone, Billi could see a lightness there. Still, her fury bubbled.

She thought of all the years he'd been cold to her, forgetting her birthdays, ignoring her when she came home crying because the other kids had teased her or she'd gotten into some stupid fight. The way he'd dismissed her achievements. Nothing had mattered except this: bringing Billi up to be his killer. She could barely look at him.

Kay, still weak from the ritual, leaned against the wall, away from her. He was afraid.

"Satan," he said. "You met Satan."

Arthur stiffened. He'd pulled the knife out of the headboard and put it on the table. "Where?"

"He'd been waiting for me at Temple Church."

"But why didn't he just come through when I was performing the ritual?" Kay asked. Billi wasn't sure if he was pleased or disappointed.

"He said that he didn't try to come through; it was others like him. Ethereals are weak when they first enter the Material Realm." Billi checked the window; the Devil was long gone. "He offered me the Silver Sword, but only if I killed you."

"And fulfilled Kay's prophecy," added Elaine.

Kay suddenly stiffened. "I've never made any prophecies. You know I can't." He glanced back at Elaine, then Billi, confused. "You know I can't." But he sounded unsure.

Elaine shook her head. "Not now, Kay. But when you first came to us . . . Should have bet on the horses back then." She laughed, but it withered as a poor joke. The sense of fear was thick in the room. "I'll explain it all to you later," she said, looking over at Kay, her head lowered.

"I never wanted this for you, Billi," said Arthur. He sounded sincere, but so what? This was the life he'd given her.

Kay touched her hand. She looked up at him, and there

was such softness in his eyes, their pale blue light reflecting such gentleness, that if Billi had been anyone's child except Arthur's, she would have wept. Kay's fingers wrapped around hers, and Billi felt how smooth they were against her own, hard and callused by years of weapons training. Poor Kay, they'd lied to him too.

Elaine cleared her throat. "What do we do next, Art?"

He smiled, but it was sad. He was beaten. He looked up at Elaine and Kay.

"You run."

They were leaving. Elaine and Kay would take the Cursed Mirror to Jerusalem. Among the Sufis and rabbis and priests, they hoped there might be someone who could bind Michael. Meanwhile, Arthur would organize a feint, an attack that would distract Michael, in the hope of preventing him from discovering that the mirror was long gone. Billi would go into hiding. With the prophecy having proved to be a failure, Arthur wanted Billi far away from the oncoming battle.

Billi helped Kay pack. Elaine had grabbed two garbage bags full of used clothing from the pile of junk she always had in the garage, and dumped it on the bedroom floor. Billi picked up a brown polyester shirt with orange stripes and held it up against the light. Had Elaine picked these vile things on purpose?

It looks absolutely—

"Don't swear," Kay said.

"I didn't say anything."

"But you thought it really hard."

Billi found a packet of thermals and swiftly stuffed them in the suitcase.

"You're leaving again," she said as she folded another shirt, then scrunched it up and tossed it on the floor. She couldn't let it end like this. She wouldn't.

"We could go together." And she *would* go with Kay. No matter what her dad said. If Kay wanted. She looked at him, hoping. But he shook his head.

"No. It's safer this way." He didn't look at her, just kept his attention on the clothes. "I *did* miss you, you know."

Billi nodded.

"You're the only friend I've ever had, Billi." He paused. "Maybe more than friends?"

Billi thought about how she'd felt when she'd kissed him at Trafalgar Square.

She smiled. "I was hysterical then; it doesn't count."

Kay put the last of the sweaters in the suitcase, then closed it. Billi could hear Elaine and Arthur getting supper ready. There were plates rattling and cutlery clanging. A kettle whistled.

"You can do it, Kay." Billi held his hand. "You'll catch Michael, I know you will." She squeezed it. "Catch him and come home."

Kay frowned. "Then what?"

Billi remained silent. Even when he did return, how could they be together? She wasn't a Templar; he was. The Order meant everything to him.

"It doesn't, Billi. Not as much as other things."

Billi raised her eyebrows at Kay. Would he quit the Order for her? It wasn't fair to ask him.

"Then maybe we'll be like normal people?" said Kay.

They both knew that was never really going to happen.

Elaine banged on the door. "Dinner's ready."

They gathered at the table as the food was served. Arthur said grace, then Elaine began ladling out the vegetable hot pot. Elaine and Arthur worked together seamlessly, him passing around food as Elaine filled the bowls.

"Y'know what this reminds me of?" Elaine looked about the table. "Passover."

Billi remembered that the Passover meal was held to commemorate the night the Angel of Death delivered the Tenth Plague upon Egypt's firstborn. Billi glanced over at Kay. See? She did pay some attention in her Templar lessons. Kay smiled. He didn't look great: the effects of the ritual had left him badly depleted.

"I don't think smearing lamb's blood over doorposts will stop Michael this time," Arthur retorted dryly.

"I know that," snapped Elaine. "It's what the blood symbolizes that's important: the blood of sacrifice. The most powerful magic there is. Just killing a lamb wouldn't mean anything now. The sacrifice"—she glanced at Billi—"needs to mean something." She took a tray of spinach and passed it around the table. "I used to love making food for the seder. The horseradish, all the chopped nuts and apples floating in the wine." She laughed suddenly. "Do you know what we used to do? Do you know about Elijah's Cup?"

Billi nodded. "You fill an extra cup in case Elijah comes to your door."

Elaine clapped her hands. "Exactly! When I was a child we would pour the cup, then wait. While we waited for the prophet, everyone would be watching the front door. It's an old trick, but the best. When no one was looking, my dad would knock on the table! You should have seen the way we'd jump!" She laughed and raised her fist above the table—

Bang.

Bang.

Bang.

Someone was knocking at the door. Hard, firm, and steady. Kay's eyes were fixed in the direction of the noise, his face ashen. Billi got up and looked at her dad. He half rose, but she shook her head; she'd check. He hesitated, then nodded. But not before sliding a knife across the table. She took it and tucked it into the back of her belt. Then in the silence, Billi left the room and entered the stair landing. A hot film of sweat ran down her back, clinging to her shirt.

Driven by an irresistible fear, she descended, turned

the doorknob, and slowly pulled it back.

Michael was waiting in the doorway. No threats, no sudden movements. He didn't need them. With shocking clarity, Billi knew she had lost. Truly, utterly, and completely lost.

29

He smiled at her and placed one foot on the threshold. "May I come in?"

It took a few seconds to force her mouth open, and a huge effort to speak.

"No." It was all she could manage.

Her eyes focused on the mezuzah in the doorway.

Could it stop him? Elaine's dwelling was guarded by dozens of wards; the mezuzah was one of the most powerful. Maybe—

Michael smashed the box with his fist. He pulled out the delicate scroll and held it between forefinger and thumb. The paper spontaneously combusted. It was ash within seconds.

Like all Billi's hopes.

"You couldn't stop me at the reliquary, what makes you think this"—Michael shook the ashes away—"would stop me now?" He stepped into the corridor.

She backed away slowly. A trickle of icy sweat rolled down her back; every inch of her skin shivered with Michael's oncoming steps.

"Who is it?" Elaine shouted from upstairs.

Run. She had to run. They all had to run. Run! She couldn't get the shout out. Her throat was dry, tight.

She backed up the stairs toward the open door. She didn't dare take her eyes off him as he came after her, matching her step for step. But when she walked through the apartment door, she shot a look over her shoulder; her terror-filled eyes all the warning necessary. She turned and ran, stopping between her dad and Kay.

Michael paused by the entrance. He surveyed the room.

"Hugues de Payens would surely be disappointed to see the Knights Templar sunk so low."

"Sometimes we enter the filth to find our enemies," said Arthur. He held a carving knife. Billi didn't think it would do much good. Kay stared at Michael, his face pasty. He was leaning heavily on the table and looked ready to collapse. Elaine had her hand on the biscuit tin. Michael moved into the center of the room, savoring his victory. Billi had no doubt he'd kill all four of them with little effort.

"It's best this way, firstborn. Give me the mirror and I'll finish you fast and painlessly." His eyes didn't leave the tin. "The plague's not pleasant. Not pleasant at all." His eyes shone with anticipation. "At dawn, with the crowing of the cock, all those infected by it will die, and I will watch London be reborn. From up on high."

"You can take your offer and shove it where the sun don't shine," Arthur snapped. He slipped his hand into Billi's. Michael saw it and laughed.

"How sweet, Arthur. I didn't think you were that sort of man."

He wasn't. Billi felt him squeeze with his first two fingers. Once, twice, three times. A charge. She would break left and distract Michael while Arthur charged him. With a carving knife. Suicide didn't even begin to describe it.

"No," she said. Her dad tensed but didn't move. Billi stepped forward. "Look, Michael. You know it's wrong. You can't bring people back to God like this. This isn't what it's about."

He laughed. "Ah, is this an appeal to my better side? To my humanity?" He pushed himself off the wall; heat and light radiated from his body, waves of hot air trembling between them. "You forget, mortal, I have no humanity."

Kay lowered his head, groaning. The plates and cups on the table shook and jumped about, spilling tea over the yellowing tablecloth. Billi, still holding her dad's hand, stepped away, drawing her own weapon. Then Kay screamed.

The dining table catapulted across the room, smashing Michael against the wall. Plaster tumbled from the ceiling as the wood exploded, sending jagged splinters across the room. Billi caught a few on her face before diving behind the sofa. A moment later, that too flew into the air and crashed into Michael.

"Run!" shouted Kay. He stood in the center of the room as chairs, plates, knives, spoons, and practically everything that wasn't nailed down flew around him like leaves in a hurricane. Billi's knife was wrenched from her hand, and even the floorboards creaked and groaned, their nails rattling as they dragged themselves out of the floor, summoned by Kay's will.

Michael rose, brushing off the dust, then turned to face Kay. Heat erupted around him, and Billi gasped as though she'd been pushed against an open furnace. Flames flickered along the wallpaper and the edges of the flapping curtains.

Kay glanced at the kitchenette. The drawers flew out, and a shower of steel knives, forks, and skewers burst across the room into Michael. He stumbled as the blades tore into his body, sprinkling the walls with his blood. But he did not fall.

Billi wanted to help, but Arthur grabbed her arm and fled, ripping her off her feet and through the door. Elaine was a second behind her, biscuit tin clutched to her chest. Their ears popped with an implosion of fire and wind. The floor rippled and the walls slid half a foot sideways. The entire building shook violently.

Billi covered her head as more chunks of plaster tumbled down. The stairs lurched and cracked. The door at the bottom was in front of them, but the building seemed to be sucking them in. The ground tilted, and she fell forward, her dad saving her from tumbling headlong down the flight of stairs by grabbing the back of her shirt. Broken chips of brickwork spat on her face, stinging her cheeks. She didn't know which way was up. Elaine rolled into her, and they knocked heads. A deafening wind howled down the staircase, loud as if they were downstream of a jet engine.

Get up!

She threw herself at the door, which was already half out of its frame. It crashed open with a jolt. Half crawling, Arthur and Billi lifted Elaine from under her armpits, and together they fled out onto the street.

Elaine's apartment was a blinding white inferno. The roof was a frame of black skeletal ribs, and half the walls had fallen.

"Kay!" Billi shouted. She'd thought he'd be right behind them, but she couldn't see him. He was still in the apartment! She turned, but her dad grabbed her, his fingers digging deeply into her biceps.

"It's too late, Billi! It's too late!" His face was deathly white—frantic—as he pleaded.

"No!" She fought him, screaming and swinging her fists. She had to save Kay. Arthur ignored the blows and wrapped his arms around her.

"It's too late."

He pulled her away from the blazing building. Half a dozen people dressed in pajamas, dressing gowns, or hastily tossed-on coats stood on the road staring at the flaming building. Some took photos.

The final explosion threw them all off their feet. The ground rippled, breaking the black tarmac into thousands of chunks. The air filled with a blaze of white fire, and Billi couldn't get up. All she could do was try to gaze into the awesome light.

Michael walked down the street, stepping over the people writhing in pain. His clothes smoldered, and ribbons of smoke twisted off him. He was caked with blood, and there were still knives jutting from his body, like some hideous statue of Saint Sebastian.

The biscuit tin lay a few feet away, where it had rolled out of Elaine's grasp. Billi tried to stand, but the air seemed oppressive and dense, like some invisible weight was holding her down. She couldn't move. She couldn't stop him.

Michael picked up the tin and tore off the lid. Light from within bathed his face

"At last." He ripped off the bubble wrap and lifted the Cursed Mirror above him. "At last!" Golden light poured out, brighter than the sun and cloaking the archangel in a nimbus. First, they whispered. Then they sang. Then the watchers trapped beyond screamed as they poured their energies into the Material Realm. The heat doubled, then trebled, multiplying second by second as the portal to Limbo opened. Billi covered her ears before her eardrums burst from the devastating noise of countless choirs. The light was unbearable, and she buried her head under her arms. The tarmac beneath her began to melt and steam.

A thunderclap ended it. The heat was so intense that the air just exploded. The final shock wave passed, and Billi realized she wasn't dead. The sky rumbled and the first spitting drops of rain landed on her face. She raised her head cautiously.

Michael stood in a blackened crater of molten tarmac with the other watchers gathered around him.

They appeared as hazy shadows trembling against the fiery light, slowly taking form and substance. Each one screamed as it tore its way through the final barrier between realms and returned, at last, to this one. Billi watched them stumble, naked and exhausted, and collapse on the ground, black vapors rising off their still-forming bodies. Dozens and dozens took the same journey, and soon the street was littered with white, tattooed bodies. Michael walked to one and helped lift it up. They stared at each other, their golden eyes filled with ethereal power. Michael embraced him.

"Araqiel," he said.

The others stood. The shadows rippled and wrapped their bodies like dark cloth. Against this their white faces shone with angelic light. Dark angels, indeed. Michael moved among them, welcoming them back.

The Cursed Mirror. Michael dropped it now that he no longer needed it. Billi crawled toward it, hoping that having it might give them a chance. She stretched out her hand.

Michael saw Billi and picked it up again cupping the disk in his hands. It melted like butter through his fingers, and long strands of glowing molten copper dripped onto the street, hissing and solidifying into a formless blob.

He then bent down and gently lifted Billi's face. Those eyes that she'd once thought so beautiful and brilliant were now the eyes of a pitiless hunter. They reflected no warmth, no compassion. He lowered his face and kissed her. Billi flinched, but his fingers clenched her jaw, holding her fast. It felt like she was pressed against a boiling kettle. She wanted to scream, but his lips held hers shut. Then Michael dropped her.

The other watchers gathered around him.

"Come, we have God's work to do," he said. They turned away and vanished into the darkness.

Billi got up, took a few steps, then collapsed as her head spun and the ground swayed. She turned toward the sky, desperate for some cool rain on her face, but she was burning. She felt as though the raindrops were boiling off her skin the moment they landed. The air turned thicker, making it hard to breathe. The noise became a high-pitched endless buzzing, and the ground gave way. Hands grabbed her as she fell, and her dad was shouting at her, his eyes wide with terror, but she couldn't hear what he said. Steel nails raked her belly, and she doubled over, bile gorging her throat and spilling out of her mouth. Elaine rushed to help, and her hands passed over Billi's eyes, just briefly.

She saw the cloud of black crystalline necro-flies descending on her. She screamed as they infested her face, crawling over her mouth and her eyes, their drone echoing deep in her skull. She thrashed wildly, trying to fight them off, but they swarmed thicker and thicker around her until she was covered in them, and her eyes filled with darkness.

The plague was unleashed.

30

I'M DEAD.

Kay's dead.

We're all dead.

She floated in the air, warm and weightless. She felt safe and secure, something she hadn't experienced in years.

If this was death, it wasn't so bad.

But as Billi's senses returned, so did the pain. Each breath was like dragging broken glass down her throat, and white-hot needles dug into every joint.

Wasn't all that meant to end when you died?

"Billi?"

Her dad was close, looking down at her. He was carrying her in his arms. He hadn't done that since . . . when? Ages and ages. He wiped her face with his sleeve.

"Don't cry. We're almost home."

Home? Where was that?

She looked up into the dark sky, and floating above him were two knights riding a single horse. The Knights Templar.

My God, the Templars have a heaven all to themselves.

Just great.

She'd thought once she was dead she'd have a break from all that. But as her eyes focused, the two knights became a small black iron statue atop a plain, white, stone column.

Home. What other home did they have?

Temple Church.

Elaine threw her coat on the pedestal at the foot of the Templar column, and Arthur laid Billi on it. Drizzle tickled her face, its coolness dampening the red fever boiling her skin.

From here crusades had been declared. From here the greatest military order of medieval times had made holy war. Nobles, princes, and even kings had come here on bended knee and trembled under the gauntlets of the Knights Templar.

Now it was a fire-blackened shell. The windows were shattered and the doors were boarded up with plywood. The rain smeared great streaks of soot down its white walls. Distant flashes of lightning lit the thick black clouds that loomed over London. The air trembled with thunder.

But there was another sound, almost drowned under

the violent sky. Billi lifted herself onto her side, straining to distinguish the noises.

Church bells. The city echoed with them. The noise rose as more and more bells joined the summoning. The black clouds seemed to shake with anger and thundered back. For a brief moment, Billi hoped. She hoped that something would happen . . . anything.

The bells were summoning the faithful. The fearful.

The rain beat down hard, and wind screamed across the courtyard. Billi could no longer hear the bells. She sank back onto the hard cold stone. What good would it do them? Michael had won. And tomorrow all the firstborn would be dead.

Kay was dead. She'd be dead.

Arthur sat down beside her and stroked her hair. He leaned against the column and smiled weakly. There was a gentleness there that she hadn't seen in years. He looked so different.

"Art," said Elaine, pointing into the darkness ahead.

They came. Black silhouettes moving cautiously through the wall of rain. Arthur stood up and pulled out the carving knife.

The watchers. They'd come to finish the job. A half dozen or so, but that would be more than enough. They each moved with a warrior's confidence—not rushing, but approaching with a deadly sureness.

Arthur stepped forward.

"Close your eyes, Billi," said Elaine. She bunched up her bony fists, determined to fight till the last. Billi wanted to laugh; she wanted to cry. Elaine hadn't been a Templar in life, but she was going to die one.

No. Billi would not go with eyes closed and on her back. She forced herself up. Her muscles spasmed, but she forced them under her control, gritting her teeth. If this was the end, she'd fight. The black shapes came closer.

"Art?"

She peered into the darkness. Hold on. . . .

"Gwaine?" said Arthur, his voice tinged with hope. He took a cautious step toward the nearest figure.

He walked out into the weak pool of streetlight. Gwaine's face had aged—his cheeks were sunken and more deeply grooved then before. But his eyes shone wetly. He stopped an arm's length from her dad. Billi watched as the others appeared. The air about them went still, and she held her breath.

"Arthur." Gwaine's lips locked into a grim line as he took Arthur's right hand in his and went to his knee. "My Master."

They'd come. They'd all come. Bors, Gareth, old Father Balin, and the others. Pelleas hugged Billi, squeezing her until she couldn't breathe. Even Elaine got kisses from Bors, and Billi watched, laughing in relief.

They'd come. They were few, but to Billi, she realized at last, they were everything.

It was inevitable. She'd tried and fought against it. She'd quit and almost abandoned them, but this was her life, her destiny. Kay was gone and this was all the family she had now.

31

"BUT I'M COMING WITH YOU," SAID BILLI. SHE SAT ON a stool with a brown woolen shawl over her shoulders, feeling a hundred years old. The pain had turned down from unbearable agony to merely unbearable. Maybe here, deep in the temple catacombs, the bones of the ancient Templars were better wards than all the magic Elaine could manage.

"No, you're not," answered Arthur. He raised his arms up as Elaine checked his bandages. He looked ghost-pale and gaunt, but he was Master and would lead the Templars. He beckoned to Pelleas, who had a chain-mail hauberk slung over his shoulder. Arthur wrapped a padded silk tunic around his chest, knotting short red bows under his left side.

"Gwaine will take Bors and lead the feint. I'll take the others and spearhead." Pelleas lifted the hauberk over his head like a sweater. Leather cords ran down from the nape to the mid shoulder blades. Pelleas knotted them while Arthur loosened the neck opening.

Gwaine. She couldn't believe it.

"You'll give that job to Gwaine?" she asked.

"He's seneschal. Why shouldn't I?"

Billi leaned closer and whispered, "Dad, after what he did? He betrayed you."

Arthur's eyes met Pelleas's as he bound his master's waist with a broad leather sword belt. "The seneschal has my full trust." But the words didn't reflect the icy stare Arthur shot at Gwaine, who sat across the armory, fixing the bindings to his battle-ax. It wasn't over between him and Gwaine, but it could wait.

Arthur rolled his shoulders and settled into his armor. "How do I look?"

The thousands of polished mail links glittered in the low light. The shirt was short, ending just below the hips, infantry style. The cuffs and neck opening were lined with leather, and Arthur wore it with a pair of black combat trousers and shin-high hiking boots. He selected a heavy sword with a plain cross guard and a walnut-shaped pommel. The meaty blade wasn't long, and it looked more like a machete than the elegant blade of a knight, but Billi knew it wouldn't blunt easily, could deliver awful wounds, and was her dad through and through. Sharp and brutal. He slipped it into a scabbard on his left hip. On the right were a pair of narrow-bladed fifteenth-century Milanese stiletto knives.

"Dressed to kill," Billi croaked.

Still sitting on her stool, she glanced around the armory. Elaine wandered around the dimly lit catacomb, mouth open. She stared at the collection of bones in the alcoves, the weapons and armor. She tested the weight of a sword, and her face swelled red with the effort.

All the Templars could fight with any style of weapon, but each had a favorite. Gwaine used an ax: a modified fireman's tool, steel-hafted, and just as useful for smashing as chopping. Gareth strummed the tight bowstring of his composite bow like a lyre, then ran his palm softly over the black eagle fletching of his arrows. Bors had a pair of short swords strapped across his back. Father Balin sat under a table lamp, carefully using a toothbrush to scrub any dust or grit from the flanges of his mace. Finally Pelleas, the classic duelist, had a rapier and main-gauche. He stood in the center of the armory floor, eyes closed, slowly reaching down to his toes, stretching his back. Thin black leather gloves were tucked into his belt.

The Templars were ready for battle.

"What about me?" Billi thought out loud. She hadn't meant for anyone to hear it, but Arthur did. He put his weapon down and walked over. He sighed and crouched beside her. "Listen, Billi. You're to stay here with Elaine."

"You're taking Father Balin and not me? He can barely lift that mace."

Arthur looked over at the old priest. Billi knew she was

right; he was knocking on seventy, and he hadn't been much of a warrior to begin with. She could see that her dad didn't like it either.

"Balin's made his choice."

"But how are you going to beat the watchers?"

"They've just arrived, so won't be at full strength. We'll strike hard and fast. Maximum damage in minimum time."

"What about Michael?"

Arthur's hand tightened around his sword hilt. "I've beaten him once already."

"But Dad, that was then. Now he's got all the other watchers—all his power. He can't be beaten. What you're planning is suicide."

Arthur turned to her and hissed through gritted teeth. "So we don't even try?" He leaned on the table, his head bowed. "What else can we do but fight?"

"Even when it's hopeless?"

"Especially when it's hopeless."

"Why, Dad?"

He smiled. The sudden warmth took Billi by surprise. *"Deus vult."* He took hold of her hand. His palm was coarse and hard from years of handling heavy weapons; thick calluses lined his thumb and fingers. Billi had a few like that too. "Billi, I've ruined enough of both our lives believing in Kay's prediction. All those years I couldn't tell you how I felt, just to make you strong. You can't imagine the fear I've lived with." He kissed her forehead. His lips rested against it, and Billi felt tears slowly trickle down from his cheeks onto hers. "You're everything to me, Billi. I can't live without you."

He stood back and looked at her. Not like a master would his knight, but as a father would his daughter. Arthur's eyes gleamed.

"Billi, I'm so proud of you. I always have been."

Gwaine stood discreetly nearby, Arthur's leather jacket over his arm. "We're ready, Art."

Arthur wiped his eyes. He took the jacket from Gwaine and pulled it on. Billi stood up as the other knights gathered by the door.

"Where to, sir?" asked Bors.

Arthur looked at Billi, his eyebrows raised.

Where else would he be? Michael had as good as told her.

I will watch London reborn. From up on high.

"Elysium Heights."

Elaine brought Billi a bowl of soup. Steam rose from the tin pot, and she sprinkled coriander over it before handing it to her.

"I'm sorry about Kay," she said, taking the seat beside Billi. She put her bony fingers on Billi's hand. Elaine had loved Kay too.

Billi closed her eyes. The hot soup was making them water, and she didn't want Elaine to think she was crying.

Kay.

He'd only just come back, and now he was gone. There was a black hole deep inside Billi, and she stood at the edge of it, scared to look down, lest the lonely darkness take her. That hole was made the moment Kay had left. She loved him. She'd spent a year alone, and now that would be forever. She looked up at Elaine, who just nodded.

"He was a valiant knight," she said.

They found some camp beds and old blankets and set them up in the corner of the armory.

Elaine shifted uneasily under her covers. "Don't like sleeping with the dead," she said, jutting her chin out at the pile of bones sitting nearby.

"I doubt even your snoring will wake them," Billi said.

She wrapped the blankets around her and closed her eyes. It didn't take long for Elaine's snorting snore to fill the darkness. It rebounded off the walls until it seemed to be coming from all directions. Despite her exhaustion, Billi couldn't sleep. Sharp knives prodded between her bones, and one moment her body shivered, the next it was dripping with sweat. No matter how much she drank from the water bottle next to her, she was constantly thirsty. And the buzzing . . .

The noise of the flies echoed in the dark chamber. She couldn't see them anymore, but she cringed at the idea that they were crawling over her. She lifted her blanket over herself, pulling it tight. Maybe the flies couldn't get her down here. She turned this way and that, eventually sinking into sleep.

Kay.

Images rolled in her dreams: the flames bursting from the apartment, Michael crushed under the sofa, and Kay. The way he smiled at the world.

Kay.

She missed him. Missed him more than she'd thought she would. That hole grew inside her.

I'm here, Billi.

They'd kissed. She'd never kissed anyone before.

Come outside; I'm waiting.

Her fingers tingled as she remembered running them through his hair, silver in the moonlight.

Please, Billi. I'm waiting.

Billi blinked open her eyes. It had sounded like he was right beside her, whispering to her. Just a dream. She rolled over.

Not a dream, Billi.

"Kay?" she whispered, not believing it could be him.

Yes, Billi. It's me. Come outside.

It sounded like Kay. She shook her head. Delirious. That's what it was; she was delirious. The Tenth Plague was affecting her mind.

How stupid are you? Just look outside!

Now that sounded like Kay.

Billi stumbled barefoot up the stairs and paused. Beyond the boundary of the armory, what little protection she had from the effects of the Plague would be gone. Even now she could feel the pain pulsing stronger and the red-hot claws scraping at her insides. She glanced around the courtyard, afraid it was all a dream—that he was never coming back.

Then she saw him standing under the cloisters. He leaned against a column, arms crossed, without a care in the world. Ignoring the creeping illness that was polluting her veins, Billi stepped out into the rain. It flew down in dense sheets, and the cold winds stunned her face, but she didn't care. She shuffled forward, though it felt like she was walking on broken glass. Even in the weak lamplight his skin shone brilliant white, his hair like spun platinum. The blueness of his eyes made her heart leap.

Kay.

32

BILLI DRAGGED HERSELF UNDER THE COVER OF THE cloisters and rested against a column. She wiped away burning tears and stared at Kay, afraid to come too close in case this was a dream and he disappeared.

"How?" She moved forward, but Kay took a short step away.

"I was . . . saved." Kay frowned, and dark lines broke the whiteness of his brow. He shook his head.

The fire. The building had collapsed.

"The fire brigade saved you?" She reached out her hand. Her fingers shook, but she wanted to touch him to see if he was real.

"No, not them." He came forward suddenly and held Billi's arms and looked at her. "I came back for you, Billi. I couldn't leave you."

He was real.

Billi buried herself against him, relishing his embrace. She wouldn't let him go—not this time.

"I thought I'd lost you, Kay." She was cold and shivering, and Kay squeezed her, his warmth surrounding her. "Where have you been?" But she didn't care; he was here now.

"I did it for you," he whispered desperately. Billi felt him sob. She pulled back and looked up at him.

"It's okay, Kay. You're okay. It'll be all right now." But the fear in his eyes made her hesitate. He broke away from her and passed his hand over his face.

"I did it for you," he repeated. What was he going on about? He looked over to the corner, and Billi followed his gaze.

It lay against the wall, bright, deadly, and silver. Her blood turned to ice.

The Silver Sword.

Billi walked over to it. Even without touching it she could feel its power. Slowly her fingertips touched the hilt, and her hand gripped the weapon.

The spike of energy was stronger than before, a mainline of ethereal power straight into her heart. Every atom of her burst with strength, and the Tenth Plague evaporated instantly, burned off her by the sheer brilliance of the shining sword. Satan had told the truth after all; the sword did make her invulnerable to Michael's powers.

She turned to Kay.

"How did you get this?" Fear inched its way through her, and she tightened her grip around the hilt.

"How d'you think?" Kay reached out, pleading. "I did it for you, Billi."

"How, Kay?"

"It's me, Billi." Kay was a few feet away, but Billi could see the caution in his movements. He didn't want to get too close. He was afraid.

Oh God. Billi felt her chest and pulled off her crucifix. She threw it on the flagstone ground between them.

"Pick it up, Kay. Please."

Kay bent down onto his knees, staring at the silver cross. Billi watched him, her heart tearing apart.

"Please pick it up." If he picked it up, everything would be okay. They'd be okay.

Kay reached out. As he got within a few inches, his fingers started shaking. They curled up, and he drew his hand to his chest, cradling it.

"What have you done, Kay?" But she knew. He'd given his soul to the Devil. For her.

"It's still me, Billi." He stood up, and a change came over him. The light was gone. Billi could see nothing but a reflection behind his shining eyes, and that smile that had once seemed to be in love with the world was just a few stretched muscles. He kicked the crucifix away. "It's still me." He repeated it again as he strode forward, trying to persuade her it was true. Trying to persuade himself.

He grabbed her sword wrist, and the other arm went around her, holding her fast. His face hovered above hers, and Billi saw the terrible struggle in the emptiness of his eyes. His hunger was already rising, and a feral growl came from deep inside him. His body stiffened, but his lips peeled apart, and his teeth, already subtly sharpened into a row of razor-sharp points, glistened.

"It's. Still. Me." His smile was tight, and his body shook with the lie.

"I did it for you, Billi." Then he sank his teeth into her neck and showed her what happened.

TERROR

when the ground collapses and Kay tumbles down two floors, blinded by the dust and flames. He summons his will, and floorboards tear away, hurled up at Michael like giant flaming spears. Michael rips down a wall, and Kay dives between two half-collapsed beams. He covers his face, and the smoke smothers him, and he curls up, deafened by the roaring inferno around him.

PAIN

as the hairs on his neck crinkle, and blisters swell and bubble on his skin, and he knows he's going to burn to death. He coughs as the smoke tries to crawl down his throat, and he is afraid. His shirt catches fire, and the agony blanks out his mind as the building falls down, and he's held fast, unable to move, with the fire eating his arm.

AWE

at Satan's appearance. He's squatting on the burning support beam, oblivious to the fire around him. His eyes are empty sockets, and Kay knows the Devil has come to witness his death. He must be brave and die a martyr. But he smells his arm burning, and with it the sickening odor of fat and roasting pork.

ANGER

when the Devil says he admires his courage. Kay is a true Templar and will be remembered as a martyr. Satan has no wish to deny Kay his glorious death.

FIRE

eats at Kay's limbs, and wave upon wave of agony crashes over him. He's breathing in shallow petrified gasps, but he grits his teeth. He must bear it for a little longer, and then it will end forever.

PEACE.

But what of Billi? asks the Devil. At least Kay chose *to martyr himself. Poor Billi will die, like the other firstborn, in sickness and agony till the last. The deaths will be countless, and there'll be no martyr's headstone for her. She will go into a mass grave, dumped into the cold soil with thousands of others, nameless and forgotten. A mere statistic. She will not die easily, but over the night; each moment will be a fresh eternity of pain as the Tenth Plague gradually consumes her.*

DOUBT

worms its way into his mind.

What of Billi, indeed? asks the Devil. He reaches out his hand. Take it, Kay. If not for you, then do it for Billi.

BILLI.

Kay takes it.

"No!" Billi screamed and tore free. She clutched her neck low on the shoulder, and her hand came away red and wet.

She stared at him. "Oh God, Kay. What have you done?"

"I did it for you, Billi!" Tears swelled, but they were thick scarlet. He saw the horror on her face and suddenly understood. "Jesus, Billi, I didn't mean it. I didn't mean it." He took a step forward. "I wouldn't hurt you. I'd never hurt you."

"Get away from me!" The Silver Sword was in her hand, the tip pointed directly at Kay's heart. "Why?"

He stepped back, the pain on his face turning into anger. "Oh, did you think he'd just give it to me? D'you think I'd have chosen this, if it hadn't been for you? I did it for you!" His eyes blazed like two gems caught in a furnace. He watched the deadly blade hovering between them. "Now you're going to kill me?"

She wanted to say no, but the word caught in her throat. A flicker of . . . what? Fear? Doubt? Sorrow? crossed his face.

"He saved me, Billi. Saved me. You left me there, dying in the flames. I saw you run—you, your dad, and Elaine. You left me." Kay spread out his arms. "But . . . I forgive you. I do. Look, Billi, it's me. It's Kay." But all Billi could see was the blood in his mouth and the wild hunger in his eyes.

No, this wasn't Kay.

Not anymore.

"Let me help you," she said, stepping closer. She had to do something, but didn't lower her weapon.

"How? Ease my suffering?" He thrust out an accusing finger at the Silver Sword. "With that? I've given you everything, Billi. Everything." He was backing away, fading as though the darkness were sucking him in. He halted, his body blending with the shadows. He stretched out his hand, reaching for her, but Billi didn't move. The hand recoiled, and Kay stared at her with his white face stretched into a bestial snarl. "You treacherous bitch."

Then he ran into the night. It was a long time before his screams faded.

33

FIVE IN THE MORNING AND THE STREETS WERE PACKED. Dawn was less than an hour away. Billi had the Silver Sword wrapped in a sheet, tied across her back in what the squires called "ninja style." She had truly lost Kay now. There was only one place to go . . . one thing to do. She gazed up into the sky and saw it above her, not far now.

Elysium Heights.

A woman sat on the edge of the curb, rocking back and forth, slapping her head. Her face was fixed in a silent scream, her eyes screwed tight but void of tears.

She looked mad with that dumb repetitive rhythm. It was only when Billi passed in front of her that she realized why.

Cradled in her lap, still dressed in a pair of Winnie the Pooh pajamas, lay a limp baby. Dead or alive, Billi didn't know. She pushed herself back into the crowds, away.

Billi walked through the people, the abandoned cars, the screaming children and hysterical parents. Headlights illuminated the bedlam as thousands took to the streets. Horns beeped endlessly, siren wails were ignored, and hundreds upon hundreds of despairing mothers and fathers cried, yelled, fought for some little help, some little hope.

The roads to St. Paul's Cathedral were gridlocked. Cars were abandoned in the middle of the road when they couldn't get any closer to the church, so people climbed over them, carrying semiconscious children in their arms. The entrance was under siege; hundreds of people crowded around and tried to clamber over hastily erected barricades while exhausted priests and policemen attempted to hold them back. Above them the skies echoed with church bells and thunder.

Billi stared around, bewildered.

Michael's masterpiece.

The gates into the Elysium Heights site lay crumpled in the mud. The Templars' van had been driven through them and left a dozen yards farther, engine still running and its front crashed into the side of a Dumpster.

The rain and wind attacked Billi with greater ferocity; now the elements seemed determined to keep her from entering. Even though the heavens roared with thunder, she could still hear the screaming cries and the clashing of steel.

She threw the sheet off the Silver Sword and entered.

Her heart pounded. The sprawling site, dominated by the immense black tower, was dark and full of cold, fathomless shadows, any one of which could have been hiding a murderous angel. Huge bulldozers, countless cabins, and storage containers seemed to have no logical order, creating a maze. The mud squelched and sucked at Billi's boots, forcing her to drag herself, foot by foot. She tightened her grip around the hilt as she turned a corner into a small opening.

Father Balin was propped against a wall. Rain dripped off his white hair, and his chin rested on his chest. His clothes were filthy with blood and mud. Billi knelt down beside him and touched the wide gash across his torso. The mace lay on his lap, and his crucifix hung from his right hand.

He hadn't been much of a fighter. She looked at the wrinkled face; his eyes were closed and a faint smile remained. It wasn't tears running down her cheeks; it was only rain. Only rain. She kissed his forehead and left.

The clouds above boiled and spat down lightning, momentarily shocking the sky white. Ahead Billi could just make out figures moving through the half-assembled tower, encircling a band of men.

This was it, then. For seven hundred years the Templars had kept the darkness at bay. They had fought, they had died, and it had come down to this: a fight to save London's firstborn from Michael, fallen archangel of the Lord.

This was their last stand. Their last hour.

And their finest.

Gareth, atop a truck, was calmly notching his bow. He launched arrow after arrow of black-fletched death, unerringly seeking out hearts and necks and eyes among the bright and shining and howling angels.

Bor, wild and savage, used his pair of short swords like a butcher's chopper, while Pelleas was fighting back tooth and nail, even though he was almost submerged beneath clawlike hands and white bodies.

Gwaine stood bloody, battered, and defiant to the last. His left arm hung uselessly, ripped open to the bone, but he fought on, waving his ax in wide circles over his head.

And Arthur.

They said Arthur brought nightmares to the monsters, and now Billi saw how.

He stood on top of a steel storage crate the size of a double garage. His heavy jacket was torn and the steel mail beneath tattered. Blood ran from a dozen cuts across his arms, chest, and legs, and his face was a mask of berserk fury, his lips torn into a snarl as he raised his sword and howled.

"C'mon!" he cried. About him lay the dead, and around him circled the living. Two watchers, each armed with machetes, leaped a dozen feet across the air. The first didn't even land; his torso was sliced by Arthur's sword in midair, so the neat halves of him tumbled to the blood-drenched mud beneath. The second faltered, stunned by Arthur's savagery, and that hesitation cost her everything. Arthur swept his weapon across her machete, knocking it away. The angel turned to flee, but Arthur grabbed her golden hair and snapped her back. She didn't even have time to scream as he drove his blade through her.

Still weak, having just entered the Material Realm after centuries of imprisonment, the watchers didn't yet have Michael's supernatural ability to survive the blow of a mortal weapon. The knights were causing a dreadful slaughter, but the watchers fought hard and had numbers on their side. They just needed to hold off the Templars for a bit longer. Dawn was coming, and then all the firstborn infected by the Plague would die.

Billi stood still. The noise, the terror, and the chaos of the battle was overwhelming. She didn't know what to do. Should she help her dad or protect Gareth? Or aid Bors? Each moment could be their last, could be *her* last, and panic and uncertainty gripped her.

Watchers scuttled like insects along the black steel beams and columns. There were dozens of them. Lightning erupted again, and silhouetted against the raging white was a lone figure poised on the highest point of the tower's frame.

Michael.

She knew. It was down to her. It always had been. She was a Templar, and that meant fighting evil till the bitter end, because someone had to. And if this was to be the Knights Templars' last hour, it would be hers too. She knew it and, finally, was not afraid.

You shall keep the company of martyrs.

Had this moment always been planned? This was where she would fight? Would die? Kay's prophecy? A freak meeting on the train? Destiny?

No, simpler than that.

Supernatural energies coursed through her from the weapon as it trapped the sparks of lightning and blazed. Billi raised the sword high and cried:

"Deus vult!"

She ran now, straight for the goods elevator. The other Templars saw her, and understood. They broke their way out of the attacking watchers to rally around her. The dark angels sensed it too. They screamed and howled, leaped from steel girder to girder, but she was there, the knights already forming a protective ring. She threw herself into the steel cage as Arthur reached her. Their eyes met, and he smiled. She stood up, steady despite the way the fragile steel cage shook in the tempest. Arthur didn't speak—there was nothing to say. He merely nodded. Then he stepped back and slammed the gate shut.

Billi twisted the red handle, and the elevator rattled and sprang upward. She gazed down into the swirling battlefield as the Templars formed a circle around the bottom of the scaffold. Around them, merging into the darkness, were dozens of Michael's followers. Billi stared down until they were lost in the rain.

34

THE ELEVATOR JOLTED AS IT STOPPED. THIS WAS THE end of the journey. Billi dragged her sleeve across her face, wiping away the blinding rain. She tightened her grip around the Silver Sword, feeling its energy pulse through her, then rolled open the door and stepped out.

"Billi, how appropriate," said Michael. He stood on the very top of a steel column barely wide enough for both feet. Despite the wind screaming around him, he did not falter, but waited, perfect and balanced. He wore only a pair of black jeans, his torso bare, glistening like silver. His elaborate tattoos writhed like serpents over his white skin, alive and eager. The two long scars on his back were bleeding heavily now.

"Come down," she said. Her eyes were set on his, but she did not tremble under their unearthly gaze.

A Templar does not tremble.

"And what?" He smiled contemptuously from his high perch.

"Engage in an orgy of violence." She stepped out into the center of the half-concreted floor. "It should be most cathartic." She held the sword in both hands, but low. "Or are you scared?"

Michael sighed deeply. "What do you see out there?" He held a sword in his own hands and pointed it westward.

Toward St. Paul's Cathedral.

Lights. She saw thousands of lights, even from so high up. The city that had twinkled the first time she had looked down from this very spot was now flooded in a flickering yellow haze of light.

"Beautiful, isn't it?" he said.

But Billi knew what those lights were, what they meant. Each one indicated a family with a dying child. Someone they loved was going to die at dawn.

"See, Billi? See how I've brought God back into their lives? They will never again stray from the path of righteousness."

"And what of the millions you'll kill?"

"They will pass into Heaven. They are my sacrifice."

"You are beyond insane. You haven't brought God into their lives; you've only brought fear."

Michael smiled to himself. "Fear is the beginning of faith." He gestured to the eastern sky. Despite the dark storm clouds, there was the faintest hint of color, just a thin dash of gray and purple. "Not long now."

Billi tapped her sword tip against the floor; she'd had enough. "Come down and die."

He spread his arms and dropped.

Gravity didn't take him; Michael was made of something other than crude flesh, bone, and gristle. He was a being of light, and glided onto the floor, his toes first brushing the surface before settling himself firmly down.

"Remember this?" he said, holding the Templar Sword aloft and slowly turning the polished blade. It had changed. Billi couldn't see the difference, but she felt it. Power radiated from it; it was no longer mortal-forged steel, but something more, imbued with angelic energies.

Billi raised her own weapon. "Remember this?" she asked.

Was it her imagination, or did Michael go pale?

"The Silver Sword. It's been a long time since I've seen that. How did you get it?"

"The enemy of my enemy is my friend," Billi replied.

Michael opened his mouth in a silent "Ahh" and nodded. "Satan. How ironic that you should make treaty with the Morning Star to destroy me."

She stepped over a crossbeam, wary of the gaps in the concrete floor, carefully shifting her weight from one foot to the other, eyes never leaving Michael's.

The swords touched, deadly edges stroking each other,

testing for that first opening. Billi's heart hammered with concentrated adrenaline, and tiny jewels of sweat rose on her forehead as she sized up her opponent.

Saint Michael.

The archangel of the Grigori.

The Angel of Death.

God's killer.

A cold tentacle crept up her spine. Those golden predatory eyes trapped her, and Billi felt—

Stop it.

She was freaking herself out. She couldn't let fear win this battle.

Fear makes the wolf seem larger.

Michael flicked her tip aside and swapped grips, then instinct took over. Billi didn't even see the attack, but turned her wrist and the steel screamed. Flying sparks leaped from the killing edges as they both fought to drive their tip into each other's flesh. Michael's hot breath washed her face as they butted together, then sprung apart.

His offensive was unrelenting. The sword caught her arm, but she barely felt its sting. She backed away, deflecting attacks that came on like an avalanche. Michael's blows smashed against the Silver Sword, and her arms ached from each assault.

Their hilts locked. She tugged hard, hoping to rip the weapon from Michael's grip.

Michael grinned. "Is that the best—"

Billi screamed and head-butted him. Michael's legs wobbled just for a second, but it was enough.

As he fell, Billi grabbed his sword wrist and drove her knee into it. There was a jolt—it was like kicking a tree—but his fingers loosened. She twisted her sword hilt, and the Templar Sword slipped free and spun away.

Michael roared, ignoring the Silver Sword as it ripped across his ribs, and grabbed Billi's head. Iron-stiff fingers covered her face. Muscle, bone, flesh, all flexed under the viselike pressure. White-hot pain swelled in her skull, and her eyes bulged. But she wouldn't quit. She hissed, consumed with battle madness.

The Silver Sword touched his stomach, and she pushed deeper and deeper. Even as her jaw cracked and nerves screamed, she pushed.

Michael let go. He stumbled back, clutching his side. Billi gasped, suddenly free of the crushing fingers, and the ground rocked unsteadily as she tried not to faint.

Michael's hands were sticky with his blood, but the stomach wound wasn't fatal. His eyes searched for a weapon. He moved toward the discarded Templar Sword like lightning.

But Billi was faster and slammed the pommel into his face. Michael crashed backward into the fallen debris, splashing into a puddle. She stumbled forward, holding the quivering sword tip directly at Michael.

He looked up at her, face frozen into a twisted grimace.

The Silver Sword touched his chin and bobbed above his throat. He snarled.

"So here you are. And now you intend to kill me?"

"As you killed the Egyptians." She raised her sword, steeling herself for the killing blow.

Michael smiled. "Not quite." He raised his hand. "Help me, my friend."

The darkness beyond the strange forest of girders quivered like a heat wave off tarmac. Billi thought she heard something, but under her own heaving breath she couldn't tell from which direction. Then she heard it again and realized it was in her head.

Billi.

She turned abruptly and saw Kay standing there, partially hidden behind a column.

35

KAY SMILED. BILLI'S HEART CLENCHED AS HE STEPPED closer. *He's changed so much already.*

His skin shone like pearl under the ghostly light, smooth, translucent, flawless. His eyes burned bright and sharp with desire, with hunger.

With hate.

"I'm happy you're here, Billi. We can spend your last few moments together," he said.

"Kay—"

He roared and charged. Billi dodged sideways but caught her foot on uneven concrete and crashed down hard. She raised the sword, but Kay slammed his boot into her wrist, making the nerves scream, then go numb. Tears swelled, and through the blur she saw the Silver Sword hurtle away.

Too fast; how did—

His foot hit her chest like an iron sledgehammer. She gasped, breathing in jagged ice and fire; her ribs had cracked.

"Kay, please," she murmured. Her head was tumbling, her legs loose like wet rope.

He's too strong.

I can't stop him.

"Kay, don't." Billi lay at the edge, half-falling, the wind pulling hungrily at her. She turned over slowly, every bone shouting in pain, and was crawling away on her hands and knees when Kay blocked her path. He squatted down and turned her face to his.

"What, don't you like it? Why not? All this is thanks to you." He lifted her up, one-handed. "Because of you."

He gave an insane laugh, then lowered his head against hers and whispered, "I can't bear it." He raised his head and grinned maniacally. "Help me. I want to kill you so much." He punched her in the face.

Billi blacked out for a minute.

She could taste the metallic-edged blood—her blood swilling in her mouth. She opened her eyes, but her vision reeled and the sky above spun around and around. She couldn't get up. "Kay, I'm so sorry." She slid out her hands, hoping to find something to help her up. Her right palm touched steel—cold, hard, familiar.

The Silver Sword.

Slowly, they both looked at it. A stream of power dribbled through her palm into her arm. Her grip firmed.

Then relaxed.

"I can't," she said.

Not Kay.

"Take it, Billi." He stared at her, eyes blazing with madness. His fingers were hooked like talons, and he snarled, "I can't stop myself." He grabbed her, and Billi witnessed the struggle within him. "You have to do it," he whispered. "Stop me."

Kay had been true to her—to them both. He'd given his soul, damned himself to save her—to save them all. In that moment she looked at him and understood what the prophecy meant.

She will sacrifice the one she loves to save the children.

It wasn't about her dad.

It was Kay.

Billi's hand tightened around the sword hilt.

"Forgive me, Kay."

The groan escaping his lips rose like a banshee wail. The sky turned white with lightning, and she saw Kay as close and clearly as she'd ever seen anyone.

The soft gentle contours of his jaw, the downy white hairs on his chin, his lips. She could still feel his touch on hers.

Billi closed her eyes; there was warmth from the blade, the pain receded, and dawn was coming.

"Finish it!" screamed Michael to Kay from the far side of the floor.

Kay dropped to his knees. He cradled Billi and wrapped his hand around hers—and the sword hilt.

Billi settled in his lap and looked into his eyes. She had to be as brave as Kay if the firstborn were to be saved. If Michael were to be stopped. A sacrifice was needed.

They looked at each other, and he touched her lips with his.

"Do it, Billi," he whispered.

Billi's hand trembled, but Kay helped her to hold the sword steady. He pulled her tightly against him, squeezing his lips hard against hers.

"Good-bye," he said.

Billi pushed the sword into Kay's heart.

Blood erupted from the wound, and Kay's body went limp. Billi pulled the sword out, and it slipped from her fingers as she cradled his collapsing body. She pressed her hands over the wound.

"It's okay, Billi."

Thick sticky blood coated her hands and soaked his shirt. Kay choked. Frothy red bubbles burst from his mouth and nostrils.

It's okay, Billi.

"Kay," she whispered. His scarlet hands cupped her face and held her steady. The bloody handprints were warm against her face. Handprints like her mother had left on her bedroom door. She looked into his eyes, willing him to hang on. It didn't matter how long, but every second was one second more.

"I'm sorry, Kay," she said. He was dying, but she wanted to feel every last moment.

He stared back, eyes clear, focused. His bloody mouth split into a smile—that secret smile.

Beautiful

His last breath was just a sigh. She stared, waiting for him to breathe just a little.

Just a little.

Please, Kay.

Just a little.

Billi squeezed his body and kissed him, tasting the salty blood, vainly hoping for the slightest breath.

But nothing came.

She looked at him, but Kay was gone. Those big blue eyes faded, open but empty. He wasn't looking at her anymore. She heard the scrape of metal sliding on the stone floor, and the creak of a foot on timber. A shadow fell over her. She didn't look around. She didn't have the strength.

"What d'you think he sees, with eyes so wide?" she asked. She'd tried hard, but it was over.

The cold silver blade touched her cheek. "You'll know soon enough," said Michael.

Billi slowly raised her head. Michael held the Silver Sword to her throat. He looked at her not with triumph, but a strange resignation. As if he'd always known it would end this way.

Billi touched her cheek and felt the sticky blood marking it. So much like her mother had done. She stared at the dark red stains on her fingers, and stopped.

Her mother had known how to defeat Michael. He hadn't left Billi alive on purpose that night he'd come to their home ten years ago, not out of his own choice. He couldn't reach her. *Jamila had marked the door with the blood of sacrifice.*

Back then, her mother had died to protect her, and now Kay had. She pressed her bloody fingers against her lips. Kay had died to prove his prophecy, and now it was her turn. But if she was wrong, she would die. Strangely, she didn't mind.

Kay would be waiting.

"It's better this way," said Michael.

"Just do it."

The sword bolted up and swept down. Billi held Kay against her heart as the blow struck.

The Silver Sword shattered into thousands of sparkling lights, a silent eruption of diamond stars that blew bright, then gently vanished, gone before they touched the ground.

There was a sting on her neck, and she could feel the warm trickle of blood rolling down her cold skin.

She touched the wound; a small shallow cut. She turned toward Michael. He stared blankly at his hand; the sword utterly gone.

"How?" muttered Michael.

Sacrificial blood. The greatest magic there is; that was what Elaine had said. Michael stumbled away, shaking his head. The Jews of ancient Egypt had protected their homes with the blood of sacrifice, and the Angel of Death could not cross.

The watchers' one immutable law.

"You should have passed over, Michael," Billi said as she cradled Kay. Michael had tried to cross a barrier protected by Kay's sacrificial blood. "You broke covenant."

The look of horror said it all. Michael raised his offending hand and wailed. He tore at his rain-sodden hair and ran his nails deep into his cheeks. Throwing his arms up toward the heavens, he pleaded, "Forgive me! Forgive me!"

Lightning ripped apart the dense curtain of clouds. The sky filled with unbearable brightness, and the roar was deafening. The wind almost threw Billi over as it swept across the city. Deep within this cyclone, Billi heard a million voices crying, and caught in the center, she saw Michael, his essence evaporating as knife-edged strips were carved off him. He stumbled and cringed beneath the onslaught. Down on his knees, he begged.

"God Almighty!" he screamed, and then it consumed him, his scream dying away into the chorus of the damned tempest.

Billi hugged Kay as the storm raged, but its brightness, too fierce and too powerful to linger, sucked into itself, and when she finally opened her eyes, it was dawn—true dawn. The storm had passed, and through the clouds she saw daylight at last. She looked into the sun, tingling with the warmth of a new day. "God Almighty indeed."

Somewhere, on some small city farm, a cock crowed.

And a million children slept on.

36

THEY BURIED KAY A WEEK LATER AT A SMALL NORMAN church on the coast of Kent. It sat on a cliff overlooking the still and silent sea. White-winged seagulls circled against the sharp blue sky. Percy, Berrant, and Balin had been buried in London, but Billi wanted something special for Kay.

He'll like the view, she thought.

No family, and the stone just had his name, birth, and death, and a brief epitaph:

A POOR SOLDIER.

Elaine stood at the head of the grave. Billi had thought Arthur would give the eulogy, but knew Elaine had been a mentor to Kay in a way her warrior father never was.

"We're all poor soldiers," said Elaine. "What's life but bitter struggle and pain? You have to be a soldier to bear it. To bear witness to what life brings: loss, despair, defeat. Our victories are few, and fleeting." Billi watched the tears sparkle on the woman's wrinkled cheeks, sliding down the deep grooves. Elaine continued. "We have to have faith. Faith that something good comes out of our sacrifices. I think we can say Kay proved just that." Billi took her dad's hand, and he gave hers a brief squeeze.

"Kay wasn't a warrior. But when he was called, he was not found wanting." Elaine's hands covered her eyes. "We can only hope that his reward is a just one."

The sun shone on the polished oak coffin lid as the other knights lowered it into the grave. They were all there. The Poor Fellow-Soldiers of Christ and the Temple of Solomon. The Knights Templar.

Four weary men and Billi.

Bors and Pelleas stood on one side of the coffin while Gwaine and Arthur stood on the other, holding the ropes slung under the coffin. Her dad was sweating, grimacing from the pain of his stitches, as inch by inch they lowered Kay to his final resting place. Billi closed her eyes and saw the lingering ghosts of Percy, Balin, and Berrant.

And Kay.

She felt hollow. This morning her heart had leaped when she'd seen a tall skinny blond boy. For a fraction Kay was alive, but the boy turned and it wasn't him.

Kay is gone. The thought shriveled her insides; how could he be gone so quickly? She'd cried in the morning, shocked she couldn't remember everything about him. She couldn't bear to think her memories might fade, so she forced herself to recall every single feature. His pale skin, the silvery hair, the soft bristles of his beard just gathered around his chin. And his eyes. They were the one thing she'd never forget.

Blue—they were very blue.

The coffin scraped the bottom of the pit. The knights reeled in the ropes.

Don't leave me, Kay.

The others lined up, and each paused by the grave, giving a silent prayer, a final farewell. Then it was Billi's turn.

I can't do this.

Arthur stopped and looked at her. She blushed with shame. He'd buried his wife, and it hadn't stopped him.

How could she do less? And what else would Kay expect of her?

"Say good-bye, sweetheart," Arthur said.

But she couldn't move. She stared at the coffin; a tiny patter of loose earth dropped onto the lid.

Don't go.

Billi

She jolted, glancing around, heart suddenly pounding hard and rapid.

"Billi." Arthur held out his hand. "Let him rest." Then he walked away down the green slope. She looked into the dark hole and undid her crucifix chain. She held it over the edge, then let it slip and clatter onto his coffin.

The others lined along the gate as she walked. She looked at each, and one by one they nodded in greeting. This was where she belonged. Arthur stood last. He put his arms around her and pressed her close to his heart. She heard it beating fiercely against hers. Her father kissed her tear-stained cheeks and whispered softly:

"Welcome to the Knights Templar."